what i MEANT...

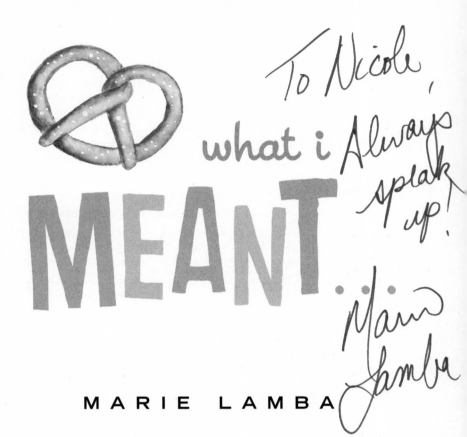

MEANT...

MARIE LAMBA

*To Nicole,
Always
speak
up!
Marie
Lamba*

RANDOM HOUSE ⌂ NEW YORK

Text copyright © 2007 by Marie Lamba
Jacket illustrations copyright © 2007 by Cindy Revell

Grateful acknowledgment is made to the following to reprint previously published material:

Sanga Music, Inc.: Excerpt from "Where Have All the Flowers Gone?" by Pete Seeger, additional verse by Joe Hickerson, copyright © 1961 (renewed) by Sanga Music, Inc. All rights reserved. Reprinted by permission of Sanga Music, Inc.

Special Rider Music: Excerpts from "The Times They Are A-Changin'" by Bob Dylan, copyright © 1963 by Warner Bros., Inc., copyright renewed 1991 by Special Rider Music. All rights reserved. International copyright secured. Reprinted by permission of Special Rider Music.

www.randomhouse.com/teens

Educators and librarians, for a variety of teaching tools, visit us at
www.randomhouse.com/teachers

Library of Congress Cataloging-in-Publication Data
Lamba, Marie.
What I meant— / Marie Lamba. — 1st ed.
p. cm.
SUMMARY: Having to share her home with her demanding and devious aunt from India makes it all the more difficult for fifteen-year-old Sang to deal with such things as her parents thinking she is too young to date, getting less-than-perfect grades, and being shut out by her longtime best friend.
ISBN: 978-0-375-84091-3 (trade)
ISBN: 978-0-375-94091-0 (lib. bdg.)
[1. Family life—Pennsylvania—Fiction.   2. East Indian Americans—Fiction.
3. Aunts—Fiction.   4. Interpersonal relations—Fiction.   5. Schools—Fiction.
6. Pennsylvania—Fiction.]   I. Title.
PZ7.L1676Wha 2007 [Fic]—dc22 2006010898

To

Baldev, Adria, and *Cari*

for their faith in me, and their love

And to my parents,

Santo and *Louisa Busterna,*

and my brother,

Stephen Busterna—

the funniest storytellers I know

what i MEANT...

1

"What *exactly* did they say?"

"To call." I give my aunt a faint smile.

"What did they say? You must think."

That *is* what they said, you stupid old cow! I want to scream this, but of course I don't. Okay. Let me backtrack a bit. I know this doesn't sound good, but I'm a nice person. Really. And I'm totally loving to my family. And, true, my aunt is part of my family, but from the Indian side. She's my dad's sister-in-law. Normally I love my Indian relatives, though I don't see them that often, but normally my Indian relatives are all sweet and nice and ask me questions about how I am and smile. Sadly, there is nothing normal about my aunt. Because she's my dad's brother's wife, I'm supposed to call her "Chachi," but that sounds all affectionate, like she's someone who would hug me and make sticky sweet *rosogullas* for me and tell me to eat them all because I'm so skinny. Right. I guess that's the idea we all had when we turned our lives upside down to let Chachi live with us. It'll only be two years, my father had reasoned. Just long enough for my cousin to finish his undergraduate degree, and now, with my brother, Hari, at college, we have a bedroom free, so . . .

"You must tell me every word this person is saying," my aunt says. She is scowling now. As if I am hiding the answer to her problems. As if the entire universe is out to get her. I smile at this.

"Eh?" she says in a sharp voice. Her black eyebrows are raised, and she looks like she'd be happy to smack my knuckles with the portable phone she is waving at my face. Really, it'd be so easy to snatch the phone from her bony hand and whack her on the head with it. Not a hard whack, you know. Just a friendly rap. Just a way of saying, You asked the question and I answered it. Listen and move on!

My little sister Doodles comes running into the kitchen: "It's gone!" She looks panicked. Since Doodles is only eight and tends toward the dramatic, I figure she's lost something goofy, like her bubble-gum-wrapper collection. But she says, "All my money. Gone!"

"Don't interrupt," Chachi says.

"Wait," I say. "Doodles, are you sure?" She's been saving money for Christmas presents since the end of the summer. When she last showed me, her purse held a surprising thirty-eight dollars.

"My purse was hanging on the back of my door. Now it's gone."

"And?" Chachi demands. "How does this concern me?"

I take a deep breath and remind myself of all the reasons my parents say I should be extra nice to Chachi. Because she is family, and family takes care of family no matter what. (This is my dad's way of thinking.) Because she's been all alone in America since her husband died and her only son has gone to college. Be a good person and just try to be patient. (This is my mom's view.)

"It was a lot of money for Doodles," I try to explain. "This means a lot to her."

Chachi frowns at my sister. "It is gone now. You go too."

Tears brim in Doodles's eyes as she rushes from the room.

"Why did you have to be so—"

"Tell me," she says. "What was said, *exactly*?"

Patience, Sang. Lots of patience. "The woman said, 'Is Kajal there?' I said no. She said, 'Can you have her call Carol at Copy Stop?' I said, 'Sure, what is the number?' And she said . . .'" I look at the pink message slip I filled out, and I read the number back to her. "She said, 'Thank you.' I said, 'Sure, goodbye.' She said, 'Goodbye.' *Click.* Dial tone."

My aunt bunches up her eyebrows. I'd like to say they're bushy, but no. They're delicate. She's younger than my mom, and actually quite pretty, with her long black hair and heart-shaped face. Anyway, I used to think she was pretty before I got to know her better. So my aunt bunches up her eyebrows and says, in that harsh accent of hers, "No. Think again. I must know."

I long to scream, LEAVE ME ALONE! THE TRUTH ISN'T SOME MULTIPLE-CHOICE TEST! IT IS WHAT IT IS! For one terrible moment, I think I might actually do it—yell in that tone I only have the nerve to use on my mom, who has to love me no matter what. I tighten my mouth, holding back the words. The tension between my aunt and me is palpable. Electric.

ZEEP-ZEEP!

We both jump, for the phone in her hand has sprung to life. My aunt answers it, saying in the softest, kindest voice, " 'Allo?"

Forgoing the snack I'd originally journeyed to the kitchen to find, I take my cue and sprint through the living room and up the steps leading to the bedrooms. My sister is sitting on her bed, her back to me, arms crossed.

"Doodles? You okay?"

She doesn't turn around, or even move. I realize she's trying hard not to cry.

"Don't let her bug you," I say in a low voice.

"Sangeet!" Chachi shouts. "Telephone!"

In my own room, I grab my phone and say, "Hey," just as I close the door and pop the lock.

"It's me," Gina, my best friend, says.

I sink onto my bed and twirl a lock of my black hair round and round my finger. "What did you do now?"

"What's that supposed to mean?"

"The phone?" Gina usually meets me online after school. A phone call means she's grounded for something. No Internet. No radio. Somehow her parents never consider the phone as a privilege to be taken away. Probably because Gina never touches it—unless she's grounded.

"My mom's totally going nuts on me today. Like there's some sort of unspoken deadline for when things should get done."

I make a sympathetic sound while I stare at my ceiling. Glossy pictures of Orlando Bloom as an elf and Orlando Bloom as a pirate stare back at me as if I'm the one he's fighting for.

"I told her I'd clean up my room, right? She didn't say it had to be today, though, did she? No. I said I'd do it, and I would've if she'd just give me a frickin' chance. God. Parents want everything yesterday. Like we don't have anything important to do ourselves. You are *so* lucky you aren't me."

I glance around my own pristine room and think Gina doesn't know how good she's got it. If I had as much as a towel on the floor, the world would come to an end. Gina? Her room is loaded with towels and shirts and books and magazines. She has wall-to-wall carpeting, but for the life of me I can't remember what color it is.

"So," Gina continues, "she starts, like, screeching at me, and I'm all like, 'Calm down, already,' and whatever, and then . . ." Her voice sounds all choked and emotional.

I sit up. Gina's not the emotional sort. She's more like a tough girl with a hidden heart of gold. Something's happened. Something huge. "Gina, you can still go tomorrow night, right?"

Silence.

Ohmygod. This can't be happening. I feel my ears ring and I know I'm panicking. How am I supposed to go on this date without Gina? I'm not allowed to date. Not until I'm sixteen, even though I tried to tell my parents that fifteen is definitely old enough and that I'm mature enough and that only complete geeks with nerdy parents aren't allowed to have boyfriends. Gina had it all planned out. How she and I would go ice-skating together on Friday and just have Jason and his friend Glen secretly meet us there, and how my parents couldn't get mad, because it wasn't really a date, and how it wouldn't be weird because it wasn't like it was just Jason and me, which would freak me out completely anyway, and how, best of all, my parents would never know anything about the boys being there. It was perfect. I've spent all week deciding what I'll wear, and I've almost narrowed it down to my final choices, and if that pimple on my left temple would just go away, the world would be perfect—except now everything is falling apart.

I'm clutching the phone tightly. "Clean your room."

"But—"

"Clean it. Gina, if you call yourself my best friend, you will clean your room starting this instant and won't stop until every last candy wrapper and soda can and CD case has been tossed, arranged, or otherwise organized, and you will say, 'Sorry, Mom. Please forgive me.' "

Silence.

"Please!" I practically shriek.

There's a sigh. "Only for you, Sang. But you owe me *huge.*"

Noticing I've been holding my breath, I suddenly let it out. "You're the best, Gina. The *best.*"

"Yeah, right."

"Can I help you clean?"

"Got a bulldozer?" She gives a grim laugh. "I think I'd better go it alone for a while. Besides, you don't want to encounter yet another Baldarasi explosion."

Over the years, I've seen a few of these. I think back to the time Mrs. Baldarasi was making Easter dinner for her extended family, simmering pasta and a vat of sauce. Everything was fine until the timer went off and Mrs. Baldarasi drained the pasta in the colander over the sink only to find she'd picked up the wrong pot and had poured an entire day's work worth of homemade sauce down the drain. "Explosion" seems like too tame a word for what happened next.

"Good luck," I say. "And thanks."

"It'll be fine, Sang. You'll see."

I hang up the phone and lie back on my pillow and sigh. My zit will disappear, and I will wear the perfect outfit, and I won't say anything stupid, and Jason will be totally sweet and romantic. I imagine his hair a little longer than it is—sort of blond, in a ponytail—and he's wearing one of those white blousy kind of shirts a pirate might wear. He'll pick me up when I fall on the ice, and it'll be the best time of my life. In three weeks, when

Hari is back from college and home in good old Doylestown, Pennsylvania, for Thanksgiving, I'll tell him all about it, and he'll meet Jason and see how cool and great he is, and make Mom and Dad see that this sixteen-years-old dating rule went out with the Neanderthals. I look up and tell Orlando, "Everything will be perfect." I give him a deep smile, the type I've practiced before the mirror, stopping at just the point where the dimple on my right cheek appears. Orlando looks back at me, his one eyebrow raised as if he's saying, Are you sure?

*S*kating *with Jason* . . . It's a few hours later, and I catch myself chewing on my pencil and staring off into space again. Nine p.m. Time for my favorite show. I look at the notebook and textbooks and papers spread all over my desk. I shrug. I've got my homework under control, haven't I?

Actually, I'm not sure. I start to rustle through my papers, looking for my datebook-organizer, but stop myself. There's no use looking. The book's been missing for the past two weeks. This is a major disaster, because my datebook is the secret to my good grades. And it's not like I can just run out and get myself a new one. This organizer is special. I write in it every project deadline, assignment, quiz, and test. And I fill in reminders to study certain sections of my notes a week prior to a big test. But that's not the special part. See, every year since I was in seventh grade, my favorite uncle has sent me one of these books from India, with a note that reads *To my scholar girl, with love.* The book always has a soft leather cover, it always has my name in gold script running across the bottom, and it always *always* gets me straight A's. I figure there must be some mystical Indian mojo thing contained in its pages. And without that, I'm totally lost.

Oh well. I suppose I'm managing okay, considering. I can finish up my math in my history class tomorrow, and I don't think that English essay is due till next week.

I stand and stretch, and glance at the clock again: 9:03. Better hurry. I arrange my books into a tidy pile and put my chewed-up pencil back into my drawer. There. Now everything looks under control. I shut off my lights before stepping into the hall.

"Sangie?" Doodles wants more of the bedtime story I've been telling her.

"Can't tonight. *Sweet Guy* is on." I head past her door.

"Sissy?"

I stop. She knows that gets me every time. I mean, she's not nearly as little and sweet as she used to be, but somehow, when she calls me "Sissy" like she used to when she was just two, my heart melts. It reminds me of when she used to tell everyone her name was Cheese because her real name, Cherise, was too hard for her to say. I've been calling her "Doodles" ever since.

In the glow of the night-light, I see her shifting around her pile of teddy bears to make room for me to sit beside her. Predictably, her favorite, Taffy Bear, is on top of the stack. For a little kid, Doodles is kind of serious.

Always scrunching her brows together and thinking, thinking, thinking, like she's doing right now. Tonight her shoulder-length brown hair is a tangled mess, giving her a mad-scientist look.

"Where do you think my money went?" she asks.

"It'll turn up."

"But we looked everywhere."

"You want the story, or you want to talk about your money all night?"

"Both," she says.

I roll my eyes and begin. "Remember how Rani was going to visit the palace? Well, first she gets lost. Then she finds the way and everything's better. Now she marries the Maharaja's son, and all is fine with the world."

"That's it?" Doodles frowns. "That stinks."

"It does not. Now good night."

"No." She crosses her arms and glowers.

Hmm. I know how this'll go. If I leave now, she'll only follow me and complain, and Mom and Dad will wonder why we're fighting, and somehow Doodles will make it all my fault. Rotten little twit. I sigh. "Rani needed to get to the palace, for she knew her one true love awaited her there, but the journey was so hard. Could she make it?" I look at Doodles, who has now settled onto her pillow. "The elephant she rode was a gentle beast who swayed to and fro and tossed his ears in the hot sunshine." My sister nods. I know she is remembering the elephant ride we took in India three years ago, the last time we visited family there. The surrounding countryside was dusty-dry as we made our way up toward Amber Fort, set in the hillside. The palace was decorated with bright tiles and ancient paintings and delicate mirrors. The elephant's feet made a soft swishing sound on the pavement as we rocked from side to side on the seats strapped to its back. Monkeys lounged on the palace walls, staring as we made our way past.

"And?" Doodles prompts me.

"Well, a terrible thing happened. The elephant entered a village. It was a messy and filthy village, and its roads were covered with junk."

"What kind of junk?"

"Doesn't matter. The important thing is that the elephant couldn't see where it was stepping. Its foot got stuck in a deep pothole and it fell over."

"Did Rani die?"

"She was okay. But the elephant"—Doodles's eyes are wide, and she's clutching Taffy Bear tightly—"the elephant was okay too, but refused to go another step ever again. To this day it still lives in that village. That's it for tonight."

"But it can't be. What about Rani?"

"Tomorrow," I say, standing and feeling slightly guilty because I know that tomorrow night I'll be out, skating with *him*. "Now go to sleep before you get in trouble." I scooch out of the room, expecting her to coax me back, but all she says is, "G'night, Sissy."

I race down the steps that lead to the living room, make a sharp left, and zoom down the next flight into the family room on the ground floor. To my horror, there's my dad in his white cotton pj's, watching a dull dull dull news show. "Dad, it's Thursday."

He doesn't react. He's concentrating on what some pasty-faced old man is saying on the TV. My dad's hand is on his chin. This is bad.

"Dad, you know I watch *Sweet Guy* every Thursday night at nine."

He lifts his hand from his chin, gesturing at me to stop talking. His eyes never leave the set. This is very bad indeed.

I plop onto the couch beside him, wondering for the zillionth time why we only have one TV. Okay, so I understand that cable is a waste of money and all that, but an extra TV would hardly cost anything. I know what my parents' response would be to such a proposal, because I've tried it often enough: If we get more televisions, we'll watch more. Like that's such a big problem. Actually, I'm not sure if my parents are mostly cheap or mostly technologically phobic. I mean, I must be the only tenth grader in the U.S. without a cell phone. Anyway, I try not to push the TV issue too much, because last time I brought it up, my dad started going on about how we use the computer and the Internet too much and how there should be limits to that too.

So I sit on the couch, my arms crossed tight, trying not to think about how this is finally a new episode of *Sweet Guy* and about all the great stuff I'm definitely missing at this very moment. I am itching to change the channel. Oh, I'm going nuts sitting here, trying to be patient. Trying not to interrupt his show. It should be my show! It's so unfair. I'm about to snap. I decide I'd better put some food in my mouth. I head upstairs, and stop when I notice the kitchen light is already on. My "Aunt Alert" is on full response. I've definitely learned avoidance, and most often this means not going into the kitchen until she's evacuated. On the bright side, I've lost about five pounds in the past three months. I turn, and I'm about to sneak back into the family room when I feel her coming up behind me.

"Hey, Sang."

I stop and twirl. "Oh, Mom. I thought . . ."

"It's just me," she says, and she gives me one of her usual warm hugs. My mom and I are pretty close. I can tell her anything, and she is one of the nicest people I know. She's always working on charity events, raising money for the poor, doing clothing drives—that type of thing. She's too nice, really. I think that's how we got stuck with Chachi. I mean, Mom's American, so she wasn't raised with all this "You have to take care of family no matter how awful they are, and respect your elders even if they're complete jerks" stuff they believe in India. Yet she agreed to take Chachi in. My mom lets go and wraps her arm around my shoulder. "So what's up?"

I point to Dad downstairs. *Sweet Guy.*

She tilts her head to one side. *I think so.*

"No, Mom. *Sweet Guy* is on now. Do something." I'm feeling desperate. What's the point of rushing through homework—well, almost through it—and cutting stories with elephants short if I'm stuck watching the pasty-faced-old-man news show?

Mom pats my shoulder. "Not to worry," she says. I nod. I know she'll handle it. Dad always listens to what Mom wants. "Wait here a moment. And whatever you do, don't talk."

I nod again. My dad hates when I argue with him. According to him, in India teens never argue with their parents.

After a moment of quiet conversation with my dad, my mom tells me to come down to the family room. She says, "It's yours at the next commercial break." See? Mom's the best. Now if only I could convince her to talk to Dad about this idiotic no-date rule.

3

So I'm feeling all fuzzy because Jake on *Sweet Guy* had hurt his girlfriend Jessica's feelings, but he felt really bad about it, so he decorated her entire house with those tiny white Christmas lights to show her what a bright, sparkling part of his heart she is. My own eyes fill a little with bright, sparkly tears because he is so sweet and because, after all, the name Jake really sort of sounds like Jason, doesn't it? My Jason will be even better, because he's real, not just an actor. And who knows? Instead of Christmas lights, maybe he'll rent a snowmaker and create a snowstorm just at my house because I'm so cool, or something like that.

Anyhow, I find Mom already in bed in her green-and-red plaid flannels. It's a great color combo on Mom. The red plays up the auburn of her wavy hair, and the green brings out the olive tones in her hazel eyes. I sit beside her, and the fluffy white duvet puffs around me.

"Mom?"

She holds up a finger while she finishes reading a sentence in her book. Tonight it's *Zen and the Art of Motorcycle Maintenance*. When she's finished her sentence, she raises her brows at me.

"Is it good?" I ask.

"Amazing. You're definitely reading this one next."

"Sure. I'll get right to it as soon as I finish *Angela's Ashes, The Joy Luck Club, The Once and Future King, The Scarlet Pimpernel,* and *Dinner at the Homesick Restaurant.*"

"Oh," she says, and sets her book on her night table. "Guess you've got some catching up to do. So what's up?"

"Did you notice how I didn't bother Dad about that show? I mean, I could have argued with him—told him it was my turn, which was perfectly true. But I didn't, did I? I was patient. I let you handle it."

My mom smiles. "So you did."

"So don't you think that shows how I've, you know, grown up? Matured?"

Mom nods. "Definitely. I'm really proud of you."

"So I should date, then."

"What's his name?"

I stall. "What?"

"His name. Must be somebody. You've only brought this subject up every day for the last two weeks."

"Why does it have to be all about some guy?"

"Exactly." She nods wisely, as if she's won the argument.

"What? No. What I mean is, I'm talking about *me*. My rights. Don't you think your daughter, with her straight A's and her nice friends and her clean room . . ." For a moment I think of Gina.

"Yes?" My mom tilts her head, waiting.

"I mean, I'm a good kid, right? Mature and all, don't you think? Even for fifteen? There's plenty of girls who aren't anywhere as mature as me, and they are allowed to have boyfriends."

"It's ridiculous, isn't it?" My mom gets out of bed and goes to her dresser. She takes a pair of thick white socks from the top drawer and starts to put them on. She's always complaining about having icy fingers and feet. "What *are* those parents thinking?"

That's so not the point! "Mom, just talk to Dad for me. Okay?"

Mom seems about to say something, but instead takes out another pair of socks. She stares at them for a moment and throws them back into the drawer. She climbs under the covers. "You're lucky you don't live in India. Your father—"

"Please." I fall back on my dad's fluffy pillow. "Must I always hear about how Dad didn't date? How nobody dated? How they just let their precious little mommies and daddies arrange a match for them? That was like, what? Ten million years ago?"

"Twenty," my dad says as he walks into the room. He's got a *New Yorker* rolled up under his arm, and his face is covered with black-and-gray stubble, his ten o'clock shadow. By morning he'll look like a homeless person, with his pajamas all crinkled, his stubble worse, and his short hair sticking up like a Kewpie doll's. "Anyway, my mommy and daddy didn't pick *her* out." He points at Mom and smiles, lifting one side of his mouth. "You're in my spot," he says to me.

I move to the foot of the bed as Dad climbs under the covers. "You mean they had another wife picked out for you?"

"I mean they had nearly a dozen supposedly ideal Indian women selected for me to choose from. But what choice did I have? Your mother practically stalked me. First going to the same university as me. Then moving into the same apartment building after graduation."

"Me? Stalking you?" my mom says, looking amused. "I had no idea who you were. Then you show up at the door of my apartment with my mail."

"I was merely being polite. What else could I do when the mailman insisted on putting your letters into my mail slot? Good manners, right?"

"And it was good manners that made you ask me out to dinner?"

"Of course." He gives my mom a mischievous smile. "You know me. Always being proper."

This gets me thinking. My dad was the only guy in his family to cut his hair (something his Sikh religion frowns on) and to ditch his turban. He was the first in his family to move to the U.S., and the only one to marry someone from another country. "Dad, you're a total rebel."

"Not exactly," he says, though he looks a little pleased at the thought.

"I bet your family freaked when you told them you were engaged to Mom."

"Let's just say your grandparents had concerns."

"They kept asking me if I drank lots of alcohol, smoked, and if I'd been divorced lots of times," Mom says, and laughs.

"Well, you can't blame them," Dad says. "American women did have a crazy reputation in India. Something to do with the TV programs they started getting there. *Santa Barbara* and *Dallas,* and things like that. Still, they loved your mother the moment they met her."

Mom says, "I suspect they were relieved your dad was finally being responsible and settling down."

Dad gets comfortable and opens his magazine.

I nudge Mom's foot and give her a look. She shakes her head. But I can't wait anymore. I mean, the date is *tomorrow.*

"So, Dad," I say, "don't you agree that a person should be rewarded for being responsible?"

"Absolutely."

So far so good. "And don't you agree that if somebody is mature, they should be allowed to do things a mature person is allowed to do?"

His brown eyes dart to my mom before he answers. "Uh, depends."

"She wants to date," Mom says.

"She's just a child," he says.

Okay, Mom. Now's the time to let him have it.

"I told her she has to wait till sixteen," she says, and hides behind her book.

What is she doing to me?

"Sixteen!" he says.

Whoa. Now I get it. Mom is using that whole reverse-psychology thing. "I know," I say. "Sixteen. That's like nine months away. Isn't that ridiculous?"

"It's horrible," he says.

By now I'm smiling so hard, my dimple must be as deep as a belly button.

"You should wait until you are finished with your studies," he says.

"Till I'm done with *high school*?" I say. My dimple has disappeared.

"College is more like it," he says, and opens up his *New Yorker,* holding it high so he can't see the icy glare I'm sending his way.

"Mom?" I say. She clears her throat and turns the page of her book.

My mouth is clenched tight now. I'm holding back a big ugly rush of words about how stupid and narrow-minded parents can be. About how I want to be all open and honest with them, but they are so impossible that they are forcing my hand. But how can I say any of this to a book and a magazine? Instead, I only pound my fist on the duvet—which shows restraint, if you think about it.

My dad jerks away from me and drops his magazine. His eyes are fierce. I didn't know his foot was there. I didn't mean to pound it. But before I can even say I'm sorry, he's yelling at me. I don't even hear what he's saying, because I'm so furious, it's like my ears are filled with sirens. He points toward my room. My mom continues to read. I HATE YOU ALL! I think, but I don't say this. Instead, I stomp out of the room, flick on my light, and close my door. I don't mean to let it slam, but before I can apologize for that, it's my dad's turn to come stomping to my room. He throws open my door all rudely, without knocking, and says, "How dare you be so fresh!"

"Eh? Op-kee megange hore-hay?" Chachi is yelling something like that from her attic bedroom.

Times like these, I'm glad I never learned Punjabi. Times like these, I wish it were Hari up in that room. I wish he were here to come into my room later to see if I am okay. I wish he were here to talk to Dad for me.

"Nothing! It's nothing!" my father shouts to Chachi. He turns back to me and says, "Lights out, right now!"

"But—" I want to tell him I need to finish my homework, brush my teeth, have a date.

"No arguments, you hear me?" He's pointing now. "And you'd better learn to control yourself, young lady, or you'll wind up in serious trouble one day."

"Fine." I go to my bed and lie down. Just before I shut off my light, I see Orlando staring back at me. He doesn't look too impressed.

4

"The line for these was out the door. Here," Gina says, and holds up two luscious powdered doughnuts she bought for breakfast from the cafeteria—just one of the perks of *finally* being in high school. I say *"finally"* because, even though we're sophomores, this is our first year in the high school building (our middle school went all the way up to ninth grade). The high school is *huge,* and I still don't know where everything is. At least now I can find my classes, can usually find a bathroom, and can make it through the lunch line without feeling like a complete moron who doesn't even know where the condiments are.

Right now, Gina and I are hanging out before the first bell. Kids are swarming all around us, and lockers are banging shut. "Thanks," I say, taking a doughnut. "Hey, that skirt looks so great on you." It's hot pink, and matches the pink bands in her braces. She rolls her eyes but smiles, and I'm thinking of how fantastic she's going to look in a few weeks when her braces come off.

"Just think, Sang. You. Jason. Pretty soon I'm going to be a third wheel around here."

"Shush," I say, glancing around. Ella Jenkins is right behind us at her locker, but thankfully she's busy talking with her friend Lauren.

"Relax, no one heard," Gina says. "Your secret's safe with me. And you know why?"

I nod, and together we recite, "Best friends keep best-friend secrets." It's our own goofy little motto. Gina has been my very best friend since second grade. We're like sisters. I know, we look totally opposite. I'm five foot six and she's barely five foot two. I'm darker-skinned and have long black hair, and she has short dirty-blond hair and is pale enough to get freckles on her shoulders and nose in the summer. So we don't share clothes, or hair products. So what? We're still a team. She comes up with the big ideas, and I try to find a way to make the less crazy ones really happen.

"I just don't know *why* you want it kept secret," she says. "If it were me, I'd be telling everyone."

"There's nothing to tell. Besides, this whole date thing will probably bomb."

"The whole date thing won't bomb. It'll be great. Now if only we had a diabolical scheme to get me my own guy."

"What about Jason's friend? The guy coming skating with us?"

"Naw. Too tall." She bites her doughnut and chews thoughtfully. "Let's see. I could become a stripper. That always turns some heads. Don't they have some kind of pole-dancing class at the night school?"

"I don't think so."

She looks down at her not-so-well-endowed chest. "Maybe you're right. Okay, how about this? I keep my clothes on, but stuff my bra."

"Ah, but what if you're successful and some guy falls in love with your chest, and then things, you know, progress. . . ."

She whacks me. "You have a dirty mind, you know that? Wait." Gina rubs her chin. "I've got the answer. Breast implants."

"Gina, you are not getting a boob job."

"Why not? Think about it. A permanent change for the better."

"First of all, your parents would never let you, and second of all, you can't afford it. Anyway, you don't need it. You're gorgeous and funny, and—"

"Short and flat." Before I can argue with this, she adds, "And I do have money. My untouched birthday savings account. I should have enough to buy at least one boob."

"Now *that* will get you noticed."

"Interesting." She rubs her chin again.

I push her hand away. "No."

"Wait!" somebody says. I turn and see Megan Chung calling to a scowling senior wearing faded jeans. He faces her, and Megan stares at him with those large black eyes of hers. They're just like the eyes of baby harp seals, those impossibly adorable little white creatures that fur hunters belt over the head with a shovel.

I brace myself for what I'm about to witness. See, Megan is really nice, but she's an absolute disaster around guys.

"My name's me," Megan says to the guy, and gulps. "I'm hi."

"Well, that explains a lot," the senior says with disgust.

"N-no. Not that kind of high. I just wanted to say, I'm pants."

"Right." The guy backs up. "Whatever. Just stop following me." He hurries away.

"Nice pants," Megan says to herself. "That's what I wanted to say. NICE PANTS. Arrgh!" She whacks herself on the forehead.

"Megan, get over here," Gina says.

Megan shuffles up to us.

"What was that?" Gina asks her.

"What do you mean?"

"That. You. Over there. Trying way too hard. Why don't you just be yourself?"

"But, Gina, I *am* being myself. That's the problem."

"Just try to relax," Gina says, brushing some powdered sugar off the edge of her skirt. "What's the big deal? It's just some guy."

"Guys *suck,*" Ella Jenkins says to us, slamming her

locker. She takes a vicious bite from a chocolate bar and marches off.

"She and Anthony just split," her friend Lauren tells us in a confidential voice. We all make sympathetic sounds, and Lauren scurries after Ella.

"At least she *had* a guy," Megan says.

"So will you," I say. "You'll see."

"Sure," she says in a glum voice. "You guys coming to History?"

"In a minute." I hold up my doughnut. Mrs. Finelli doesn't allow food in class. When Megan heads off, I say, "Okay, Gina. Please please please tell me your room is clean so this date thing can actually happen."

"Oh."

The way she says this makes me want to scream NOOOOOOOO! I take a huge bite of the doughnut instead.

"Well," she says, running her tongue over her braces, "I think it'll be fine."

I want to ask for details, but my mouth is jammed with doughnut, so I just nod, as if to say, Tell me more. . . .

"It'll definitely be fine. Perfect," Gina says. "I've got it all worked out. Now I know you love to worry about things, but don't, okay? You know I won't ever let you down." She pats my arm reassuringly. "Oh, hey, Jason." She's looking over my shoulder.

I shake my head. Gina's always teasing me like this.

But she's not teasing, because a moment later I hear his gruff voice say, "Hey."

Oh God. I'm like a stuffed suckling pig, because no matter how much I chew and chew, I can't get this damned doughnut to go away.

"Hey, Sang," he says.

I turn and nod. Oh, he looks totally sizzling hot. He's wearing baggy jeans and a short-sleeved blue T-shirt, and his arms look pretty strong, and he's definitely taller than me. I wasn't sure about this, because I usually see him sitting in the cafeteria or just in passing. And he's got these hazel-green eyes and shaggy brown hair and one small diamond earring that if my dad saw, he'd surely flip. Oh, this may be love. I wonder yet again if he's really interested in me. Me? But Gina made triply sure that, yes, he was interested in me, Sang Jumnal. In their gym class, he told Gina he'd noticed me with her from time to time. Said I looked interesting. Exotic. Oh, how I floated after hearing that.

"How's it going?" he asks, and I *so* want to answer him. You know, say something that makes me sound interested but not too interested. But the powdered sugar is starting to tickle the back of my throat, and I'm trying to control my breathing through my nose so I don't sneeze. I hold up my half-eaten doughnut as if this will explain my lack of response. Man. Did I really stuff half that thing in my mouth at once?

It seems like he's going to walk away. Don't! Stay just a little longer. I try to smile, though I suppose, since my

cheeks are bulging with doughnut, that my dimple is no-
where in sight. I flick my eyes at Gina. Help me!

"See you tonight, Jason," she says, then gives me a
quick pat on the back and goes.

"Yeah, see you," Jason says to her. Now he's looking at
me. Staring, all distracted-like. I feel my cheeks tingle.
"Sang?" he says. His hand moves toward my face. He is
going to touch my face.

Ohmygod.

I tilt my head toward his hand. My heart starts to race.
Ohmygod ohmygod!

But suddenly he pulls his hand away. And he says,
"You've got, like, crud on your nose."

The bell rings.

I swallow.

Everybody races to their classes, including me. Even
through my horror, my mortification, my body still can
respond with robot-like reflexes. Even with a booger
hanging from my nose and my life at an end, I can still
obey the rules. Just before I dash into History, I have the
good sense to swipe at my nose. The back of my hand
shows a dusting of powdered sugar, not snot. Well, that's
something, isn't it?

5

"Now try this one." Gina holds a red-and-black-striped top against me and squints. "Naw. You need something more, I dunno, sexy."

"How 'bout some powdered sugar?" I say, and sink to the floor.

"You know what the secret to good dating is?" Gina sits beside me and she's got my attention. See, while I'm the oldest girl in my family, Gina's the youngest of three. While she hasn't actually had a steady boyfriend yet, she's definitely got advice to dispense. "The secret is a good sense of humor."

I groan. "That's something ugly girls say."

"Thanks."

I elbow her. "Come on. You're not ugly. You're the farthest thing from it." Gina looks away from me. "You're so thin and pretty and so great to hang with."

"Guess that's why the guys are beating down my door." She glances at me.

"What I meant was, if a girl doesn't have nice looks, people tell her she can make jokes to get attention, or something pathetic like that."

Gina gives me an "Are you for real?" look. "Sense of humor," she says. "Learn to laugh. End of statement." She twists the shirt she's holding into a ball. "So listen. I'm thinking about trying out for spring track."

I laugh.

"I'm not that bad a runner."

"You're a great runner," I say. "But I stink. Face it. It'd never work. It'd be like the newspaper, only in reverse." Gina and I had signed up for the school newspaper in September only to discover that even though I kind of liked interviewing people and writing, Gina hated it. She didn't like taking pictures either. So we both quit. I mean, it wouldn't have been fun without her anyway.

"Yeah, I guess you're right. It was a stupid idea." She drops the shirt on the floor and stands. "Think she's out of the kitchen yet? I'm starving."

I fold the shirt neatly and stick it in my dresser drawer and follow her down to the kitchen. "You sure your room will be clean in time?"

"Don't sweat it," she says, and opens the fridge. "It's like you don't you trust me or something."

"Of course I trust you. Don't be stupid." Gina's kept every single secret I've ever told her. And really, she's never let me down when I've needed her. It's just that, well, sometimes she can be a little disorganized.

Gina surveys my aunt's wall of Tupperware filled with sprouting beans. "Disgusting. There's nothing to eat in this place." Then she turns and surveys me. "No wonder you're dropping pounds."

"You don't know the half of it. You play lookout, okay?"

I remove box after box of Tupperware. Behind it all is a prize.

"Pudding!" Gina says.

"Shhh," I say. "My aunt hides them here so no one else will eat them."

"That's vile."

"I know." I hand Gina a spoon. "Eat fast."

6

My mom places her icy-cold wrist on my forehead for the third time. "You sure you're okay, honey?" She's staring at me with concern.

I try not to swat her hand away. "I'm fine. Eyes on the road."

"You feel a little warm," she says, but her eyes do return to the road, which is good. When someone is driving you to your first secret date, it's better if you don't get into an accident on the way.

"I only feel warm because your hands are always frozen."

Mom nods. I hope she drops the subject completely, because the truth is, I do feel a little sick—but not because of the flu. I'd better take it from the beginning. Things started off pretty good this afternoon. Gina and I were able to eat the pudding and dispose of the evidence just minutes before my aunt appeared, slamming the pressure cooker onto the stovetop to make her usual *chawal* and *dahl,* better known as rice and beans.

With chocolate pudding pumping through our veins, we were inspired. We quickly put together a great outfit for me to wear: jeans, and this really cute light blue sweater with white snowflakes embroidered here and there. Even the zit on my temple seemed to relax, becoming not so much a bump as a small red spot. A bit of cover-up and I was good to go.

"See that?" Gina said. "You're perfect."

"Right," I said in a skeptical voice.

She grabbed both my arms and shook me. "Perfect, you hear me? Frickin' perfect. Say it."

"I'm not going to—"

"Say it now," she said, shaking me harder.

"I'm frickin' perfect!" I shouted, and I couldn't help but smile.

"There." Gina let go. "That wasn't so hard."

Gina was all set to spike the rest of Chachi's pudding with Ex-Lax, but I insisted she go home to finish her cleaning, because everything depended on this. Before she went, we scanned the Net one more time to see if Jason was signed on. No trace of IMonFIREtwo. Gina said he was probably spending hours in front of his own mirror and that's why he couldn't chat. I told her she was crazy, but secretly I thought, Wow. Could it be?

Anyhow, dinnertime was pretty weird. But then again, it always is these days. We don't talk at the table much anymore. My aunt was busy slurping up her soupy dahl, her eyes never leaving her plate. She occasionally took a bite of a raw beet, which she ate whole, like an apple. You know, I used to like Indian food. Like spicy chicken curry followed by warm, sweet *halvah* for dessert. But lately I've lost my taste for anything Indian. Good thing Mom usually makes plain old American stuff.

"I got all my spelling words right today," said Doodles, daring to break the silence.

"That's great," my dad said. My mom nodded and smiled. Chachi bit her beet.

"Oh, and can somebody take me around to sell candy tomorrow?" Doodles stared at me when she asked. I stared at my plate. She has to sell chocolates to raise money for her Girl Scout troop. Not exactly my idea of fun.

"I'll take you around," Mom said.

"And guess what I figured out?" Doodles sounded excited. "Did you know we can actually go down to the bottom of the field during recess? Used to be you'd get yelled at, but today Eileen and I were—"

"My room is cold," Chachi said.

Doodles took a deep breath and began again. "Today Eileen and I were looking for—"

"Turn up the heat," Chachi said. "I will fall sick."

"Eileen and I were looking for acorns and—"

"I cannot fall sick. I need more heat."

My mom held up her hand. "Just a minute, Doodles." She turned to Chachi. "I can turn the heat up tonight."

"See that you do," Chachi said.

My mom and dad glanced at each other, and we all went silent for a while. "So, Doodles," my dad said. "Continue with your story. What happened next?"

"I forget," she said in a gloomy voice.

"Come on," Dad said. "I really want to hear."

"No you don't. Nobody cares about my stupid day." Doodles ran from the table. We heard her door slam.

My father wrinkled his brow. "I'll talk to her."

My mom patted his arm and said, "Cherise will be okay. She just needs a little time."

Throughout all this drama, Chachi continued to shovel food into her mouth. I stared at my plate, trying to pretend she wasn't there, trying to tune out the chomping of beets, the slurping of dahl. I pushed my brussels sprouts and chicken cutlet from side to side. I dug my fork into my mashed potatoes, making the brown gravy flow out of the little pit I had made. It's a sight that usually cheers me, but tonight, somehow, it held no joy.

"You're not eating," my mom said. She notices everything. How would I ever get away with this whole secret-date junk?

"I am," I said, and to prove it, I poked a brussels sprout with my fork. It was dripping with gravy, which was kind of gross. But Mom was watching closely, so I was determined to eat it. The sprout slipped off my fork and splashed gravy on my sweater. My perfect sweater! There was a huge blotch of gravy right over my left boob!

Chachi looked up and grinned. Beet juice covered her teeth like blood.

I can fix this, I thought, but despite paper towels and mild soap and dabbing, I couldn't. Back in my room, I rummaged through my drawers, desperate to find something, anything, to wear, when something truly horrible happened. The phone rang.

I closed my eyes, thinking, Please please let it not be for me. Then something even more horrible happened. I heard my aunt's harsh voice calling up the stairs. "San-geeeeeet?"

It was Gina. "She's totally unfair. I can't believe I'm related to this woman."

For a moment I thought Gina was talking about my aunt, but then I realized who she was really talking about. "You can't come," I said. It was a good thing I hadn't actually eaten dinner, because if I had, I'd have lost it at that moment. Gina was grounded for a week.

"What am I gonna do?" I said.

"See if Megan can go, or Franny or somebody."

"Right." I headed for my keyboard, but groaned. "No one's around. They're all doing that Ella thing." To help Ella Jenkins get over her breakup with Anthony Casamoni, a bunch of people were treating her to the movies, then to dessert at Applebee's. Apparently there's a waiter there Ella always thought was cute.

"Crap. Okay, reschedule. Do it next week. I'm sure I can go by then. See if he's online."

He wasn't. Calling him was out of the question. Nobody calls anybody. Unless they both have a cell phone, and there's absolutely no chance of having to talk to somebody else's parent when you call. I'm completely deprived and definitely don't have a cell. I don't know about Jason. And anyhow, Jason only talked to Gina about the date. He and I never actually talked much at all, but tonight all that was supposed to change. I was in a panic.

That's when Gina came up with her plan. It seemed perfect. I'd tell my mom I was meeting Gina at the rink, and I'd get dropped off and picked up by my mom because Gina's parents were too busy to give me a ride. Perfect, except for the part where I'd be the only one there with two guys. Gulp. I settled on wearing a maroon sweater, and in the mirror I could see the zit on my temple had grown. I dabbed concealer on it, but this just made it look like a huge tan lump. I parted my hair on the side to cover it.

All systems were go until my mom started asking me why Mrs. Baldarasi couldn't drive one way at least. Then Mom wanted to give her a quick call and I found myself telling my mom that Mrs. Baldarasi wasn't home. Nobody was. They were all out at some special celebration, at which point my mom said she would gladly give Gina a ride home, then, if it'd be easier for Mrs. Baldarasi. Gah! I thought. Stop being so nice!

So now we're pulling up to Ice World. Lots of people are going in, some with skates hanging from their shoulders by the laces. It'll be fine. Great. I'll tell Jason that Gina is still coming, so it won't seem too weird. . . .

Mom drives up to the entrance. My heart is pounding in my throat. "Bye, Mom," I manage to say.

Mom looks past me at the people walking into Ice World. "I don't see Gina. Let me park and walk you in. I'll wait with you till she—"

"No!" I look out the window. "There she is." I wave to nobody. "Okay. Bye, Mom."

"Be good," she says.

My cheeks flush. I give her a quick kiss and I'm out the door. I walk up to Ice World, unable to look back at my mom's car. I just pray she's gone. The doors to Ice World slide open. Inside, the lobby is neon-bright and refrigerator-chilled. I dare to look around. There's some people lining up to buy admission tickets in front of a glass booth; to my left, a few middle schoolers are hanging out by some arcade games. No sign of Jason or his friend. I'm shivering a little now, whether from the cold or my nerves I can't say. I dig my hands into the pockets of my coat and look to my right. Some parents have herded a group of kids about my sister's age into a corner. The boys and girls are all clutching birthday presents. Every one of those kids looks excited, bouncing on their toes and smiling.

I decide to stand near the ticket booth.

"Are you waiting in line?" a mother asks me.

"No. Sorry," I say. I move more to the side. God, this is awkward. This would be so much better with Gina here. We'd talk and giggle, and I wouldn't look so pathetic and—

"Hey," he says from behind me.

I twirl around to see Jason, a huge dimpled smile on

my face. But it isn't Jason. Instead, it's a man wearing an Ice World T-shirt. "You're blocking it." He points to the glass doors leading to the rink.

I shuffle over more. And wait. I shift from foot to foot. The doors whoosh open and shut. People buy tickets and enter the rink. I'm still alone. Something horrible plays in my mind, over and over and over again: *You've got, like, crud on your nose. Crud on your nose. CRUD ON YOUR NOSE!*

I involuntarily wipe my nose. It's feeling a little bit sniffy. Like I might cry. But that's stupid. I look at my watch. It's 8:27. I've been standing here for twenty-seven minutes. I sniff again.

"Sang?"

This is it, I think. I take a deep breath and turn. But it's not Jason, or his friend what's-his-name. It's Dalton Dreyfus, another guy from school. He's wearing a pointed party hat with bright polka dots on it. He seems suddenly to realize this, because he pulls it off so fast that the elastic gets tangled in his glasses. He flushes and fixes them, waving the hat around.

"My sister's party. I'm helping." He shrugs.

I smile, relieved to not be standing alone for the moment.

"Dalton, come on. We're going in," a little girl calls. The partygoers crowd toward the glass doors that lead to the rink.

Dalton shrugs again. "Guess I'll see you inside." He

gives me a goofy salute and follows the party, but before he gets to the rink's door, he tosses his hat into the trash.

I'm alone again. Then it hits me. DUH. Jason must be inside. He's inside, skating around, wondering what the heck happened to me. Maybe he thinks that I stood *him* up. That's a terrible feeling, I think as I rush to get in line. I buy my ticket and enter the rink. The ice is a mass of swirling people and cheesy 1980s dance tunes. I try to spot Jason, but everyone is moving too fast. I don't see him in the bleachers. He must be on the ice somewhere. The only way to find him is to get myself out there. At the counter, I hand over my sneaks and get a pair of granny-like brown skates in exchange. Blech. Still, everybody seems to have the same ones. Resigned, I sit on a bench and start lacing. A moment later, Dalton is next to me, lacing his own skates.

"Who you here with?" he says.

"I'm meeting friends." Which is true, I hope.

"Cool." He tightens his laces. "You any good at this?"

I think about the whole dating thing. "I don't think so."

He smiles, and for the first time I notice he has a dimple too, on his left cheek. He's actually not so bad-looking, but Dalton's just one of those guys who is always there, in my history class or at the lunch table. You don't really notice him too much, because he's a little on the quiet side, and a little on the nerdy side too. I guess that's why I feel so comfortable sitting here with him. If I was sitting beside Jason, well . . .

I glance around. "I'd better get going. See you." I stand.

"Not if I see you first," he says, and points like he's shooting at me.

"Oh, okay," I say. I take a few wobbly steps forward and look back at Dalton. He has his face in his hands. Maybe he has a headache or something.

So now I'm on the ice. At first I'm working hard to not look like a total idiot, because I never know when Jason will skate right up to me. Finally I get my rhythm going enough to look up, and now I'm gliding around the rink. There are people everywhere. Little kids are wiping out left and right, which makes it hard to look for Jason since I really have to watch what's going on in front of me. But after I've been around the rink twice, an awful feeling starts to grow. A horrible, rejected, crud-on-my-nose, zit-on-my-face sort of feeling. I stop and hold on to the side, pushing the feeling down and away. I stay there and watch the skaters go round and round.

Now I'm seeing the same people again and again. The chubby woman who giggles and clings to a chubby man as they wobble past. The twenty-something guy in the hockey skates who cuts through the crowd with smooth crossover strokes. A huddle of birthday party kids knocking each other down and laughing.

Every so often, Dalton skates by. The first few times I look another way, pretending not to see him. I mean, I'm supposed to be meeting friends, right? Then why am I all alone, like some pathetic loser?

"Disco Duck" is now playing, like my own personal

loser soundtrack. On about Dalton's fifth time passing, I look away again, and I feel something simply horrible. My lip. It's trembling. All stupid hopes are gone. Jason's not here. Of course he's not. He was never coming. I am such an idiot.

I face the wall, and grip its edge tight. My breath catches as disappointment fills me, as tears well up in my eyes, as everything becomes blurry.

"Hey, you get hurt or something?"

It's Dalton. I shake my head. I wish he'd go away.

There's a long pause.

"You want some cake?"

I can't answer.

"Cake," he says, as if he's disgusted with himself.

This makes me look up at him. I don't dare blink or the tears in my eyes will surely spill out. "What's wrong with cake?"

He shrugs and looks at the skaters. At that moment three girls from his sister's party glide by. They wave at him and he nods. They giggle to each other and whisper behind their hands as if they've just seen Daniel Radcliffe from the *Harry Potter* movies. It's obvious they all have a fabulous crush on him. Dalton rolls his eyes and sighs. "Some Friday night, huh?"

7

Hurt. Devastated. Empty. Ugly. Miserable. Ridiculous. Foolish. These are just a few words that describe some of the bitter sorrow inside of me. My mom picks me up. I lie to her and tell her that, no, Gina doesn't need a ride because she was picked up already. Lie (again, again) that I had a really fun time, and that it just doesn't sound like it because I'm super-tired because I skated so much. I wish I could tell her this was one of the most humiliating nights of my life. I wish I could get one of her hugs. . . . My mom keeps asking me questions, as if she wants to know every last detail. I'm running out of fake answers, and after a while I can only shrug in response.

Now I'm back in my room. I take off my maroon sweater and chuck it in the laundry even though I want to toss it in the garbage. In fact, I wish I could toss everything into the garbage. My hair straightener and my jewelry box, my magazines and my phone. Even my computer. I wish I could scream and kick things.

I put on my pajamas and rummage in my closet. I know it's not very mature, but I want my Fuzzy Bear. I find her, covered with dust bunnies, behind an old backpack. I brush her off and hug her and lie on my bed.

I look up at Orlando. He seems sympathetic. I'm surprised I'm not crying. All night I've felt I was on the verge of tears. Well, not *all* night. Dalton and I did have some laughs teasing his "fan club" about how he wanted to marry one of them, and the cake was pretty good. . . . Anyhow, all night I've been on the verge of tears and now, when I can finally bust loose, I'm not sad anymore. I'm angry.

Furious, in fact. I realize I am strangling Fuzzy, and loosen my grip. Okay. I decide to get organized. Why am I angry? Because, number one, Gina let me down. Would it kill her to be a little neat? I mean, some best friend, right? Number two, Jason is a complete jerk only pretending to be a nice guy. Number three, none of this would have happened if my parents didn't have this stupid stupid dating rule. I would have been able to tell them everything, and right now I would be with my mom, spilling my guts instead of hiding in my room.

Suddenly I am glad that I didn't destroy my computer. I log on and scan my buddy list. Gina's not on. Duh. Her mom probably hid her keyboard again. Jason's not on either. I'm not sure if I'm sorry about this or relieved.

Maybe he had a really good reason for not showing up, I think. But I had a really good reason not to, actually several, and I did anyway. What's that say? (Can you spell "loser"?)

The computer blips.

HARIMONSTER: sup?

It's my brother. I can imagine him sitting in his dorm room, the glow of the computer screen lighting up his round smiling face. I'm suddenly missing him like I haven't missed him since the week after he left. True, he's three years older than me and obviously a boy, but still, we used to be able to talk about anything. Time to spill my guts.

SINGSANGSUNG: i hate my life!!!!!!
SINGSANGSUNG: ur so lucky
SINGSANGSUNG: u get to do wat u want
HARIMONSTER: true!
HARIMONSTER: gtg cya soon

And he's off. I feel stung. Would it kill him to chat for one minute? The phone rings. I snatch it up. "Hari?"

" 'Allo?" The voice is scratchy and muffled. Immediately I know it is from India.

"Yes," I say in a loud, clear voice. "Hello."

"Ah. Sangeet, my little darling, is that you?"

"Yes, Taoji. How are you?" It's my favorite uncle,

phoning from New Delhi. I imagine him sitting in a wicker chair on his balcony, with a view of the trim gardens two stories below. I imagine him pressing his portable phone tightly to his ear so he can better hear me through the wrap of his turban.

"I am wonderful," he says. "And how is my little scholar girl doing? Hmm?"

While younger-brother uncles are *chachas* and their wives are *chachis,* older ones are *taojis* and *taijis.* It's all pretty complicated. Believe it or not, in India there are even different names for aunts who are your father's sisters and their husbands, and for aunts and uncles on the maternal side of the family. But since my dad doesn't have any sisters and my mom's family isn't Indian, I don't remember what any of these are called. This taoji is my dad's oldest brother. As the oldest, he takes a fatherly and ambitious view of us all, and that means he expects me not only to get good grades, but to someday be a Rhodes scholar. No pressure, right?

"Getting all A's, then?" he asks.

I think about my lost datebook-organizer, about the trouble he must go through every year to purchase it and have my name put on it and ship it. How can I tell him I'm the farthest thing from a Rhodes scholar? That I'm so stupid *I actually lost the book?*

Fortunately, before I even dare to speak, he says, "That's my good girl. And how is your sister doing? And your chachi? Is she settling in nicely?"

"We're all fine," I say. Liar.

"And did you have a nice Diwali?"

Huh? "Um, yeah?" I lie again. I'm not sure why.

"You don't know Diwali? The Festival of Lights?"

I twist some hair around my finger. "Not exactly, Taoji."

"Well, make your papa tell you more about it. All right? Promise?"

"Sure."

"Good. I so look forward to seeing you for Thanksgiving."

"You're coming? Really? That'll be so great." This is the truth. Taoji really cares, and he's always fun and silly, and we haven't seen him in over a year, since the last time he came to New York on business. "Is Taiji coming too?"

"Not this time, darling. This is just a quick trip. Now put your father on so I can give him my program."

So I find my dad and give him the phone, and return to my room. Nineteen days until Taoji comes. Taoji might make Thanksgiving with Chachi almost bearable. Twenty days until Hari comes. Hari and I will spend tons of time together. I picture Hari punching Jason in the nose, and Jason crying. Somewhat cheered, I shut off the computer and say good night to Orlando.

8

It's a crisp and sunny November morning. I'm riding my bike to the cemetery to meet Gina, like I do every Saturday, for our run/ride (she runs, I ride). Even though Gina is totally grounded, I know she'll be there. Mrs. Baldarasi believes that exercise is essential for teens, making them less hyper and less obnoxious.

I zoom past Fonthill. That's a castle built in Doylestown in 1912 by this rich guy, Henry Mercer. It's a museum now, but seeing it all set back on its massive lawn, with morning dew sparkling in the grass and a bit of fog lingering in the hollows beside it, I can imagine someone still lives there. And not some rich crusty old geezer either. I can imagine Orlando inside, throwing open the top windows and gazing across the grass and seeing, well, me.

Oof! The speed bump in the road catches me by surprise, but I pedal on. I find Gina stretching her quads beside the Elmer family mausoleum. Before I even come to a full stop, she grabs my arms. "You're alive," she says. "You okay?"

See? That's what best friends are all about. Here I thought I'd have to go through all this painful explanation of my misery and humiliation, but Gina just takes one look at me and she *knows*.

"Thank God. I thought I'd never see you again," she says.

I set down my bike and nod, suddenly feeling very brave. Some girls might have stayed in bed, refusing food, but here I am, out in the world.

"Who was worse?" Gina says, rolling up the sleeves of her huge white hoodie.

I puzzle over this for a moment. Gina did blow it with the room non-cleaning thing, but she's here now, supporting me. But Jason—God! "He was, Gina. Of course."

"I knew it. Did he pull all that 'When I was a boy I would have never done such a thing to my parents'?" She says this while rolling her shoulders, then her neck. It's all a part of her warm-up stretch, but looks like she's doing the Chicken Dance.

Her words sink in. "Huh?"

"Your dad. Guess he's going to send you to school in India now, right?"

"Why exactly would my dad be sending me to India?"

She's on the grass now, doing straddle stretches over Lucy Lindquist's tomb. "Well, your mom was certainly pissed enough. You know, when she called last night to ask my mom if she could give me a ride from the rink too, and then my mom said—"

"My mom *knew*?" My stomach sinks to my feet. "She knew and she didn't say a word?"

"The silent treatment?" Gina nods. "Guilt city."

"No, Gina. Not silent. Worse than silent." I'm pacing around Gina and Lucy Lindquist trying to make some sense out of it all. "She pretended nothing was wrong. But she kept asking me questions," I say, remembering her banter. Her 'So did you buy any snacks?' and 'Did you see anybody you knew?' And, most deviously, 'Did Gina have fun?' "Ohmygod ohmygod ohmyGOD!" I sink onto the grass.

Gina stands and straightens her sweatpants. "Sang, calm down. What's the worst that can happen?"

I imagine myself living in a female monastery in India. I'm 90 million years old and still not old enough to date. I swallow hard. "I'll just apologize."

"Now don't talk crazy. We just have to think," Gina says, and runs down the paved path lined with tombstones.

I grab my bike and follow. If anybody can figure out a way to fix this mess, it's Gina.

9

 s usual, Gina comes up with a bunch of ideas, from the lame (take what's coming to me) to the extreme. And, as always, the extreme involves a plan Gina calls "the Pretzel," which is when we empty our bank accounts, take the train to Philly, get a cheap room, and make a fortune selling pretzels to tourists. So now I'm cycling back to the house, ready to try Gina's most reasonable plan: Evasive Tactics. They can't talk to me if they can't find me, right? That could work. I'll be in the bathroom when Mom and Dad are around. I'd suggested to Gina that I can claim I have this wicked diarrhea bug. I'll bring all my magazines and maybe my homework in with me too (where the hell is my datebook-organizer???). Gina thought this whole diarrhea scheme was inspired. Actually, she seemed a little disappointed that she didn't think of it herself, but I assured her I never would have found such an ingenious solution without her guidance and inspiration.

Now I'm riding past Fonthill again. The dew's dried up and the fog's faded away, and it looks kind of broody and cementy, not nearly as romantic at all. I pull on my brakes, and my bike squeaks to a halt at the edge of the long, sweeping lawn.

Okay, I know Orlando Bloom is definitely not inside. Probably only an old lady named Myrtle is, waiting to guide visitors on a "quite fascinating" tour of the interior. I feel the whole Jason humiliation thing flooding back to drown me. But Gina said he probably mixed up the nights. That he probably was really sick, maybe even in the hospital. I imagine myself nursing him back to health. Feeding him Jell-O. Swabbing his diamond stud earring with a Q-tip. He might be dying even as I sit here. Wishing he could say some parting tender words to me. Maybe someone's called, like Jason's friend Glen—or was his name Gary? I'll get home and everyone will be like, Where were you? There's an urgent message for you! Hurry to the hospital before you lose your one true love!

I push on my pedals and ride home. As I pull up to our split-level, I see both cars in the driveway. I don't know whether to be glad about this (I'll need emotional support when they tell me about Jason, not to mention a lift to the hospital) or bummed (Evasive Tactics would be a heck of a lot easier if the parents were not home).

I park my bike in the garage and go into the house.

Tinny Indian movie music is coming from the family room. My dad must be watching the Saturday matinee Bollywood movie on Channel 35. He always makes fun of the goofy guy-gets-girl, guy-loses-girl, guy-gets-girl-again plots and the hokey dancing. But he tries to watch it every weekend. When I was little, I used to put on my red-and-gold printed *salwar kameez,* a traditional Indian outfit with a super-long shirt over baggy pants, and I'd drape the golden *chuni* scarf around my head and dance to the *chunka-chunka* beat of the Bollywood music while my dad laughed and clapped. Doodles now has the chuni. I don't know what happened to the little salwar kameez, though.

I tiptoe past the entrance to the family room, and Dad doesn't notice me at all. There's a clear path up the stairs to my bedroom. I know I should take advantage of the moment, but two things tell me otherwise. First of all, my heart. If there's a message for me about Jason, it'll be by the phone in the kitchen. Second of all, my stomach. I'm starving!

I slip off my sneakers and go into the kitchen. No note by the phone. I should be relieved he's okay, right? I frown and pull open the fridge. Behind that wall of disgusting bean-filled Tupperware is pudding. I know there's at least four left, if she didn't suck them all up already. It's amazing, really. She's always sticking her nose up in the air about how perfect her diet is, all beans and roots and crud, but if we have a box of cookies in the house, it's gone the next morning. My aunt must do midnight munchie raids or something.

I remove some Tupperware and see it. Chocolate pudding. Oh yeah. I take one, shove the beans back, and shut the fridge. I eat a few spoonfuls, but don't feel any better. I mean, Jason's not in the hospital. That could only mean one thing. He chose not to come. It was the crud on my nose, or maybe he saw the zit, or maybe once he got a close look at me, he decided I wasn't all that exotic and interesting after all.

I swallow another mouthful of pudding, wondering if I should go ahead with the diarrhea ploy. Ugh. Now the last thing I want is gloppy chocolate pudding. I shudder and drop the half-eaten container into the trash.

"EH?"

I'm busted.

Chachi rushes to the garbage and retrieves the container, holding it high. "What is this you are wasting? Who told you to invade my personal food? What have you to say? Eh?"

I wince. Why doesn't she just shout, Hey, Lena and Akash, here's Sangeet! Come and get her! "I just thought I'd try—" I begin in a whisper.

"You thought? You thought? You thought you would steal from me, eh?" She shakes the pudding, and a blob gets on her hand.

I close my mouth tight. I close it super-tight so I won't say that she is the one who takes from us all the time. Eating our food. Using our house. Taking away all the laughter and joy with her nasty face and mean ways. Hiding food from us when we have given her so much.

"Eh?" Her eyes are so black and hard. I sense rather than see her pulling her arm back. "Answer me, you—" Her arm moves forward, and I can hardly believe it. She's going to *hit* me?

"Kajal?" my mom says to my aunt. "Is something wrong?"

My heart is thudding. Forget avoidance. I step close to my mom.

Chachi's thin lips curl into a grin. She lowers the pudding and shows it to my mother. "See?" she says. "So much waste. I was just telling Sangeet not to waste."

My mother looks at me for a moment. I give her a meaningful stare back.

Chachi stares at the pudding. "What I wouldn't have done to have such a treat as this when young," she says, her voice taking on a sad, soft tone. "No sweets for Kajal. At times no breakfast or lunch. Weak tea only."

I swallow. "So you went—" I'm about to say "hungry" when Chachi's eyes flash at me with cold fury.

"Yes, I went into the kitchen to find this." She shakes the pudding at me like she'd love to throw it in my face. God, it's so clear how much she hates me.

Mom is nodding her head and giving Chachi a gentle smile. "It is a shame," my mom says.

"But, Mom, I didn't . . ." Well, I did throw out the pudding, but that's not the point. "She was going to . . ."

I want to tell my mom about the slap I almost got, but she's giving me an odd look. Does she think I'm going to lie? Again? I'm speechless, and there's a triumphant glimmer in Chachi's eyes. I can't bear it. I clench my fists and run to my room. I'm smoldering. I sit on my bed and stare at nothing.

It's not long before my mom is in my room, looking all annoyed. "You know, it wouldn't kill you to be a bit more polite to your chachi."

"AAARRGH!" I flop onto my back. Orlando looks like he wants to help. I bet one of those Elvish arrows would do the trick.

"I know this is difficult," Mom says. "And that it's hard for you to understand how she is. Think of it this way: Your childhood has been easy because you've always had everything you need. But things weren't always easy for Chachi. She didn't start off poor, but when she was a child, a relative stole from the family business and ruined them."

I sit up. "Really?" So maybe stealing is part of some family tradition. Generations of thieves, hundreds of years ago, sneaking around by torchlight, pocketing gold coins and *pakora*s. It's kind of funny in a ridiculous way.

"Yes, they struggled for years for the most basic comforts."

Oh. Not so funny. I sigh.

"Now she needs our caring," Mom says. "She's all alone in the world."

Because she's horrible. Does thinking this make *me*

horrible? I mean, if Chachi weren't such a nightmare, then I would feel sorry for her. Really. But . . . "Does she have to live here?"

"Sang, we've been over and over this. You know the rest of her relatives are back in India. She wasn't in this country for long before your uncle died, and she never really got used to life in America. It was okay when your cousin Raj was still around to help her manage, but now, with him at college—well, imagine how she must feel. Her son's away, her husband's dead."

Talk about laying on the guilt. Sure, my uncle passed away and it was sad and all, but that was like a zillion years ago. Anyway, probably he stole her pudding and she slit his throat. I swallow hard. Chachi was going to hit me. "Mom, there's something you should know."

Mom tucks her hair behind her ears as if this will make her hear what I have to say better. I realize she's expecting me to make a full confession about last night. Only I'm not exactly ready to give it, and anyway, it's not my fault their rules are so screwed up. And where does she get off yelling at me for being rude to Chachi? To Chachi, the rudest person on the planet? How screwed up is that?

I pick up my new copy of *Teen Ink* magazine and rush past her. "Diarrhea" is all I say before locking myself in the bathroom for a long, long read.

10

*a*fter a weekend mostly spent hiding in the bath-room with some novels, I'm back in school. I am standing by my locker, shoving my coat in as quickly as possible, hoping I don't see *him*. I pull out my history textbook and my notebook. I slam my locker shut and turn face-first into a poster board.

"What d'ya think? Will Fish Face give stupid me a B?" Gina's holding up a project about the guns of the Revolutionary War. It's the visual for a presentation we all need to make sometime after Thanksgiving. My topic is Molly Pitcher. Whoopee.

I give Gina's poster a scan. It's not too bad, aside from a few typos and a pool of glue on the bottom corner. "You're not stupid, and it looks good. What are you doing? Actually working ahead?"

"Thought I'd at least get it in on time for once." Mrs. Finelli, aka "Fish Face," marks assignments down an entire grade for each day they are late. Gina once got an F minus. "Where's yours?"

I freeze. "Mine? The visual's due today?" I move to find my little datebook, but of course it's still lost. "Crap!"

Gina nudges me with her elbow. "Hey, Jason," she says.

This time I believe her. I feel him hovering behind me, and all I can do is wipe my nose just in case and turn slowly around.

"See ya in History, Sang," Gina says, and before I can grab her arm, she's gone.

So I look up at Jason. Not a zit in sight, and he's got this all-knowing smirk on his face that makes the bones in my legs get all rubbery. "S'up?" he says, all cool and hip.

"Nothing," I say, and shrug, trying to be equally cool and hip but feeling all sweaty and dorky.

"Did you go Friday? I didn't."

Whoa. What's up with this? Maybe he didn't think it was a date at all, maybe he thought it was just some take-it-or-leave-it event with lots of people going. Or is he mocking me? He's smiling, but not in a mocking way. And he's resting an elbow on the locker just by my head. It's a pose I've seen a zillion times before beside Sara Harding's locker. Some hunky football-player type, wearing his hunky football-player jersey, would rest his elbow against the locker just before he would lean down and start sucking face with her. What a slut. But then, she sucks face with a wide assortment of guys, and I wouldn't be sucking face, I'd be kissing, and just with Jason.

"Sang?"

I blink. Earth to Sang. My cheeks burn. "Yeah. I'm okay." I'm FABULOUS, in fact. He's still here. Still pretty close.

"So?"

"So," I croak. He's actually asking permission to kiss me. Permission totally granted, I think, and tilt my chin toward him.

"So did you go skating?"

"Oh," I say. I drop my chin and clear my throat. "No, no I didn't. I—I was busy."

This is obviously the right answer, because he nods his head and keeps staring at me. I give him my dimpled smile. I can feel the bell about to ring, but if it would just wait a few extra seconds, Jason will surely lean closer and . . . I tilt my chin up toward him again. Just a few more seconds . . . My heart is pounding. Our eyes lock. I can practically feel the warmth of his body coming closer. Just a second more and he'll—

"Hey, Sang." It's Dalton. He nods at me and his glasses slip down his nose.

"Oh, hey," I say in a breathless voice. I give a wave, hoping he'll just move on by, but he doesn't. He seems determined to speak with me, wrecking this whole intimate locker scene Jason and I have got going. Sure enough,

Jason takes his elbow off the locker. No! I could just *kill* Dalton.

"That was great the other—"

"Dalton!" I give him a poke. He looks stunned, but I can't worry about that. I mean, Dalton almost told Jason I was at the rink. That would make me not just a loser but a lying loser. "You'll be late for class," I say, and open my eyes wide. Get the hint, dude, I think.

He does get the hint, and to tell you the truth, he looks kind of hurt as he walks away.

"I'd better go," Jason says, and winks at me before he heads toward his own class. Yes!

I wave and collapse against my locker. The bell rings, and, in seconds, classroom doors slam shut and I'm the only one left in the hall, but I don't care. I don't care about anything but Jason.

11

I'm determined to not let anything sink the cloud I'm floating on. Not even when, in History, Fish Face gives me a stern warning about being late to class, then collects the Revolutionary War visuals and asks me twice where mine is. Later, while I'm helping Franny Withers with some Jefferson notes she missed because she was out sick, Fish Face calls me up to her desk. I notice Dalton watching me.

Fish Face's eyes look particularly fishy behind her thick glasses. "Sangeet," she says in a voice just above a whisper, "is there something wrong?"

I'm trying to find a subtle way to explain to my teacher that I had the runs. After all, this lie did work with my parents.

"Something wrong at home, perhaps?" she adds.

I think of my aunt, of my mom catching me in a lie, of that horrible dating rule. . . . "No. Not really. Why?"

Mrs. Finelli flips open her grade book. "Well, when a top student goes from straight A's at the midterm report to a C average, and then forgets an assignment that will bring her grade to—"

"Mrs. Finelli, excuse me," I say. "I thought I heard you say I have a C average."

"Well, yes. And this poster could have brought your grade at least to a B minus."

There's a wailing sound in my head. Something like *AAAAAAAAAAAAAAAH!!!* How could this happen? Sure, I did miss a few summary assignments and bombed that quiz last week. Maybe my game has been a bit off, but a C???? My parents are convinced I'm Ivy League genius material. My uncle is convinced I'm a Rhodes scholar. Ivy League geniuses and Rhodes scholars do NOT get C report cards. "Mrs. Finelli, I've never gotten a C. I haven't even gotten a B since like seventh grade. I was sick over the weekend. I'll hand the poster in tomorrow."

She takes off her glasses and sets them on her grade book. Now she looks less like a fish and more like a kindly grandmother. "I'm sorry you were ill, Sangeet, but your poster project was assigned two weeks ago. I have to mark it down a grade for every day it's late. Any other way wouldn't be fair to others in the class who have worked so hard to get things in on time."

I glance at Gina. "Okay, I'll turn in the poster tomorrow, then. But, Mrs. Finelli, I really have to get that A. If

I ace next week's quiz and then the end-of-section test, could I still have a chance?"

"Hmm." Mrs. Finelli taps her glasses on the desk. "There is a group extra-credit project you could join."

"Come on, Sang," Gina says. "It'll be fun."

We're on the bus riding home, and Gina's ecstatic because if she does well with the extra-credit project, she has a chance to bring her grade up maybe to a B, something she rarely achieves. It's not that she isn't bright. I mean, she did get into Honors History. But she's just not that into following things through. I'm happy for Gina, but I still can't help but feel sorry for myself. I feel like my entire academic career is unraveling before my eyes. And it isn't just History. I bombed today's pop math quiz. What's up with that? "I just wish we got to pick who was in our extra-credit group," I say, and dart a glance at slutty Sara Harding, who is several seats ahead of us and leaning over Tommy McCoy, whose eyes are riveted on her cleavage. "How did she get into Honors History, anyway?"

"She had that young-guy teacher last year," Gina says. "Instant A's."

"Ugh. This is going to be horrible."

"Oh, forget about her. The others in the group aren't too bad."

She's right. In addition to my very best friend in

the whole world, there's Megan Chung, and Dalton's in the group too. Actually, I'm kind of surprised Dalton is doing extra credit. He's usually Mr. Straight A. But then again, I'm doing it. . . .

"Anyhow," Gina says, "it'll be a breeze."

I roll my eyes. "I hardly think a forty-five minute presentation on the sixties and seventies will be a breeze." We have to meet at the library tomorrow to divide up the work. I bet Slutty Sara doesn't even show up. "And why the sixties and seventies? Why not the Revolutionary War? It's what we're studying, and we've got tons of crap on that. It just doesn't make sense."

"Maybe she wants us to show a more modern revolution. Whatever. But it'll be easy. I mean, just think." She taps her temple. "When did our parents grow up and go to school? In the sixties and seventies. And what do parents love to do more than anything else in the world?"

"Torture us."

Gina grimaces. "Okay, the second thing they love to do, then. Talk about the good old days. So the way I see it, we ask a few questions and before you know it we've got firsthand accounts of what it was like to grow up then—what the music was like, the clothes. . . ."

"You're brilliant," I say.

"Yeah, right," she says. "So just nose about your parents' old stuff—you know, their music, scrapbooks, that kind of thing—and ask them a few questions."

"Hmm." I cross my arms. "If they'll even talk to me."

"Ohmygod." She grabs my arm. "I just had the best

idea. We can do a sixties-and-seventies fashion show. You know, platform shoes and miniskirts. That kind of thing. I think my mom still has a pair of fluorescent hot pants somewhere in her closet."

Gina and I look at each other. The thought of huge-hipped Mrs. Baldarasi in hot pants is simply too much. We explode with laughter.

12

olly Pitcher gave water to the soldiers and then, when her husband was hurt, she took over firing his cannon. That's what my poster is going to say, anyway. So I'm printing out Internet pictures of cannons, water jugs, and women in Colonial dress. I'm cutting and pasting text onto construction-paper backings and decorating the whole poster with red, white, and blue marker. Shreds of paper are everywhere, and my hands are sticky with glue, and this is taking forever but it has to be perfect because I absolutely have to get an A on it, which will actually make it a B for being one day late.

Doodles is in the room with me, coloring and gluing paper onto her own poster board because she's so young she doesn't have enough homework of her own and actually wants to be doing junk like this! "Sang, tell me more of the story."

"I can't. I'm really, really busy." I'm cutting out a map that shows where the Battle of Monmouth took place.

"Please, Sissy?"

I snip off more than I intend to, and growl in frustration. Back at the computer, I've got to find and print out the stupid map again.

"Sissy?"

"Not *now*!"

Doodles stomps out, which is fine by me. I start typing, when *bloop!* An IM pops up.

IMonFIREtwo: hey

I stare at the screen, my heart pulsing faster than the cursor. Jason's on!

SINGSANGSUNG: hey
IMonFIREtwo: sup?
SINGSANGSUNG: just workin
SINGSANGSUNG: u?
IMonFIREtwo: listenin to music
IMonFIREtwo: turn on Q102
SINGSANGSUNG: k

I leap to my radio and tune to the station. Someone is screaming out a song. Something about "Can't stand me. Hate me. Hate me." It's like some kind of tantrum.

IMonFIREtwo: cool?
SINGSANGSUNG: yeah
IMonFIREtwo: my fav group

The singer is shrieking about how much he smells. Now someone else is shrieking. It's my dad.

"Sangeet! Turn off that noise pollution."

I shut off the radio. "Sorry, Dad."

"Your sister is going to bed now, so no noise, right? And she is waiting for you to tell her more of your special story."

I glance at the computer screen. "But, Dad, I'm really busy."

"Make it a short story, then. You should always make time for your baby sister." That's what he used to tell my brother when I was younger. Hari was a terrible storyteller, but he could always sing beautifully. And his songs weren't about hate and bad smells, they were about rainbows and sunsets. Of course, that was when I was like ten. More recently, when he'd be up in his room and strumming his guitar and humming along, I'd just sit in my own room and listen. It was nice, you know?

I'm about to insist that there's no way I can make time for a story tonight, but I don't want to get Dad angry. For some reason, he and Mom still haven't punished me for that whole skating thing, so I don't want to push my luck. "Tell Doodles I'll be there in a few minutes."

"That's a good girl," my dad says. "And clean your room. It looks like a trash bin."

Back to Jason.

SINGSANGSUNG: wat group?
IMonFIREtwo: Stinkin Monkeys
IMonFIREtwo: we should see them sometime

Ohmygod. He's asking me out on a date for real this time! I want to type, *That will be nice.* No. Sounds nerdy. *I'd love to?* Too desperate. *I love you?* Please.

SINGSANGSUNG: cool

I hold my breath waiting for the details. The cursor blinks, but nothing happens. Maybe he's blown away that I said yes. Or maybe he's getting some details. Or maybe he's so happy, he doesn't know what to say.

"Sissy!" Doodles calls.

"Just a minute." But a minute passes, and nothing happens on the screen. Where is he? I bite my pinkie nail. Maybe I sounded too eager. Maybe he didn't mean it like a date, just like a suggestion. You know, like *everybody* should go and see the Stinkin' Monkeys. Maybe he's not really interested in me in that way at all and I'm just making it all up. Anyway, what was I thinking? If he really asked me to a concert, I'd have to tell him I can't go to concerts (my parents have just started to let me go to the mall with my friends) and, worst of all, I can't go out with him anywhere.

Might as well face it. Jason is gone. I sigh and start to walk out of my room when *bloop!* I race back.

OUTOVCNTRL8: meet at library 2morrow @ 7

Wow, I think. Now that I can do. I imagine Jason and me holding hands in the quiet area just beside the romance and mystery novels. I'm about to reply when I notice this is definitely not Jason.

SINGSANGSUNG: who's this?
OUTOVCNTRL8: Dalton
OUTOVCNTRL8: sry

Frustration wells in me. Not that Dalton isn't nice, and not that we didn't have some fun at the rink, but he pretty much busted up Jason's and my moment at the lockers, and now he's butting in, asking me to come to the library. Well, actually, that's kind of sweet, but he should know I'm not interested in him in that kind of a way. I'm thinking about how to let him down easy when . . .

OUTOVCNTRL8: bring any stuff u got
OUTOVCNTRL8: u no, old records
OUTOVCNTRL8: yearbooks
OUTOVCNTRL8: stuff like that

Oh. He means for the extra-credit project.

SINGSANGSUNG: k

I wait a moment, but there's nothing more from Jason or Dalton.

"So Rani must walk to the palace, but the journey will take her years and years, even though for most people it's only a few days' walk."

"Why?" Doodles looks up at me from where she's snuggling, in the crook of my arm.

"Because there is a powerful curse on her."

"From a witch?"

"I don't know if they have witches in India." I think of Chachi. "Maybe they do. But let's say the curse was cast by a wicked genie. Because of this curse, Rani cannot reach her love for at least nine more years."

"Why?"

"Well, the genie thought Rani wasn't old enough to date her love, even though she obviously was."

Doodles frowns at this. "Date? I thought they were going to get married."

"Whatever." I wave my hand. "So poor Rani began her long, hot walk across the hot, parched desert of Rajasthan. By the end of the first day, she was staggering from the heat, and so, so thirsty. When she was about to collapse, she came upon the most extraordinary thing. A stinking monkey."

Doodles bursts into laughter.

"I know," I say. "Rani laughed too. 'A stinking monkey,' she said. 'What can you do for me?' 'Well,' said the monkey, 'if you can stand to sit by me for one evening, I will speed you on your way to your one true love.' "

"So the monkey talks?"

"And stinks," I say. "So Rani agreed, and sat beside the monkey for three long, smelly hours. Her eyes watered from the stench. She breathed through the fabric of her snowy-white chuni to filter the air, but still, that monkey really stank. But in the end it was worth it, because the monkey waved its filthy paw toward the east. 'Go this way, Rani, and you will reach your love in only eight years.' "

"But I thought this was a powerful curse. How can a monkey change it?"

"Hey, anything's possible." I stand. "Good night." I tweak her nose and click off the lamp on her night table.

When I reach her door, she says, "Sang, do you really believe that anything's possible? Not just in stories?"

I think about the way Jason looked at me by the lockers. "Sure," I say. "Why not?"

13

I've finished my poster, finally, and spent what seemed like just as long cleaning up all the scraps of construction paper and empty glue sticks. I decide to do a quick search for stuff for my extra-credit project, and I step out of my room. The light is off in my parents' bedroom. I glance at my watch: 11:05.

In fact, the house is completely dark except for a band of light coming from under Chachi's door, upstairs. I don't think she ever sleeps. It's like she's a vampire or something.

I close my door most of the way so my light doesn't disturb my parents and make my way downstairs to the family room, where I click on a lamp. I pull out the really ratty photo album, the one from Mom's high school days. I flip through it and chuckle. Mom doesn't look that different, but her hair is super-long and just hanging around her face. And what's with all the turtlenecks? And the plaid shirts? Dork City. I turn a few pages. There's a guy with brown hair, near a car. On the next page, Mom is with another guy—this one has a black 'fro, and it looks like they're going to the prom. After a few pages, it's Mom with yet another guy, and it looks like they're going to another prom because now her gown is blue and she has flowers in her hair. Now she's skiing with another guy. This one looks hunky, with blond hair and blue eyes. What's this? A third prom? Her dress is purple and it has a slit that goes way up, and this guy has light brown curly hair and glasses. I close the album. So, like, how many guys did Mom date, anyway? There's no sign of Dad, because they didn't meet until college and this album only goes through high school. But how far *back* do the pictures in her album go? This gets me thinking.

I dive into the cabinet again, pushing aside albums till I find the stack of my mother's yearbooks way in the back. I open my mother's middle school yearbook and I'm staring at a picture of her from when she was an eighth grader. The year was 1976, and she's wearing this hideous plaid shirt with a giant collar, but still, she does look a lot like me. Or rather, I look a lot like her. Of course there's no Indian in her, so her eyes are lighter and her lashes don't have that permanently mascaraed look mine have. Her skin's a bit lighter (her grandparents were from Italy), and although she's smiling, she doesn't have my dimple, but otherwise . . . For the first time I can kind of imagine my mother being my age, having my worries.

Maybe she *does* understand why I lied. Maybe she *will* just drop it.

I start reading what kids wrote to my mom. There's the typical "You're a great kid" and "Have a great summer" stuff, but there's also stuff about some guy named Bill. *Hey, Lena, good luck with Bill,* someone named Cathy wrote. A kid named Pete scrawled, *You and Bill will be giving out cigars in nine months.* Whoa. This Pete must have been a real jerk. Another *Good luck with Bill.* But wait. Someone named Mike wrote, *Hope you make it with Alan!* Another says, *Lena, good luck with* him. Him? Who, him? Bill? Alan? I turn the pages, looking for some explanation, and on a page near the clubs I find a long entry from Bill. God, he was crazy about my mom, going on and on about how much he loves her and how much she means to him and how he'll see her all summer long. Next to this, someone else wrote:

Billy + Lena
2 B
+ 2 Gether
4 Ever

I close the book, stunned. I have learned something very important tonight. Mom was as young as thirteen and dating at least one, maybe two, boys. I try to imagine Jason writing things like that in my yearbook, but somehow I just can't picture it. I drum my fingers on the book. Surely I can use this information to change my own situation. I'll reason with Mom that, hey, she dated when she was thirteen, so shouldn't I date at fifteen? That's the best argument so far. Maybe she just forgot about it because it was so long ago, but when I remind her, I'm sure she'll be willing to convince Dad to let me do the same. Of course, I do have to work out that whole ice-skating-rink mess with her first, but I'm not too worried. Seriously. I can just feel that things are going to work out.

I grab the photo album and the yearbook to bring to the library tomorrow, and flick off the light. Damn. I've forgotten the rest of the lights are out in the house, except for the light in my room, and my door's mostly closed. I feel my way up the stairs, onto the main level, and that's when I notice a glow coming down the steps that lead up to the bedrooms.

It's Chachi, with a flashlight. I hold my breath and shrink back down the steps to the family room. Maybe she's coming downstairs to sneak some food. Mom just bought a bag of chocolate chip cookies. I'll bet anything they'll be gone in the morning. I don't want her to see me, yet I can't help but peer up the steps. I imagine how ridiculous she'll look sneaking back upstairs with the cookies. I play with the idea of springing out at her when she does so and crying, "Aha!" Even though I know I won't dare, I'm so amused that I bite my lip to keep from chuckling.

But what's this? She isn't heading toward the kitchen at all. Instead, she is by the living room couch, fiddling with something. I squint my eyes. I can hardly believe what I'm seeing.

Chachi has pulled the wallet from my mother's purse. She's poking her long bony fingers into the wallet and pulling out bills. She studies the bills under the light, selects a few, which she tucks into the waist of her pajamas, and stuffs the rest back in. Then she tosses the wallet into the purse and places the purse back beside the couch.

The beams from her flashlight skim over me as she turns. I hold my breath till she heads back upstairs. Hugging the album and yearbook tight against my chest, I think, Okay, make that *two* important things I've learned tonight.

14

I shut my locker before taking out my stuff. I just can't concentrate—it's like my mind is jumping all over the place. I mean, catching Chachi stealing. She'll definitely get booted out. There's no way my parents will put up with that. And when I remind Mom that she dated when she was younger than me, well, she'll surely talk to Dad, and then . . .

I pull open my locker (again) and glance left and right. If I don't see Jason now, I won't see him all day, except maybe in the cafeteria. What if he sits with me at lunch? Ohmygod. I'd better not buy a fish sandwich or anything else smelly. Now I wonder about my breath. I cover my mouth and exhale into my hand, then sniff my palm, but all I smell is hand soap. Why don't I ever carry mints? I pull out my rolled-up history poster and books and slam my locker shut.

"Look!"

I jump. You'd think I'd be used to Gina springing at me by now. She's holding up what at first look seems like a red washcloth.

Gina gives it a shake. "These are them. My mom's hot pants."

"No way," I say, and take them from her, also giving them a shake, expecting them to unfold or something. But no. They're microscopic. "Your mom used to wear these things?" Nothing against Mrs. Baldarasi, but one of her thighs is as big as my entire waist.

"I know. They fit *me*." Gina takes the hot pants back. "She was *my* size." She picks at her braces and stares off into space.

"That's great. Then you can wear them for the fashion show."

"No, it's not great, Sang. Don't you get it? She was *my* size." Gina stares at the hot pants. "*My size.* And someday *I'm* gonna be *her size.*"

"Oh, you are not. Gina, you are not your mom. You're totally different. For starters, you run. When's the last time your mom went for a run?"

I expect her to giggle at this, but she just nods.

"Hey, you okay?"

"Yeah. Yeah, I'm fine," she says, though she doesn't exactly look fine. She looks distracted, and kind of pale. I decide telling her about my discoveries will have to wait.

o   o   o

At lunch, Gina sits in front of this great meatball sub she brought from home, but doesn't eat a bite of it. And when she pulls from her lunch bag a pack of Ho Hos, which is one of her very favorite snacks, she holds it up and says, "Any takers?"

Now I know she's not well. "I don't have to come over," I say, "if you're not up to it." Even though she's still grounded, when Mrs. Baldarasi heard I'm helping with an extra-credit project that might bring Gina's grade up, well, I was immediately extended a dinner invitation as well as a lift to the library afterward.

"You kidding?" Gina stuffs her sub back into her bag. "You have to come."

She's right. I really need her help.

15

'm pacing up and down my bedroom. I had planned to talk with Gina first. Get some of her sage advice before I talked to Mom. But now I don't know. I mean, Mom's downstairs, Doodles is over at a neighbor's house, Chachi's locked in her room, and it's a perfect time to let everything out. It's no big deal, right? Problem is, how do I talk about the dating issue without telling her the truth about last weekend? And how will she believe what I have to say about Chachi if she already thinks I'm a liar? And how do I tell my mom that I'm a liar? I bite my pinkie nail and tell myself that this is the least of my problems, because really, she already knows I'm a liar. Okay, okay. Just do it, I tell myself, and set my feet toward my door.

Mom's in the family room, folding towels and placing them neatly in a stack in a white plastic laundry basket.

"Mom, we have to talk."

"Oh." She drops the towel she was holding and tucks her hair behind her ears.

"Well," I say. "You see," I say. I lied about the skating, I think. "It's Chachi," I say. "You know how she hides treats in the fridge? And how all the cookies and snacks keep disappearing? Well, I think—"

Mom holds up her hand. "Sang, before you say another word, your chachi's told me everything."

"She has?" Now I'm the one tucking my hair behind my ears.

"And quite frankly, Sang, I'm very concerned about you."

"About me?"

"The way you've been eating up all the desserts. You aren't, well . . ." Mom grabs my jaw and examines my teeth.

I pull away. "What? Flossing?" I give a laugh, but Mom looks dead serious.

"Sweetheart, if we've been pressuring you too much to be perfect, I want you to know your father and I never meant to be so hard on you. We know you are smart, that's all, and we just want the very best . . ." Mom's actually crying!

"Mom? Mom! I don't know what kind of lies Chachi has been telling you, but—"

"Lying is one of the symptoms." She dabs her eyes with a towel, takes a brochure from behind the television, and hands it to me. It says *Does Your Teen Have Bulimia? Here are some telltale signs. . . .*

"Chachi has bulimia?" I say.

"Sang," she says, and sighs. She pulls me over to the love seat and sits next to me. She takes my hand and presses it with her chilly fingers. "We'll get you help. Anything you need."

"Me?" I pull my hand away. "You think *I* have bulimia? You're crazy."

She pats my knee. "No one is crazy," she says pointedly.

"Chachi told you I have bulimia?"

"She's told me about all the food you've been taking. How you've been sneaking around. It wasn't hard to draw conclusions."

Me taking food? *Me* sneaking around? That's *it.* "She steals, you know. Just last night I saw——"

"Don't lie. No more lies." Her voice is a terrible whisper. "She told me you are taking food. All this food is disappearing, and you look thinner and thinner. And all that time you spent in the bathroom this past weekend." She grabs my arm. "But we'll get you help. I've spoken with Dr. Chung, and——"

"You told Megan's parents?" Megan's mom and dad run the Chung and Chung Clinic.

"Not both of them, just her mother. Don't worry, Dr. Chung won't breathe a word of it to anyone."

I gulp and think about the zillions of times Megan has entertained me with tales of the strange things her parents' nutty patients have done and said.

"You know the Chungs are excellent counselors and

they see this type of thing all the time. Dr. Chung recommended I first consult your pediatrician, so I popped into the office this morning and made an appointment with Dr. Dander for tomorrow, after school. He gave me this brochure, and it explains how lots of girls your age get bulimia, and how it's—"

"Mom, I *don't* have bulimia."

"Oh, sweetheart." Mom rests her hand on my shoulder. "It's nothing to be ashamed of."

"Mom, it's not me stealing the food. It's Chachi. It has to be. She steals. I saw her."

My mother shakes her head. "We have to be honest with each other."

"Don't you see? That's exactly what I'm trying to do. Chachi is the one stealing."

"You can't blame others for your problems. It doesn't help."

"I'm telling the truth. I'm no liar."

She stares at me, and I feel cornered. I think about closing my mouth tight. Disappearing into my room. But I can't. I raise my chin. "Okay. I lied about Friday night."

"Aha!" she says, then clamps her mouth shut. Then she says, "I'm sorry. Dr. Chung said we shouldn't push that issue right now. We don't want to aggravate the situation at this time."

So *that's* why they haven't punished me yet.

Mom wrings her hands and says, "According to Dr.

Chung, we need to understand the 'why' behind all the lies."

"But that's all I've lied about, Mom, I swear. You have to believe me." Suddenly I'm telling her all about Jason and how perfect he is, and how I actually think he might like me. Me! And how I wanted to tell her about trying to meet him at the rink, but how she and Dad were so rigid about me not dating and how they wouldn't ever understand. Finally, I tell her, "I was stood up, Mom."

I expect lots of sympathy and a warm hug, but Mom bites her lip and then says, "That must have been terribly upsetting. Still, there have to be other ways to deal with these feelings, instead of spending all weekend in the bathroom, doing"—she takes the brochure and reads page two—"bingeing and purging." She gives me her most worried look. "We can talk about things. We used to talk. Maybe, with the help of a counselor . . ."

"We're talking now. So listen. On Sunday I was in the bathroom, reading, to avoid you. Because I knew you knew I'd lied and I couldn't face you."

"You were reading?"

"*Dinner at the Homesick Restaurant.* It's a really good book."

"Oh, Sang." Mom squeezes my hand. "I want to believe you."

"Then believe me."

There's a long pause. Mom looks deeply into my eyes as if trying to see what I'm really thinking.

16

How I wish I were a Baldarasi, I think as I sit at their dinner table. Which of the three daughters would I choose to be? Michelle, a student at the community college, always has an "I know what I'm talking about" confidence in her voice, and she has all this freedom. She gets to drive, works in town at the coffee shop, and is always threatening to pierce her nipples (her nose already sports a ring). Pretty cool. Angela, a senior, is a bit prissy, but she's this great ballet dancer (I've been to a few of her recitals with Gina) and she has this long, elegant neck. I can totally picture her in a ball gown, dancing with some prince. Gina has a bit of both sisters. She's got Michelle's "I know what I'm talking about" confidence and a dash of Angela's style. Seriously, Gina can pull off any outfit. Too bad she's too short to be a model. And she's so lucky. She gets to live in this house full of chaos, full of clothes to borrow and phones ringing and boyfriends picking up sisters for dates and doors slamming and laughter and teasing and talking talking talking.

"What time is your library meeting?" Mrs. Baldarasi asks. Although the rest of us and Mr. Baldarasi are at the dining room table, she's still in the kitchen hovering over the stove, her plump arms working fast as she stirs and seasons and sautés. The kitchen is like something alive. Pots are steaming and hissing, eggplant slices are sizzling in a fry pan, alarms are going off (the smoke alarm alternating with the oven timer). This is proof positive that Thanksgiving is just two weeks away. At my house, you just don't feel it coming. My mom isn't much of a cook. She says she comes from a long line of women, including my aunt and my grandmother in Seattle, who can't even figure out the recipe for boiled water. And because my dad never had Thanksgiving growing up in India (duh), it's not such a big deal for us. Mom usually opts for the pre-made Thanksgiving feast from the supermarket. Warm for twenty minutes in a 350-degree oven and it's done.

"We have to be there at seven," Gina says.

Her mom peers into the oven. "Okay. I should be able to drive you by then."

"Sang, your brother home yet?" Michelle asks.

"He'll be home Thanksgiving morning."

"I bet you can't wait," Angela says.

"I bet I can't wait," Michelle says, twiddling her nose ring with her pinkie and grinning.

Angela shakes her head. "Michelle, we all know you think Hari's hot, but you're making Sang uncomfortable."

"Well, Hari makes *me* uncomfortable." Michelle fans herself with a napkin.

"Ignore them, Sang," Gina says.

"Yes," Mr. Baldarasi says in his eternally patient voice. "That always works for me."

I love this place.

After dinner, Gina and I are in her room. She's sifting through the junk on her floor, trying to find the clothes she'd gathered for the extra-credit project. I'm on her computer, Googling "bulimia." I get 3,080,000 results. Great. I tell Gina about my conversation with my mom. "So now she thinks I'm the one eating all the snacks and she's convinced I'm bulimic."

"You're *joking.*"

"I wish. And tomorrow I'm supposed to go to the doctor for it."

"Seriously? That *sucks.*" She kicks at a pile of fresh laundry, making it tumble. "Don't go."

"How can I not go?"

"Easy. Say you've got detention and stay after school. Or say you've got a big test and have to study. Or say you're sick. Wait. Forget that one. Just don't go."

"Easier said than done."

"You could always pull a Pretzel."

"Yeah, right."

"Just a suggestion," Gina says as she stuffs a pair of platform shoes into a bag.

I scan a Web site and learn that bulimics can look

perfectly normal. They often deny their disorder. Disproving I'm bulimic is going to be tricky.

I read some more, and guess what? I'm the perfect bulimic. According to this site, "bulimics tend to be high achievers. The causes are low self-esteem, feelings of helplessness, and fear of becoming overweight." Crap. That's me. Then again, that's just about every single girl I know.

"Oh, and you'll love this," I say, and turn to Gina. "Guess what I caught my aunt doing?"

While I'm telling her about seeing Chachi steal, Gina picks up her mom's old hot pants, holds them to her waist, and stares at herself in the full-length mirror attached to her closet door. When I'm done, she says, "Mmm."

"So what should I do?"

Gina's silent, but she's rubbing her chin and I can almost hear the wheels turning in her mind as she thinks this over. I mean, this is a complex problem. How does one bring this up? Confront the criminal? Involve the police? I imagine Chachi spread-eagled against a cop car, cursing in Punjabi.

Gina drops the hot pants and steps closer to the mirror. She's really staring at herself, which is kind of freaky when you consider she's not the kind of girl to primp and preen. She's more of the run-her-fingers-through-her-hair-and-go type. Now she's pursing her lips. It's like she's going to kiss herself. "Okay," she says, "let me ask you something."

"What?" I straighten up. I'm ready for her very best advice.

"Do you think this shirt makes me look fat?"

17

’m staring at the pile of sixties and seventies memorabilia on the library table and wondering, Why would Mom get so crazy about me looking at her yearbook? I mean, it wasn't exactly locked away, and she never said not to read it.

"Hel-looo?" snooty, slutty Sara Harding says. "Are you going to put it out or not?"

I find not only Sara staring at me but also Megan Chung, Dalton, and Gina. We're all sitting at a round wooden table in the children's section of the public library. It's nice and quiet because all the noisy little kids who normally are here by day are probably in bed by now. The table is littered with old newspapers and yearbooks and photo albums and an odd assortment of hippie clothing.

"Sorry," I say, and shrug. "I forgot to bring anything." Actually, I decided to forget about bringing Mom's yearbook and pictures because, considering how freaked she got when she found out I saw them, I couldn't imagine her being too pleased about anybody else seeing them.

"That's just great," Sara says, and adjusts her boobs so they look perky in her low-cut shirt.

Dalton's face flushes, and he clears his throat. "Well, that's okay, Sang. You can bring some stuff next time. Now what d'you say we divide up the work?"

Gina's hand shoots up. "I'm in charge of the fashion show."

Dalton starts to write this down when Sara says, "No way. I'm totally doing the fashion segment. It's my thing, you know." She glances down at her cleavage as if it is proof of her abilities.

"I brought all the clothes," Gina says, hands on hips.

"I'll look better in them," Sara says. "Right, Dalton?"

"Oh," Dalton says, flushing an even deeper shade of red. "Well, actually . . ." He swallows.

"Let's not spread bad feelings," says Megan Chung, ever the sensitive daughter of two therapists. "I'm sure Dalton thinks I am all equally attractive. I mean, *we*! We are all equally attractive. I mean, he thinks so. I mean— oh hell." Megan hides her face in her hands.

Dalton looks at me. His eyes say, Help!

"Maybe," I say, "we should all wear costumes?"

"Ooh." Megan lowers her hands and grabs a minidress. "Would anyone mind if I wore this?" Her large harp-seal eyes rest on me. Do I see pity in them? Does she know about all the bulimia bull?

"Hey, I wanted that dress," Sara says.

Dalton sets his pen down. "You know, I don't think we'll get very good grades for a fashion show."

We all consider this for a moment. "But what if we just wear the costumes during the whole presentation?" Gina's rubbing her chin. "And we can play disco music and burn incense, and I'm sure we have a lava lamp somewhere. Oh, and Dalton, you can wear this." She rummages through the clothing and pulls out a psychedelic tie-dye shirt with long sleeves, which she holds up to his shoulders.

"Oh," Dalton says. "I don't know."

"Wait," Gina says, digging deeper. "And these." She takes out a giant smiley-face necklace and the most hideous brown pair of platform shoes ever made.

Dalton is aghast. "No way!"

"Well, no one should force Dalton if he doesn't want to," Megan says. "Unless you want to be forced, Dalton." Her eyes grow really large. "Oh, that sounds bad. I didn't mean—"

"Oh, but it would be great," Gina says. "You definitely should wear these. What d'ya say, Dalton?"

"I don't know," he says. "What do you think, Sang?"

"I think it'll be the best," Gina says before I can answer. "And you won't be alone, Dalton. I'll be there."

"Well," I say, "if we all look ridiculous together, it could work." I pick up a pair of pink-tinted, rhinestone-studded glasses and put them on. The frames are huge.

Now Dalton's grinning too. His dimple really is pretty sweet.

"Here, Dalton," Gina says, and drapes the smiley-face necklace over his head. "Now you're out of sight, man."

We all groan.

"Okay, let's get organized," I say. Keeping the funky glasses on, I do what I do best—sorting out what needs to be done, figuring out how long each task will take, and creating a deadline for each job so we have time to pull it all together in two weeks, to present on the day before we're off for Thanksgiving. "So that's how we can work it out." I lay down my pen. Everyone is staring at me. I feel kind of embarrassed. I really didn't mean to take over. "We don't have to do it like this."

"Are you kidding?" Megan grabs my paper and studies it. "No wonder you always get A's."

Sara rolls her eyes and stands. "Gotta pee," she says, and walks away, her butt wiggling in her tight jeans.

Dalton shifts in his seat. "Okay, let's get down to business." Which is what we do for the next half hour— sorting through newspapers, taking notes, and dividing up the work. We are so involved that I don't even notice Sara is still missing until I see her walking toward us with some guy. She's pouring on her "charm," giggling and hugging herself so that her boobs stick out even farther.

"OOOOH." Megan leans toward me and practically falls over as she says in my ear, "Hot-hot-hottie alert."

I glance at this supposed hottie and sit up in shock. The guy. It's Jason. And he's totally staring at Sara and he's got that half smile on his face, and I might as well be bulimic because I'm totally gonna puke.

"I'm Megan Chung," Megan says, a bit too loudly for the library. "N-no. I mean . . . Hey, I *am* Megan Chung."

Jason raises his eyebrows at her. "Okay, then."

I can hear Dalton asking me something, but my mind is buzzing. Sara reaches up and brushes Jason's hair out of his eyes, and he laughs. I clench my teeth, unable to tear my eyes away from them.

"So can you do that, Sang?" Dalton is saying. "Sang?" he says louder.

Jason suddenly notices me, and he starts to crack up. "What the heck?" he says, pointing.

My hand brushes my nose and, to my incredible mortification, I remember that the huge, tacky rhinestone glasses are still on my face. I pull them off and flash a pained look at Gina, who tries to give me an encouraging "It's not really so bad" look back. But it *is* so bad. Not only am I wearing a high-necked shirt with no sign of cleavage whatsoever, but any slight semblance of good looks I might have has been completely erased by my super-dork glasses. I pull the glasses from my face and set them on the table.

Then I do what any grown mature exotic young woman would do—go directly to the ladies' room. I'm relieved to find nobody else in there. As I stare at the mirror, my lip quivers, and I suddenly feel like nothing ever, *ever* works out for me. Tears spill onto my cheeks. I quickly wipe them away with my sleeve.

I'm not exactly what you'd call a pretty crier. Already my nose is turning all red and my eyes are starting to look raw. I imagine trying to leave the bathroom only to find Jason and Sara and everyone pointing at me and whispering, Ew, what happened to her?

I *have* to get a grip.

So I wipe my cheeks some more. I take deep, cleansing breaths. My nose starts to return to its normal color, but my eyes are another story. I tear off some paper towel and wet it with cold water, and I'm dabbing around my eyes with it when the ladies' room door opens. Before I can dodge into the first stall, Gina's there, saying, "What the hell are you doing?"

"Fixing my hair." I sniffle and toss the paper towel into the trash.

"Get back out there."

"Sure," I say, combing my fingers through my hair. "Soon as I'm done."

"By the time you're done, Sara will be done stealing your guy. Now get out there."

"I can't." I look at my feet, waiting for a much-needed pep talk.

Instead, she gives me a push.

"Cut it out," I say.

"Fight for what's yours. Come on." She gives me another shove.

"Lay off," I say, and shove back. I'm starting to get pissed. I mean, I'm used to Gina being blunt. I'm even used to her yelling when we argue about stuff. But this new pushy routine is getting on my nerves. "Look, there's no way I'm slugging it out with Sara like I'm on *Jerry*

Springer or something. Anyway, he's not mine and I'm not his, and if he's into somebody like Sara, then he can have her. Right?"

Gina takes a deep breath. I expect her to apologize. I expect her to be sympathetic. Above all, I expect her to give me some words of wisdom. Instead, she rips into me. "You just don't get it, do you? Don't you know how many girls would kill to be in your shoes? To have your life? I mean, look at you. You're tall and smart, and, oh, let's not forget *exotic*."

"Yeah, right." I scowl at myself in the mirror.

"God, you make me sick! Don't you know how lucky you are to have a guy actually show interest in you? And what do you do? You hide in the bathroom while that pig wins! For once in your life, *do something*."

"But what should I—"

"I can't do this anymore. I just can't." Gina's pacing back and forth, running her hand through her hair. She stops and glares at my reflection in the mirror. "I'm done. Got that? Done. And you know what else? I am *so* joining spring track." She throws open the bathroom door and she's gone.

I'm stunned. That's it? That's her idea of help?

I stare at the mirror some more, and I find myself wondering what's more pathetic. Hiding in a bathroom? Or being so grateful that a guy looks my way? Or letting someone steal that guy away from me without a fight? Well, the only thing I know for sure is that a suspected bulimic shouldn't spend too much time in the bathroom.

God. Maybe Gina's right. Obnoxious, but right. I should fight for what I want. Isn't just waiting around for things to happen to me the most pathetic thing of all? I inhale deeply and make sure my eyes aren't too red. I even try to smile. Okay, I'm as ready as I'll ever be. So I leave the bathroom and walk back to the table. Jason is still there. He's looking through the clothes. Sara is hanging on his arm, flipping her hair.

I sit next to Dalton. He's talking with Megan about her outline for the project, and she's nodding and biting her lip, probably in an effort to keep from saying anything stupid.

"Hey, Sang," Jason says.

I don't know why, but I just nod at him.

Sara says something and pokes Jason, and suddenly I find myself leaning closer to Dalton, asking him in low tones to tell me again what I need to do, even though I was the one who originally told him. He turns from Megan and patiently explains it all again. I lean closer to him. I touch his arm, I don't know why. Dalton studies me for a moment.

My eyes dart to Jason, who quickly looks away from me. "Come on," he says to Sara, and Sara grabs her jacket and notebook. She smirks at me and they leave together. I immediately let go of Dalton and cross my arms. Gina stands and starts stuffing the clothes back into plastic bags with angry, jerky motions. I stand too and take a bag to help, but she tears it out of my hands.

"Gina, I just wanted to help."

"Don't."

18

Okay, so maybe I can understand Gina being disappointed in me. I didn't fight for this great guy. But if he is really so great, then why didn't he fight for me? Anyway, I'm disappointed in me too, I guess. I mean, I did try to get his attention, but obviously did a pathetic sucky job of it. For some reason, Gina's super-pissed. While we wait for my mom to give us a lift home, she answers my questions with grunts and eye-rolling. In the car, she folds her arms and doesn't speak to me at all.

Fine. Whatever. Like I don't have enough to worry about, right? But what did I do to deserve this? I mean, I could use a little support right now. And it's not like I did anything to her. So we drop Gina off at her house, and she says, "Thanks, Mrs. Jumnal," but says nothing to me. Things get steadily worse, because next my mom is answering my questions with a curt "Yes," "No," or "Don't know." It's obvious she's still pissed at me too. So I'm guilty of what? Number one, not speaking up for a guy who I never really had in the first place, and, number two, looking at a yearbook that has been lying around with all the family photo albums for as long as I can remember. And for these heinous crimes, my best friend and my own mother are freezing me out. Oh. And don't forget that I have to go to a doctor's appointment tomorrow for something I don't even have.

We get home and Chachi, the real criminal, is stomping around the house, the portable phone in her hand. She immediately gets in my face. "Did the Super Fresh manager call?"

I take a step back. "Not that I know of."

"She was supposed to call. You spoke with her."

"I did not."

"Sang," my mother cautions. "Be polite. Your chachi filled out a job application and is waiting to hear from the store for an interview. Isn't that wonderful?"

Sure. *Now* my mother is talking to me.

"The manager called," Chachi says. "You spoke with her."

"No and no," I say.

Chachi shakes her head. "Think. What did she say?"

"Nothing," I say. "Absolutely nothing. And remember how I said I didn't speak with her? Well, what I meant was, *I did not speak with her.*"

"Sang, manners," Mom warns.

"Manners? You want manners? Then tell her to stop badgering me. Tell her to listen to what I say."

Chachi's hands are tensing. Hit me, I think.

"Tell her to stop stealing," I say.

"*A-iy!*" Chachi's eyes are fierce, and she's coming at me.

"That's enough!" my mom says, and just when I'm thinking Mom's finally seeing things for what they really are, she says, "Sangeet Jumnal, go straight to your room, and you stay there until you are ready to apologize to your aunt."

There are no words to express how I feel. Nothing I can do. I quietly go upstairs, but instead of going into my room as ordered, I go into Doodles's room. The light is out and she's breathing softly, her face relaxed in deep slumber. I snuggle in beside her. I'm her big sister. I've told her anything is possible. But there's an ache deep inside of me now that tells me this is just another lie.

"Doodles?" I shake her arm. Nothing. I wish she were awake. There's more to the story.

"After meeting the challenge of the Stinking Monkey," I whisper, "after receiving the favor of one year off her wanderings before meeting her true love, Rani walked into the sizzling desert, her chuni pulled over her head, her heart brimming with joy. After all, she was on her way— the road ahead of her hot and rocky, yes, but straight. Leading, surely, to her love.

"Rani journeyed with a light step for days, but the days no longer seemed so bright. Clouds gathered in the sky. Not the much-loved monsoon clouds the landscape always longed for, with their promise of nourishing, cooling rains, but foreboding clouds, foretelling dark and evil days ahead.

"Rani slowed her pace, and finally came to a complete stop. Where was she going? And why? Wasn't there any other direction she should go? Was the prince really her one true love? What if she walked for two years, six years, eight years, only to find it was all for nothing?

"There was no one in the big, empty land as far as her eyes could see. No person to share her burden, to offer her advice, to give her comfort. Not even an animal walked the land, nor did a bird wing above. Rani was alone. Her journey stopped, and she sat on the dusty road as large drops of rain slapped her head, her feet, the ground. The drops sizzled like water spilled from a hot kettle. . . ."

In the morning I awake in Doodles's room, surrounded by pink blankets and posters of ballerinas and princesses. Doodles is beside me, lost in dream, and I carefully get out of her bed.

I've got this wicked crick in my neck that stabs me with pain every time I try to look to the right. The perfect start to the perfect day.

At my locker, I'm getting out my stuff and Dalton comes up to me and tells me Mrs. Finelli has decided our extra-credit project is due on Monday. "Can you believe it?" he says. "I thought we'd at least have another week to work on it. I mean, it's already *Wednesday*."

I try to give him a sympathetic look, but he's standing

to my right and looking at him is painful because of the crick.

"We have to get an A on this, Sang," Dalton says. "If we get less, it can bring my A average down. Extra credit will actually count against me." There's a panicked look in his eyes.

"You're already getting an A? Then why are you doing this project in the first place?" I roll my neck to ease the pain.

"Well," he says, shifting from foot to foot, "I thought it was pretty obvious." His voice cracks as he's saying this.

I'm rolling my neck for a second time, and that's when I see him over to my left, about fifteen lockers down. Jason's leaning his elbow over Sara's locker, and Sara's leaning her face up toward him.

"God!" I slam my locker shut and dash toward the classroom.

"Sang?" Dalton comes rushing after me. "I didn't mean to upset you." He grabs my arm.

I'm looking at my feet and taking big gulps of air.

At that moment, Gina comes sweeping by, pushing herself between Dalton and me.

"Gina," I say, my voice barely working. "What'll I do?"

She gives me a cool look and doesn't say a word.

19

*a*fter a miserable day of school, it's time to go home. Everybody is jostling each other, and the hall is choked with students and backpacks. Gina and I usually meet by the water fountain in the corner before going to our bus. I'm waiting. Students are streaming by. She's been in a snit all day, but I *have* to talk to her.

I can't think of anything I've done to make her so mad. The thing is, if something bugs Gina, she usually just blurts it out, yells for a minute, and it's over, forgiven, done. Like in fifth grade, when she'd told me she was going bra shopping that afternoon and I let it slip to Stephanie Steinberg, who told the world. Gina screamed at me, right in front of the teacher, "Best friends keep best-friend secrets! Got that?" And I yelled, "Yeah! Sorry!" And it was over. Since that day, I've always kept all of her secrets, and she's always done the same for me.

There she is, coming down the hall. She glances in my

direction but walks past me. "Gina? Wait." I shove my way through a mass of football players, pushing past their broad shoulders like I'm trying to score a touchdown for the other team. By the time I get around them and catch up to Gina, she's just outside the glass doors. She's regarding me with that cold, distant look again.

"Gina, wait. I have to tell you. Jason and Sara," I say. "I saw them together. He was—"

"You, you, you," she says. "No one else matters in the entire universe, do they?"

"That's not true. Gina, what's your problem?"

"See that?" she says. "You haven't got a clue."

Gina's fists are clenched.

The buses rumble to life.

Gina turns on her heel and rushes to bus 72. I know I should follow, but I can't.

The buses pull away, belching their exhaust.

I swallow hard. Guess today I'm a walker. I hitch up my backpack and begin my twenty-minute journey, heading toward the main road.

Try to forget about Gina, I think. At least for now. There's nothing I can do about her now, right?

But how can I forget? My best friend *hates* me. And she's right, I haven't a clue why. It's like she's keeping a huge secret from me or something. Oh God. What if it's something really bad? Like, what if something's terribly wrong with her and she can't bear to tell me?

I tell myself I'm being stupid. And I tell myself to

relax and try to enjoy this beautiful day. The sky is a deep blue, and the light is making what leaves remain on the trees glitter yellow and red and orange. And I notice I'm not alone, because on a day like today, lots of kids decide to walk home. I wave to the ones I recognize, and soon I'm walking with Janice Druthers and some of her powder-puff football team. They're talking about how their team is going to get crushed in their game later today and de-bating whether they should all wear French braids.

Doylestown is actually a great place for walking when your life isn't falling to pieces. You see the bookstore win-dow with the latest reads, the trendy clothes on the racks of A Special Gift, and zillions of scented candles in the Poor Richards store. There's also a miniature old-fashioned bar-bershop complete with pole, and the shoe shop where Lola the Scottie dog waits beside the entrance to play with whoever enters. Next to her is a hopeful sign: DOGS WELCOME.

By the time we reach Planet Smoothie, it's jammed with students. Megan, holding a giant smoothie in her hand, spots us through the window and waves for us to come in. Frankly, I'm tempted. After the day I've had, I could use some nourishment.

Nourishment. Oh no. The doctor's appointment is today. Right after school. Mom's probably going to think I'm late on purpose to avoid the whole thing, which will make her think I really do have an eating disorder to hide. I wave bye to everyone, and I rush on.

I'm by Nat's Pizzeria just as the door bursts open and out leaps none other than Jason, a slice in his hand. He races down the street, and I half expect a cop to be chasing him.

Great. I have to hurry home in the same direction. He'll probably think I'm following him. He probably saw me by Nat's and thought, Gah! It's that crazy stalker chick, just like in *Swimfan.*

I cross at the light, and much to my relief, there's no sign of Jason ahead. Okay. So I can just hurry on home. I won't be much later than the bus, and no harm done.

No harm done. Yeah, right. Somehow, everywhere I turn, there's been nothing *but* harm done.

The rich smell of roasting coffee beans wafts from the open door of Coffee & Cream. This makes me think of Michelle Baldarasi, who works there, which makes me think of Gina, which makes me feel really crappy.

"Can I interest you in a matinee?"

I pause. The metallic voice came from the County Theater. I turn, and there's Jason inside the tiny glass ticket booth, wiping pizza sauce from his chin with a paper napkin.

I'm totally caught by surprise, and it takes a moment for me to respond. "No thanks," I finally say. I turn away, ready to move on.

"There's a great art film opening. Very funny, very different."

His metallic voice coming through the tiny speaker,

the way he's stuffed in the little glass booth like an arcade gypsy . . . I imagine depositing a quarter, and his mechanical mouth telling me my fortune. I step closer. "I didn't know you worked here."

He shrugged. "I guess you don't see too many movies here."

"I do." Well, sort of. The County is where I saw *Bend It Like Beckham, Pride and Prejudice,* and *Monsoon Wedding.*

"I work mostly afternoons," he says, and smiles.

I catch myself about to smile back. What am I doing? Here he is, being all Mr. Nice Guy so he doesn't have to feel guilty about this whole seedy Sara thing, and I'm responding like a dog that's been given a new squeaky toy. Unbelievable! I am so incredibly gullible.

Okay. Now I'm mad. "Look, Jason. I don't really know you, and you don't really know me. No harm done, right? Later."

An elderly couple steps up to purchase tickets from him. This is my cue. I'm walking away. To my shock, I hear a voice, not metallic, say, "Hey, Sang?"

Jason's right behind me. The couple seems perplexed, peering into the empty glass booth.

"That's just it," Jason says, falling into step beside me because I refuse to stop. "I don't really know you, and you really don't know me. But I'd like to, you know, know you." He's blushing.

I stop. Now I'm the one who's perplexed. "You know Sara well enough."

"I'd like to know *you*."

"And how many girls do you want to know?" I say, and cross my arms. "On average."

He rubs his forehead. "I'm an idiot. Never mind." He's backing away. "Sorry."

Oh God. He looks really upset. What if he was being sincere? What if all along he really was interested in me and not stupid Sara? She was probably throwing herself at him and he was probably trying to get away from her without being nasty, and I was just too stupid to see the truth.

Now he's back in the ticket booth, looking flustered as he fumbles with coins and tickets. "Enjoy the show," he says to the elderly folks.

I should go home. Be the good girl. The dutiful daughter.

I'm at the booth. "Two tickets," I say, "for Friday night, if you're free."

He looks up and we both stand there, two idiots grinning at each other through the glass.

Okay, this last part never happens. Instead, I walk the rest of the way home feeling miserable and lonely, tormenting myself for being so stupid and throwing away what will most definitely be my one and only chance with Jason.

As soon as I arrive home, I am immediately driven to the doctor's office. Mom's sitting on the exam room's only chair, biting her thumbnail, and I'm wearing one of those ultra-stylish paper gowns. Dr. Dander, who has a perfectly round bald head, is starting to make me nervous.

He's smiling at me, but the smile doesn't seem to reach his gray-blue eyes, which are staring, staring, staring. Staring at the backs of my hands, my teeth, my weight on the scale, my chart. He's asking me a bunch of questions, like if I think I'm fat. (No.) Too thin? (No.) "So you think you're perfect?"

That's not what I meant at all.

"Is being perfect important to you?" he asks.

What's the right answer? I'm trying to be honest, but when he asked if I exercise and I told him about Gina and I doing our marathon bike rides/runs, he marked something on the chart.

So now I shrug.

Finally he caps his pen and sets my chart on his desk. "Okay. Here's what I think. Sangeet appears healthy. Her body image, weight, and attitude appear normal. And there's no sign of prolonged vomiting."

I nod at my mom. I want to say, See?

"However," the doctor says, "I must trust a parent's instinct, because who knows a daughter better than her mother?"

"But, Dr. Dander," I practically shriek, "you just said I'm *healthy*."

"Sang," he says, "your mother is clearly worried about you. We need to pay attention to that. Bulimia is a tricky illness. Maybe you feel out of control. Say you binge-eat. It can be all very secretive, you know. You might overdo it on sweet soft foods, like ice cream, cake, pastries, pudding—"

Mom sucks in her breath.

Dr. Dander glances at her, picks up my chart, and scribbles something while saying, "Then you purge by using enemas or vomiting."

Gross, I think, and I stick out my tongue just as he looks at me. He scribbles some more. Crap. I hope he doesn't think I was doing some sort of mini-purge.

"Bulimics also diet, skip meals, and fast," he says. "They do compulsive exercise, and—"

Now I suck in my breath. Gina. She's not eating. And she's acting so weird. And she's not telling me what's wrong. She's being all secretive. And worrying about looking fat. About growing as big as her mother. And now she's going out for spring track. It all fits. But it's too crazy to be true. And yet . . .

I notice Mom and Dr. Dander staring at me. The doctor gives me a gentle smile. "Don't worry. The condition *is* curable. Therapy, nutrition guidance, and a doctor's watchful eye will do the trick."

"But, Dr. Dander, I—"

"Now it does take time," he says, pulling some forms from a drawer. "And effort. I mean, helping a young lady to feel like she doesn't need to be perfect, and helping her feel in control again, entails—"

"I'M NOT BULIMIC!"

"Sang!" my mother says, her hand at her throat.

Dr. Dander scratches his ear. "Okay, Sang. So why don't you tell me what's going on."

"It's my aunt."

"Sang," Mom says in an exasperated tone.

Dr. Dander holds up his hand. "What about your aunt?"

So I tell him. About how crummy it is having her around, and how she steals all this food and blames me, and how I do anything to avoid seeing her, including no longer going into the kitchen for snacks.

Dr. Dander asks to talk to my mother alone.

20

"When you're a mother, you want to do anything you can to stop your daughter from getting hurt. Anything."

She's driving me home from the doctor. I want to ask what he said to her, but I'm afraid to know. Suppose he said I do have bulimia—which is ridiculous, because I don't, but what if he said I do? What if this is like those movies where everyone is convinced someone is crazy, even though that person is perfectly sane? And they throw that person into a padded cell, and there's no way out?

I squirm in my seat.

"But there's only so much a mother can do, you know? That's how mothers suffer." She gives me a kind look before returning her eyes to the road.

"So you're not still mad at me? About, you know, looking at your old stuff?"

"Not mad, Sang. It's just . . ." She purses her lips. "Dr. Dander said I should give you the benefit of the doubt. Believe that Chachi is the reason for your lost weight and the missing food. Believe that you spent all that time in the bathroom to avoid Daddy and me. So that's what I'm going to *try* to do." She nods her head, as if convincing herself.

"Thank you," I say.

"But he still wants to see you every three weeks for a while, just to make sure."

I sigh. It's not great. But it's not a padded cell either.

"And," she says, "you and I need to be honest with each other from now on, okay?"

"Okay," I say. I twiddle my thumbs. I cross my legs and uncross them. "Well," I finally say, "is there anything *you* want to tell *me*?"

"No," she says, gripping the wheel tight.

I flip down the visor and peer at myself in the tiny mirror on its back. I give myself my sternest look. *Just say it.* "What about, you know, what I found out in your yearbook?"

"Pizza!" she says, and suddenly spins the wheel. The car peels to the right, and I grip the armrest. "I just re-membered, I was thinking of picking up pizza tonight. How's that sound?" Mom steers into the lot of Spatola's Pizza, parks, and turns off the engine.

I stare at her long and hard.

She's still gripping the wheel and staring straight ahead. "I was so young," she says. "It was stupid."

"You weren't so young," I say, unclipping my belt, "and neither am I."

"What?" She whips her head in my direction. "What are you saying?" Her eyes are wild.

I try not to shrink away from her. "You weren't too young to date," I say. "And neither am I."

"Oh," she says, and pulls her keys from the ignition. Her hands are trembling, making the key chain rattle in her hand.

"You okay?"

She dabs her forehead. "Yes. Yes, of course. Let's get pizza."

I'm zipping up my jacket and following Mom to the entrance when she stops and turns. "Wait," she says. "Did you say 'yearbook'?"

Oh no. She's going to go ballistic on me again. I look around. Thankfully, no one else is here to witness the scene.

"You read about these boys in my yearbook? Not anywhere else?"

"Where else would I?" I say.

She gives a forced laugh. "Oh, where else indeed? It's just that . . ." Mom takes a deep breath and smiles. She wraps an arm around my shoulder and tries to give me her usual warm squeeze, but today it feels more like a pinch. "I'm just starving. Come on."

21

One slight improvement: Chachi actually has gotten hired by Super Fresh, which means she isn't at the dinner table tonight. For the first time in months, I don't have to face her scowl or listen to her chomping on her raw beets.

We all talk about how great Thanksgiving is going to be with Hari and Taoji.

"That reminds me," I say. "Dad, Taoji wanted me to ask you about some festival. What was it? Something about lights."

"Diwali?"

"Yeah. The Festival of Lights. What's that?"

Dad sets his pizza slice on his plate. "Oh, it's great. It celebrates the force of good driving away evil."

Immediately I picture Chachi banging on the window of a smelly old bus as it zooms off into the horizon. "Cool."

"Everyone lights candles," Dad says, "firecrackers are

everywhere, and people exchange sweets." He picks up his pizza and takes a bite.

"Sweets?" Doodles sits up. "Like those things that look like eyeballs?"

Dad almost chokes on his food as he laughs. He takes a sip of water and says, "You mean rosogullas. So you remember those, huh?"

How could Doodles forget? When we visited India last, she was five and practically lived on those things. They are round and white, and in a sugary syrup.

"I want to have Diwali," Doodles says. "Can we, Dad?"

"We've already missed it. It's too bad, because on that particular evening, Laxmi, the goddess of good fortune, is said to fly through the night. Who knows? Maybe she would have visited us."

"Wait," I say. "I thought Sikhs believe in only one God."

"That doesn't stop us from enjoying a good festival."

"So this Laxmi pays a visit to all the houses—"

"Only to the ones decorated for her, with lots of lights and perhaps a pretty *rangoli* out front. That's a pattern of shapes and flowers drawn on the front walk," Dad says. "Kind of like a fancy welcome mat. Anyway, if Laxmi sees such a home, she'll enter and bless the household with joy and good fortune for the coming year. So on Diwali, every home, from the grandest mansion to the smallest hut, sparkles with hundreds of little lights along the rooftops and in every window." Dad rests his chin on his hand and sighs.

I imagine all the houses in our neighborhood covered

with twinkling white lights and every window glowing with candles. "Why can't we still do it?" I say. "So we're a little late. So what? Maybe Laxmi needs an extra week or so to fly over the Atlantic."

Dad takes another slice from the box and says, "Well, I guess we could do our own little thing. But it wouldn't be the same, of course."

Now I imagine only our house twinkling with lights. It's still pretty, though.

"Maybe you could pick up some sweets from Patel's," Mom tells Dad. "If you're ever out that way." Patel's is this Indian grocery store about thirty minutes from Doylestown.

"I guess it's possible," Dad says. "We'll have our own American Diwali."

Doodles claps.

Dad sticks a piece of mozzarella cheese on his chin and points at her, saying, "Uncle Sam wants you!"

"Children, stop playing with your food," my mom says.

Doodles carefully picks a piece of cheese off her pizza and seems unsure of what to do next. She puts on a cheese mustache and glances at Mom, who smiles. Soon all of us, including my mom, are sporting cheese beards and mustaches, and giggling.

Giggling. It's a sound that used to fill our house all the time. Well, not all the time, but often. I'm looking at Doodles, who is banging the table, tears of laughter brimming in her eyes.

This is the way it should always be in our home. It's what is right. But Mom only wants to see the good in people, and won't even listen to the truth about Chachi. Dad's so wrapped up in tradition and family values that he refuses to see how bad things are. Or maybe he does see, but just can't deal with it. He never will tell Chachi to go. I can feel this in my gut. And in my gut I can also feel the damage being done here. Not just to me. Doodles is already forgetting how to be relaxed and happy at home. In two years' time, she won't even remember what it was like before Chachi came. She'll have almost no recollection of how much fun we used to always have together. Sure, we're having a laugh now, but Chachi will come back and the laughter will stop. Chachi will be here. Live here. Eat here. Hate here. Two long years (nine months of which I'll be dateless). Two years before she leaves. Two years before we can enjoy our home again. Two horrible miserable wretched torturous long years.

No longer smiling, I pull the cheese off my upper lip and wipe my face with my napkin. Two years is too long. I decide to get organized.

22

"Rani rose to her feet, and the sizzling rain suddenly stopped. The clouds slid away, leaving the sky white-hot, but clear. She knew what she had to do."

"How did she know?" Doodles asks. She's lying with her feet on her pillow and her head at the foot of the bed.

"She just knew, okay? Now listen." I'm sitting on the edge of the bed, and I'm feeling a bit edgy myself. Like I want to get things moving. But I have to put Doodles to bed. Mom is out sorting canned goods at the town shelter, and Dad is going to leave soon to pick up Chachi from work. Doodles has to be asleep by then.

"She knew she had to move forward toward an uncertain future. She couldn't sit around waiting for someone else to rescue or guide her. She had to guide herself. She had to trust that what she was doing was the right thing. She had to trust that love and romance would be hers, but first she had to undo the power of the evil genie who cursed her life."

"So she wants to marry the prince again? What changed?"

"I didn't say she wanted to marry the prince. But she does want to marry someone someday, right? Now stop interrupting. And lie in your bed the right way."

"I like it this way." Doodles wiggles her toes. "You know, you should buy some of this candy I'm selling. It's good chocolate. You like chocolate, right? And if I'm the top seller, I get a giant chocolate bar from the Girl Scouts. I'd even share some of it with you."

"No thanks. Besides, I'm practically broke. Now lay the right way or no more story."

Doodles grumbles, but does as she's told.

"The genie lived in a high tower. Rani had to break its enchantment and sneak inside, for within rested all the genie's powers and secrets. If Rani could seize these, she could undo all the evil done, not only to her but to many other creatures on the earth. But it was a dangerous—"

I hear the garage door opening. Dad is going to pick up my aunt. "It's your bedtime," I say.

"At least finish the sentence."

"Doodles," I warn.

She punches the pillow and turns away from me. I shut off the light, step into my room, and wait one minute, two minutes. Then I peek into Doodles's room. She hasn't moved. Asleep!

I tiptoe down the hall, the floorboards groaning.

Funny how they only seem loud when you want to be sneaky. Next I go up the stairs leading to the attic bedroom. When it was Hari's room, I'd race up the steps and bang on the door, and he'd usually tell me he was busy. But sometimes he'd let me in, and we'd hang out and talk and joke around. Those were the best times. Times when we really got along, not just as big brother and little sister.

My hand is on the doorknob. For a moment I fantasize that Hari's still in there, headphones on, tapping away at his computer, rock posters on the walls, bookshelf crammed with sci-fi paperbacks and a metal bank that, when you put a coin in its slot, has a creepy little green hand that snatches your money away.

I realize that I don't know what is behind the door now. The first day Chachi moved in, I sat on the bed for a while, chatting, trying to make her feel at home. Truthfully, I had hoped she'd become a sort of substitute for Hari while he was away. But instead of being friendly with me, she had sat at the desk, her mouth set in a grim line. After I'd talked for a while, I realized she wasn't saying a word to me. Wasn't looking at me. I rose from the bed and said goodbye. She gave me a look that seemed to say, Good. That was the last time I entered this room.

I swallow, turn the knob, and push the door open. I flip the light switch. The room is sparse without the posters and the books. The bed has a scratchy-looking quilt Chachi brought with her, replacing the flowery one my mom had purchased in an effort to create a welcoming atmosphere. There's a creepy feel to the room. Not cool creepy, like Hari's bank. More like psycho-ward creepy. The head of the bed is away from the wall by about twelve inches. The night table and lamp are now at the foot of the bed. Who does that? The desk and dresser, instead of being against the opposite wall where they fit well, are pushed in front of the window, blocking most of the view outside. Both pieces of furniture are covered with piles and piles of papers.

Okay, I'm not here to redecorate. I'm here to snoop. And I'd better move fast. Super Fresh is not that far away, and Dad will be back with Chachi in a matter of minutes. So I start rummaging through stacks of papers on the desk. There's plenty of letters from my cousin, Raj. I recognize his loopy handwriting from the envelopes that arrive several times a week. Part of me thinks, Doesn't this kid have a life? And the other part of me thinks, Why doesn't Hari ever write? Or e-mail, even? I think about how he told me I could get in touch with him anytime I needed to talk. How, on the day we dropped him off at college, he handed me a slip of paper with his dorm phone number on it and said, "Call anytime. Day or night." About how I did call. And asked for Hari. Every time, a guy named Larry got on the phone and was pretty pissed it wasn't really for him. I gave up on calling.

Maybe I should read some of these letters. Maybe I'll find Chachi's sending my cousin money and food that she steals from us. I pick up a letter. Guilt seizes me. How can I read someone's personal letters? How, for that matter, can I be snooping in someone else's room?

Be strong, I tell myself. Remember, this woman stole from your mother, lied about you, almost hit you. Right.

So I read: *My dearest Mummy: How I miss you so. How I wish I could be with you at this very moment.*

Gah. He can have her. I scan the letter some more. Lots of boring stuff about a physics final, and about how he had the sniffles, so now he wears a knit hat day and night. Dull dull stuff. Perhaps another letter . . .

CREAK!

I freeze. I'm listening, but all I hear is my heart thumping. Someone is watching. I feel it.

I turn. Eyes meet mine. I draw in my breath. The eyes are on the photo of Chachi's late husband, which is hung on the wall beside the door. My uncle, or chacha, had thick eyebrows like my dad, though my uncle's were streaked with gray. And he had a kind smile, also like my dad (when he isn't yelling at me). I step closer to the portrait. His eyes seem familiar. They are large and dark-chocolate brown, and the lashes are long and thick. With a start, I realize that they are exactly like my eyes. Was he like me in any other way? Would he see things the way I do? If he were here right now, would he be on my side?

Useless to wonder. I hardly remember him. I was probably about eight years old when we met up with him in New Delhi. He was planning to travel to America with his family to settle down. He laughed in a hearty ha-ha-ha way that made me like him, though he spent most of the visit speaking to my father in Punjabi and the only thing he said to me was "Good girl." When he moved to the U.S. with Chachi and my cousin, they lived in the Midwest, and then he was ill, so only my dad visited them.

I decide I can't do this. I can't riffle through stuff with my dead uncle watching me. I just can't. Maybe that's how my dad feels when he deals with Chachi. Maybe he feels his dead brother watching.

Okay, I'm out of here. I set the letter back on the desk, but turn when something beside the stacks of papers catches my eye. Unbelievable. It's my datebook-organizer. And on the cover, someone has scratched out my gold-script name. I flip it open to today, and my assignments are scratched out with black marker. Above it, Chachi has written: *Super Fresh 5–9:30 p.m.* In fact, all of my assignments throughout the book are blacked out.

THIS. IS. WAR.

I pull open a drawer. It is packed with chocolate chip granola bars and bags of Oreo cookies. Ohmygod. The next drawer? Sacks of chips. I'll give her this: she's organized. Just wait until Mom sees this. I pull open the next drawer, and—

"What are you doing?"

I spin toward the door. I'm holding my chest so my heart doesn't escape. "Don't you ever *ever* sneak up on me like that."

Doodles is holding Taffy Bear, and is staring hard at

me with her most serious expression. I'm using her silence to think up excuses. I could say I'm just looking for an extra pad of paper for my homework, or returning something I borrowed from Chachi, like . . . like what?

"So," Doodles says, "did you find it?"

I clear my throat. "Find it?"

"My money. I think Chachi took it."

Now it's my turn to stare. She's pretty sharp for a little kid.

The garage door rumbles.

"Quick," I say. "Before she sees." I slam the drawers shut and snap off the light. Doodles and I race down the attic stairs. Doodles goes into her room, but I remember my datebook and hurry back upstairs. I snag the book from the desktop. That's when I hear the front door of the house open. I fly back down the short flight of steps, nearly stumbling. I reach the hall to the bedrooms, and slow my pace just as Chachi is heading up from the living room. With the datebook tucked under my shirt, I pass her silently in the hall.

23

"*Y*our aunt's a kleptomaniac," Megan says, trying in vain to spear her tomato with a flimsy plastic fork. We're at our usual cafeteria table, which seats at least forty people, with a mix of kids we know well and some not so well. There's Janice Druthers and some of her powder-puff football team. Ella Jenkins looks depressed and is surrounded by girls casting nasty looks at her ex, Anthony Casamoni (who, wisely, has moved to another table). And there's Dalton, sitting with some guys I know from my English class.

Megan gives up on the tomato and manages to get some lettuce onto her fork. "Oh, he's kinda cute," she whispers to me. She's eyeing Eric Bates as he's walking by. Eric is short and wide and always looks like he's pissed off at everybody. Maybe he's mad about the height thing.

"Eric? Hi!" Megan waves her fork at him and the lettuce

flies off, hitting him on the foot, splattering ranch dressing on his black sneakers. Now he looks seriously pissed.

"Oh God." Megan covers her eyes and whispers, "I can't believe I did that. Is he gone?"

"Yeah, he's gone."

She lowers her hand. "What *is* my problem?"

"Megan, it wasn't that bad."

"You've got to be joking. I just wish I could be more like you."

"Me?"

"Yeah. I've seen you. You can actually talk to guys without self-destructing. So tell me. What's your secret?"

Should I show her how to be stood up? Or teach her how to lose a guy to a slut? Or perhaps share my tips on how to totally screw up any chances with a guy, even when he's telling you he's interested? "Kleptomaniacs," I say.

My harp-seal-eyed friend blinks. "Huh?"

"Weren't we talking about kleptomaniacs?"

"Oh. Right. Somebody who can't help stealing. It's an illness. See, there was this one guy my dad used to see who couldn't resist taking gum, especially those packets right at the checkout aisle, and one time—"

"My aunt's a maniac, all right," I say, cutting her off. Suddenly I no longer enjoy Megan's stories about patients. What if she knows about me and all this bulimia junk? What if she has a story about me? I sip the last of my cappuccino, wishing I had enough money for a refill.

You can't binge on cappuccinos, can you? I push my cup aside. "Hey, Megan," I say, trying to be all casual, "do your parents ever tell you about patients you know? Like ones who are our age?"

She looks shocked. "Never. That would be completely unethical."

Thank God.

She leans closer. "Why? What do you know?"

I lean away. "Nothing. Really."

"Oh." She slouches in disappointment. "Hey, Gina." Megan scooches over to make room for her.

"Hi, Megan," Gina says, and struts past me and the rest of our table.

We watch Gina pass the bandies' table, where the drum corps guys are tapping out tunes with their plastic knives, and pass the table of senior guys who never talk because they are all plugged into their headphones. She finally sits at a lunch table full of goths dressed in black T-shirts and metal chains.

"Whoa. What's that about?" Megan says.

I shrug, bite into my apple, and watch Lewis Fullerton the Third, supergoth, show Gina his tongue stud. Gina hands him her Twinkie. "Did you see that?" I say.

"What?"

"Nothing," I say, but I can't help but worry about why she's not eating. Is she bulimic? Or am I just overreacting? I force my attention back to Megan. "Listen, I need to frame my aunt, and it's got to be good. What I really need is a plan."

"A plan would be good," Megan says. She nods, but doesn't come up with one.

I sigh and bite my apple again.

Seeming to sense my disappointment, she says, "Well, you have the datebook, right? Isn't that, you know, evidence?"

She's right. It is my book and I found it in Chachi's room, with her handwriting in it. It is pretty incriminating. And I could show this to Mom, who is supposed to believe me now. But I don't know. My gut tells me this isn't going to work. Chachi's got a way of twisting what I do and say to make me look bad. "I think I need something better, more solid."

"Well . . ." Megan raises her brows, and just when I think I've got someone to work with, she goes all therapist on me, talking about psychological issues, counseling methods, treatment options.

"Thanks, Megan," I say, then drop my apple core into my empty cup and stand. "That helps a lot."

She beams. "Can I help you with any other problems? Like you and Gina? Or"—she pauses and glances around the table—"you and *him*?"

"You know?" I sit back down. Here I thought I'd been all cool about Jason, and Gina had sworn that she'd never mention it to anyone until he and I were official, which is definitely not going to happen now. I turn toward Jason, who is sitting on the opposite side of the cafeteria, laughing with a group of guys. Crap. He's totally laughing about me. I glance at Gina, and she's in deep discussion with the goths as she picks at a giant pile of French fries. Well, she's eating, at least. But did she tell Megan about Jason? She's totally telling everyone, isn't she? I guess that's the payback for whatever she's pissed about. I feel a hot flash as I realize the layers upon layers of terrible secrets Gina knows about me. Secrets she swore she'd never, *ever* tell because we were best friends. But what happens to those secrets if we're not best friends anymore? She knows I wet the bed until I was six. That I threw up all over her downstairs bathroom the night we snuck a cigarette from her older sister's secret stash. That in eighth grade I actually cried when I heard that Orlando Bloom had a girlfriend. But I can't really believe Gina would ever tell my secrets to anyone. She just wouldn't.

"It's obvious by the way he looks at you," Megan is saying. "You want me to talk to him?"

"No," I practically shout. "No thanks, I mean." I manage a smile, and stand. "See you tonight." Tonight we're meeting at the library again to practice our extra-credit presentation. Just me and Megan and Dalton and Sara and Gina. Yup. Should be fun.

Suddenly I hear a group of people shouting, "Eat! Eat! Eat!" and pounding on a table. It's the goths. A bunch of them are having a French fry–eating contest, shoving handfuls of fries into their mouths. Gina's doing it too. She's stuffing more and more French fries in. Her cheeks are bulging.

Now kids at other tables are shouting, "Eat! Eat! Eat!"

until Gina jumps from her seat and someone yells, "Look out, she's gonna hurl!"

I watch Gina run out of the cafeteria with her hand over her mouth.

By the end of the day I feel completely sad and lonely and totally worried. I never realized how many times each day I talked with Gina, or sent her meaningful glances in history class, or nudged her in the halls as we passed. All afternoon I've been desperate to ask her if she's okay. To ask her if she has an eating problem. But she won't talk to me.

Now that it's time to wait for her by the water fountain before getting onto the bus, I know there's no point. And I know the bus ride will be totally bizarre. Like this morning, when I got on the bus and my usual seat by Gina was taken by Jessica Posting, so I sat with Sandy, who usually has Ethan sit with her, so when Ethan got on, he had to sit in someone else's spot, and so on and so on and so on. It was completely messed up.

Fine. I'll walk home instead. No doctor's appointment today, right? And no point in worrying about seeing or not seeing Jason, right?

Not as many kids are walking today. Outside, the air is crisp, the sky is gray, and the wind whirls my hair about my head, so I pull a pencil from my bag, twirl my hair into a bun, and shove the pencil into it to hold it snug. I shoulder my backpack and march past the buses and onto the sidewalk toward the center of town.

My mind is racing, crammed with everything I would normally tell Gina about. I try to sort it all out on my own.

Number one, school. This should improve, right? I know it's stupid, but just having my datebook in my bag is helping me feel more together. I've already started filling in my assignments and tests again, and when I get home I'm totally going to pull together my info for the extra-credit project. My part is all about the politics of the hippies: What did they stand for? Why did they rebel? Did they go too far? How did they change our world? Stuff like that. So that's good.

Number two, Gina. She hates me. I can't figure out what the hell her problem is. Unless it's bulimia. What if it is? God, I should definitely talk to her. But how do I talk to someone who refuses to talk to me? And what would I say? Arrgh! I have no answers.

So on to number three, Jason. Non-issue. Forget him. This would be much easier if I weren't walking up to the County Theater and the booth where he must be working at this very minute. Hey, I can't help it if I walk this way, can I? (Come to think of it, I could have helped it. I could have walked on the opposite side of the street, or taken Court Street instead. So what does that say about me? Paaaaa-thetic.) Okay, so I can admit he's nice-looking. But so what, right? And he seemed pretty nice for a while there, but looks can be deceiving and all that. Laughing about me with his friends in the lunchroom isn't what I'd call nice, even though I don't know for sure he was doing that. Hmm. Slutty Sara, though. 'Nuff said.

So I quicken my step and rush by the ticket booth. This time no one calls my name. I'm glad, right? I sneak a glance back only to see that a woman with spiked red hair is manning the booth today. I'm totally surprised. Not by the woman or her hair, but by how disappointed I feel. So I wanted to see him? God, I'm screwed up.

I've got to get a grip. I've got to push all these things out of my mind and focus like I'm some sort of Jedi Knight. Use the Force, Sang. Use it to channel all mental energy on busting Chachi. I feel the beginnings of a plan in my mind, but I don't know if it's any good. Maybe I should wait until Hari comes home. I bet he'd be good at this. Or I could make up with Gina. Gina would be full of ideas. Face it. I *need* Gina.

I rub my chilled hands together, turn, and backtrack past a few shops. When I enter Coffee & Cream, my cheeks sting from the warmth indoors. The tiny coffee shop is steamy, crowded, and all ground-coffee-bean-smelling. I focus on the people behind the counter, who are wiping counters, pouring coffee, and bagging muffins, and there is Gina's older sister Michelle. "Hey, squid," Michelle says when it's my turn to order. "You doing something different here? Or the same old same old?"

"Same," I say, unzipping my jacket.

"So is Hottie home yet?" Michelle says over her shoulder as she steams my cappuccino.

"*Hari* is back at Thanksgiving. Any messages for him?"

Michelle sets the cup on the counter and just laughs. "So where's Dorkazoid?"

"She's kind of pissed at me." I hand her a five from my dwindling stash of babysitting money and pop a plastic lid on top of the cup. "You wouldn't happen to know why, would you?"

Michelle snorts. "Some guy, I guess." She hands me my change.

I steal a glance at the people standing behind me in line. All adults, no one I know. Still, I lower my voice. "You sure she's, you know, okay? Hasn't been going to the bathroom a lot or anything?"

Michelle twiddles her nose ring and looks at me like I'm some toilet-obsessed freak. I'm about to ask again, but that's when a guy wearing a "General Manager" tag tells Michelle to please not touch her nostril at work, and he makes her wash her hands.

I turn toward the few tables behind me. All full. Story of my life.

"I'm just leaving," a familiar voice says. Jason stands and pulls on his leather jacket.

Now my cheeks are really stinging.

He doesn't meet my eye and practically bolts out, not pulling his backpack on till he opens the shop door.

I set down my cappuccino. I set down my backpack. I set down my butt.

I pick up my butt, backpack, and cappuccino, and bolt out of the shop too. No sign of him. So he must be working, then. I hurry toward the theater, but the red-spiky-haired woman is still in the booth.

Right. Well, what was I thinking, anyway? I mean, what would be the point of talking with him? It's not like I had a plan or anything. So I sip my cappuccino and I walk on, determined to focus. To use the Force. To force Chachi out . . . Crap. There he is on the cement bench at the corner, sipping his coffee.

I stop, then I hurry to the bench before I have a chance to think or plan or anything. I sit beside him and he looks at me, all confused. I set down my bag by my feet. We look at each other and both take a sip of our drinks. My throat feels scorched. It takes me a moment to talk, but when I do, all I can think to say is, "It's cold out. You should have stayed in the shop."

"Didn't think you'd want to be seen with me." He tightens his mouth and stares at a passing car.

We both take another sip.

I sigh. "Don't you wish sometimes you could start all over? Take everything back?"

This brings a half smile to his face that makes my heart flutter. It's just like in those romance paperbacks Mrs. Baldarasi is always reading.

I don't know what comes over me. I don't know why I do what I do next, or what I expect to happen ten minutes or even ten seconds from now. All I know is that I set down my cappuccino, lean toward Jason, and kiss him. My first real kiss ever. It's long and lingering, and all warm and steamy and coffee-flavored.

Then I stammer something or other, grab my bag, and speed-walk away. What the hell—what the hell—what the HELL was I thinking?

"Sang!" Jason shouts. "You forgot your coffee!"

I just wave over my head and keep on going for about three blocks while a feeling wells up inside. I stop. Set down my backpack and look up and down the street. No one.

"YES!" I scream, and I turn a cartwheel right there on the sidewalk. When I land, I'm face to face with a mailman.

"Good day?" he says in a dry voice as he pulls a stack of letters from his sack.

I feel my face flush. "Good day," I say, meaning "Goodbye." I get my backpack and keep walking, pretending I'm a perfectly normal person.

I feel like everything is wonderful, and this feeling floats me all the way to my street and up my driveway. Before I enter the house, I step on a lopsided pink chalk drawing of flowers, accidentally smearing it. I go inside and see a paper bag marked *Patel's* on the kitchen table. I peek inside. *Burfi, jalabis,* and rosogullas, all in little foil containers with clear plastic lids.

Of course. That chalk drawing outside must have been the fancy doormat thing for the goddess Laxmi. This all means our Diwali is today. Is this the best day ever, or what? I take the stairs two at a time, head toward my room, and—

"I *hate* you." Doodles's face is all red and tear-streaked. "You aren't my sister anymore." She slams her bedroom door.

I pause. Maybe I should tell her I really didn't mean to spoil her drawing, but you know what? I'm getting a little bit sick of having everyone pissed at me. Besides, I don't want to really think about anything else but that kiss. At least for a while.

So, with a smile on my lips—what a great invention, lips—I head to my room. Oh no. Something is definitely up. My dad's in my room, his arms crossed, his face in a scowl. I'm in trouble. And this is definitely *not* about a chalk drawing.

Behind him is Chachi. She comes at me, pointed finger first, screaming in Punjabi. It's all gibberish to me. He says something back to her, also in Punjabi. Now they are both pointing at me and at each other as they argue.

My heart thumps as I drop my backpack. Doodles must have ratted me out. Told that I was in Chachi's room. What a turd. I'm frantically trying to think of an excuse.

Now my dad is pointing at me, still shouting in Punjabi, as if I can understand. He catches himself and touches his forehead. "This is unbelievable," he says.

"Doodles is a liar," I say. And a turd.

"That is all you have to say?" My father raises his bushy eyebrows. He grabs something from my floor and holds it up. "Why have you stolen from your own sister?"

"Doodles's purse," I say. "Where'd you find it?"

"You know," Chachi says. "Here." She points to my dresser.

I look from my dresser to the purse in my dad's hand. "But how did it get there?"

"Huh," Chachi says. "She lies. All the time lying. Shameful."

"Never mind," my dad tells her. "I will handle this."

"Yes," she says in an almost meek way. She bows her head, and as she passes me on the way out, I see her grin.

I shiver.

"How dare you take from this family?" my dad is saying. He's talking about how family is everything. How it is my duty to protect my little sister, to set an example. How it goes against all morality to steal. There's much more said about lying, deception, shame. "Imagine what Chachi must think of us when she finds my eldest daughter stealing. When she finds my littlest one's purse hidden in your dresser."

"Chachi found it?"

"She very kindly offered to help put away laundry, and what does she find in your drawer? Disgrace."

"But I didn't take anything."

"What do you call this?" Dad shakes the purse at me. "You have broken your sister's heart, Sangeet. I must know why."

I collapse, more than sit, on the bed. I'm wondering why too. The datebook, I think. Chachi must have missed it and guessed I'd been in her room. "Well, at least Doodles gets her purse back."

"And the money?" Dad throws the purse on my bed.

I check inside. Empty.

"Where's the money, Sangeet?"

"Daddy, I didn't take anything. I *swear*."

"And to think I drove all the way to Montgomeryville to get sweets so my darling daughters could have a special celebration. What a fool I am. Well, they are all going into the garbage, you hear me?"

"No, Daddy. *Please*."

"Please? Please tell me, where is the money you've been taking from my wallet? And from Mom's purse?"

"But, Daddy, Chachi took—"

"That is your excuse? To blame all your mistakes on my dead brother's wife? Your mother may buy your lies, but I am not so blind."

I tighten my lips, clench my hands. Hold in the words, hold in the anger. I scramble into my backpack and pull out my datebook. I open it and show my dad. "See? She took this and wrote all over it. I found it in her room. She stole it, and that's why—"

"Stop your nonsense," he says, not even looking at the book. "I shouldn't listen to your mother. Patience and understanding have no effect on you. Your chachi is right. We spoil you. Maybe I should just slap you and punish you. Maybe then you will learn."

I close my eyes.

"What are you doing with the money, eh? Buying drugs? Throwing your life away? You are breaking my heart, Sangeet," he says, his voice cracking.

My own heart feels squeezed. When I open my eyes, he is gone.

I take the purse and on shaky legs walk to Doodles's closed door and set the purse against it.

Stepping into my room, I quietly close my own door, lie on my bed, bury my face in my pillow. I am about to unleash my pent-up tears when I feel someone's eyes staring down on me. I know whose eyes they are, and before I even roll over, something has shifted inside me. Would Legolas the Elf sniffle into a pillow at a time like this, or would he set his jaw and fight to the death? Would the son of a great pirate feel sorry for himself and sit around wondering who was going to rescue him, or would he risk life and limb for truth, and justice, and, of course, love? And what would Rani do?

Just like that, the tears stop. Just like that, I turn over and see Orlando Bloom smiling down at me with approval and pride. I sit up, and pull out the pencil that was holding up my hair, and open my datebook, and start to study Chachi's Super Fresh working hours scribbled in the book.

And all I can think is, Game on.

24

"I know you're mad at me, but this is an emergency." Gina bends over her paper and writes my name, then puts a big **X** over it. **X** seems to be her new symbol, because she's inked a few on the backs of her hands—there's an **X** drawn on each fingernail, and her T-shirt is black, with a skull and crossbones on it.

So far Gina and I are the only two of our extra-credit group who have arrived at the library. "Come on, Gina. Our video camera is broken. I'll only use it for a few days."

Gina continues to mark out my name.

"Okay," I say. "If that's the way it's gotta be." Some friend she is. I just had to put up with my dad screaming at me and acting like I'm some sort of criminal, and all she can do is ignore me. I put my hippie notes into a neat pile on the circular table. I fold my hands on the top of the pile and stare at the bookshelves across the room. The library's super-quiet tonight. All I can hear is the pen scratching out my name.

I drum my fingers.

Scratch scratch.

I check the clock.

Scratch scratch.

I neaten my pile again.

Scratch scratch.

I snatch the pen from Gina. "Look, can't we talk about this? At least tell me what I've done so I can fix it. I mean, can you really be that mad about how I didn't fight for Jason? Because if that's the whole reason, I've totally got news."

Nothing.

"Or is something wrong?" I ask. "Like, do you have a problem? Because you know you can tell me anything. I'm totally here for you." I stare at her, willing her to give me a full confession. To say, Oh, Sang. It's bulimia. I can't stop myself. *Help me.*

Again, nothing.

"I wouldn't tell anyone unless you wanted me to," I say. "You know you can trust me. Best friends keep best-friend secrets. So *tell* me."

"My only problem is you." Gina takes the pen back. Turns the page in her spiral notebook and starts to write my name again, and another big **X**.

I cross my arms. Fine, I think. Forget her. I don't care. But I do care. I want to scream, or cry, or both.

The silence, plus the scratching, continues. No way

I'm telling her about the kiss. I start to wonder if Jason was really into it or not. I mean, I sort of seized him, didn't I?

Sara Harding shows up next and tosses a file onto the table. She takes off her sparkly blue ski jacket, does her usual boob adjustment, and sits.

"So how's Jason doing?" Gina asks her.

I send Gina a dirty look.

Sara just shrugs and rests her head on the table.

A moment later, Megan and Dalton come hurrying toward us. "Peace, fellow hippies," Megan says, and removes her white coat. "Totally my fault we're late. My mom took forever getting out of the house, and we had to give Dalton"—she giggles—"a ride"—giggle giggle—"so . . ."

"Blah, blah, blah," Sara says. "Let's just do this thing."

Dalton bumps into the table and dumps a pile of books onto it. "One of these days I'm getting contacts," he says, removing his fogged glasses and wiping them on his Princeton sweatshirt.

"You should totally do that," Megan says. "Wouldn't that look nice, Sang?"

"Yup," I say, opening my folder.

Megan kicks me. She lifts one eyebrow and looks out of the corners of her eyes toward Dalton.

So I look at Dalton too. He's still cleaning his glasses. There's nothing stuck to his face, so what does Megan want me to see?

"You look really nice without your glasses, Dalton," Gina says. She blushes, which is totally not like her, flips the page in her spiral, and, instead of drawing another **X**, starts doodling a flower.

What's this? Is Gina hot for Dalton? Since when?

"Right," Dalton says, laughing this off.

I steal a look at Dalton, who I decide does look especially nice without his glasses, though with his glasses he's okay too, in a harmless-guy sort of way. That's when Dalton puts his glasses back on and sees me looking at him. He starts flipping rapidly through a coffee table–sized book on the Vietnam War like he's speed-reading.

"Great. We all agree," Sara says in an exhausted voice. "Dalton is totally hot. Now can we finish this thing?"

SLAM! Dalton has knocked his book to the floor. He disappears under the table to pick it up. Megan points at Dalton, nods at me, and winks. "Make love, not war," she says. "It's a sixties saying. You know. Fight the good fight."

Huh? Whatever. "Okay," I say. "Before we start, does anybody have a video camera I can use for a day or two?"

"I think I—" Megan begins.

"I do!" Dalton jumps up and bumps his head on the edge of the table. We all wince.

"You okay?" Gina says, her voice filled with concern. "Anything I can do?"

I half expect her to place a kiss on his scalp.

"No," Dalton says, "I'm fine." He adjusts his glasses and settles onto his seat. "Anyhow, Sang, I've got this video camera you can use. Maybe I can drop it by your house tomorrow, after school?"

"Can you just bring it to school? I promise I'll take good care of it," I say.

"Oh, I know you will. That wasn't why—I mean, I didn't . . ." He sighs. "Let's get to work, shall we?"

"Thank you!" Sara says.

"F.U.," Gina mutters, then gathers her stuff and storms out.

"Gina?" Megan calls after her, but Gina's long gone. "Great. Now how are we supposed to pull this off?"

"Yeah," Sara says to me. "Your friend is totally screwing this up. You better drag her butt back in here."

"She's not exactly my friend anymore." I swallow hard. Hearing it out loud makes it sound true.

"And we're not exactly going to get an A now, are we?" Dalton says. "Gina is supposed to handle all the cultural stuff, right? The music and movies and books of the time? Does anybody know if she's even started?"

Everyone looks at me. "How should I know?"

"This is a complete disaster," Dalton says. "Damn!" He pounds his hand on the Vietnam book, which tumbles to the floor again.

"Let's calm down," Megan says, and holds her fingers up in a **V**. "Remember, make love, not war. Come on, everybody, let's see you hold up your peace sign."

Sara makes a sign with her finger, but it has nothing to do with peace.

25

Sweet Guy is on, but I just can't get into the episode tonight. How could one day go from so wonderful to so horrible? One second I'm kissing Jason, the next my dad is calling me a thief, and then Gina is crossing me out of her life.

I try to cheer myself up by dwelling on the kiss, but I can't stop thinking about the way my dad's voice shook when he said, "You are breaking my heart." Right now, Mom and Dad are "discussing" me upstairs in their bedroom. I can't exactly hear what they're saying. Their door is closed, so it's more like a muffled argument. But I know they are talking about me. After all, when you have a drug-addicted, money-stealing, bulimic daughter, you have a lot of stuff to work out. And when I went upstairs for a few moments during the last commercial, I heard my dad saying, "Just punish her . . . a whack . . . forget psychological mumbo jumbo!" This was followed by Mom saying something in a low, soothing voice.

I can't believe the only reason my parents aren't punishing me is because they think I'm "psychologically fragile" or something. I almost wish they would just ground me and get it over with.

Settled back on the couch in front of the television, I try to concentrate on the show. Jake, the star, just kissed his girlfriend, Jessica, in front of her teacher, and she's all embarrassed about it. This gets me thinking about Jason again. I kissed him right there on the corner. Who knows who might have been driving by? What if my mother was on her way to the store or something? I allow myself to wonder if Jason actually liked the kiss. If only I'd stayed around for another minute, I might know. Then again, sometimes ignorance is bliss.

Jake is now trying to write a poem for Jessica so she'll forgive him. "Oh, please," I say, and click the TV off. I make my way upstairs and hesitate by my parents' door. I can't stand being shut out like this, but do I really want to have it out with them? I raise my hand to knock, then think better of it and turn toward my room. Suddenly the door opens. Dad and I both give a jump of surprise.

I open my mouth, and because I can't think of anything else to say, I ask him about hippies. Well, I do need to know more about hippies, right?

He rubs his forehead like he's got a terrible headache and says, "We didn't have hippies in India."

"Oh," I say.

"Yes you did," my mother says. She's in bed, under the covers, with her pillow propped up behind her. A book is resting unopened on her knees. "You had the Beatles. They went to India. And what about all those people who went to India for enlightenment, to speak with holy men and people of that sort?"

"All freaky Westerners," my dad says. "I remember seeing some walking around in New Delhi. They looked all dirty and smelly and drugged-out. We thought they were strange."

"So you weren't a hippie?" I ask.

This actually gets a smile. "God, no. I was only born in 1959, so I was too young to be much of anything back then. Then again, we Indians were already wearing Nehru collars and eating yogurt and sprouts and doing yoga long before it became trendy. Well, I guess you could say we were what hippies were looking for. But they got it all wrong."

"How?" my mom asks.

"I don't know." My dad rolls up the sleeves of his pajama shirt. His pj's are from India, and, come to think of it, the shirt, with its long bottom and belled sleeves, does look kind of hippie-ish. "The Westerners thought all Indians were so spiritual. No concern for money or material things. But most Indians are just like anyone else. And the hippies used lots of drugs." He gives me a hard look.

I want to tell him I don't do drugs. I don't steal. That I

desperately need him to believe me. I want to ask him, Could we do our Diwali? Please? Even though you hate me?

But before I can say anything, Dad leaves. I hear the bathroom door close.

"Come here, Sang," Mom says, patting the bed beside her.

"I'd really better write all this hippie stuff down."

"Just for a minute."

So I stand by her bed, but don't sit. There seems to be an invisible barrier keeping me from getting too close.

"I was also too young to be a hippie," Mom says. She tells me she remembers wearing fishnet stockings to kindergarten and watching *Laugh-In* on TV. By the time she was my age, disco was big, and so were platform shoes.

"Hmm," I say.

"Everything okay?"

"What do you think?" I say.

My mom sighs.

"You know I didn't take the money from Doodles, Mom. Why would I do something like that?"

She holds open her arms. "Come here. I think we both need a hug."

Part of me wants to, but I remain still. I take one step back. Then two. "Good night, Mom," I say, and just walk away from her.

26

"Sorry it's so old," Dalton says.

Inside the bag is a black video camera and extra tapes. I laugh. "It's newer than the one we have. My parents aren't exactly into cutting-edge technology."

"And my parents are just cheap," he says. "The battery probably needs to be charged. I'm sorry I forgot to do that, but the charger is in there. It takes a few hours. And the manual is in there too. Or you could call me if you have any questions."

"You sure your parents don't mind me borrowing this?" I ask.

"Actually," Dalton says, scratching behind his ear, "I kind of didn't ask them. But I'm sure it's fine. I mean, we only use the thing on major holidays. So as long as you get it back to me before Thanksgiving, it's cool."

"Don't worry. I'll definitely return it before the two weeks are up. And I promise I'll keep it safe." I zip up my coat, pull my backpack from my locker, and loop the camera bag over my shoulder.

"You ever use one of these before? Because, if you want," he says, and clears his throat, "I could come over and show you how it works." He shrugs. "You know, if you want."

"Oh, that's okay," I say.

"Oh, okay, then," he says in an extra-peppy voice, and slips into the crowd of students heading to their buses.

"Thanks, Dalton!" I shout at his back.

"Ooooh, it's going so well," Megan says, practically leaping out at me. "Did he ask you out?"

I look up and down the hall. "I haven't seen him all day."

"Good one," Megan says, giving me a playful nudge as we head toward the doors. "Seriously, I think he will any day now. He told me he's totally into you."

"He did?" I beam. And here I'd been rehearsing this whole "I took too much cough syrup, so I was stoned out of my mind and didn't know what I was doing when I kissed you" scenario for him, just in case. "Since when have you and Jason been friends?"

"Jason who?"

I give her a playful nudge back. "Good one."

But Megan is serious. She pulls me out of the mass of surging students and toward the water fountain. "I'm talking about Dalton," she says. "Who are you talking about?"

"Dalton?" I say. At that precise moment, Gina walks by. She's dressed totally in black and is wearing skull-

and-crossbones earrings. Somehow the look actually works on her. Sort of New York artsy. Gina. Dalton. Me. Right. Now I totally get it. But is that all there is to it? She's just mad about a guy? Somehow I don't think so.

"Aren't you into him? Do you want me to talk to him to set him straight?"

"No! No thanks, I mean."

"Wait a minute," she says. "Jason *who*?" At this moment the buses roar to life. "Crap, I got to go. I'm not walking today. See ya," Megan says, and rushes to her bus.

"Stinkin' Monkeys!" someone says, and grabs my shoulders.

I jump.

"Sorry. Didn't mean to freak you out," Jason says. "The Stinkin' Monkeys are coming to Philly in a week, and they just added another performance, Saturday night. Do you want to go?"

"That's awesome," I say. Not that I'm so crazy about the Stinkin' Monkeys. I mean, they're probably great and all that, but JASON IS ASKING ME OUT!!!!! Breathe, breathe, breathe. Okay. So this means he didn't mind that kiss, and he actually likes me, and, ohmygod, does this mean HE MIGHT KISS *ME* SOON???? I clutch the camera bag. Relax. Don't think too hard. Don't go all Megan Chung and blow everything. Okay. I'm cool.

"Check this out," he says, and pulls tickets from the side pocket of his backpack. "We can take the train, and my older brother's going with us. Hope you don't mind that, but my parents have this thing about me going into the city." He rolls his eyes. "I know. It's totally dorky of them."

"Right," I say. And my parents are so dorky that I'm not even allowed to go out with you at all, never mind to a concert in Philadelphia. "It sounds great."

"Excellent," he says, totally taking my reply as a yes. "You walking today?"

"Sure," I say. I should set things straight. Tell him I can't go, no way, forget about it. Even though I want to go more than I want to do anything in the whole entire world. Even though telling him I can't have a boyfriend at all will surely send him running and screaming in the opposite direction. Still, it's the right thing to do. "Actually, Jason, what I meant to say . . . ," I begin, but then he takes my hand. His hand is large and warm, and fits perfectly with mine. Ohmygod, my bones have all turned to jelly. He pulls me outdoors. The sun glints on his diamond stud earring and he's smiling, and suddenly I don't care about what's right. Oh, I'm going to this concert. I'm totally going. "Actually," I say again, "I was wondering, do you know anything about video cameras?"

27

I step into my house expecting the unexpected. Even though the enemy is, according to my datebook, at Super Fresh until 8:30 p.m., she might have planted a bomb of sorts.

I see Dad having a cup of tea at the table and thumbing through the newspaper.

"Hi, Dad."

"Sangeet," he says, and turns the page. I stand there, waiting for him to say more. He doesn't.

Whatever. I walk toward the stairs, but stop and march back to him. "Okay, here's the thing. I didn't do anything wrong, but even if I did, couldn't we still have our Diwali?"

He opens his mouth, but before he can speak, I say, "For Doodles? I mean, why punish her?"

His expression softens for a moment, but in a blink it turns hard and cold. "Diwali is over."

"But that's so *unfair*."

He turns to his newspaper, and I close my mouth tight. I go to my room and try hard not to scream. How can he possibly think these things about me? How? I try to calm myself, remembering that soon everything is going to change. Soon he'll be all, I'm so sorry, Sang. And all, How can I ever make it up to you?

I set up the video camera's battery in the recharger. If it charges fast enough, I should be able to film all the stolen things in Chachi's drawers tonight. It's a good thing I asked Jason about the camera, because it turns out he's really into moviemaking, which is why he got the job at the County Theater. Sort of a small stepping-stone in his career. After he told me this, he kissed my hand, sending little shock waves up my arm. And I thought, This is it. The real kiss is coming. The one where he initiates and I don't run away and we linger. . . . Only the real kiss never came, which was kind of awkward. You know, just waiting for something to happen, and then it doesn't. But it's okay. One step at a time, right? I mean, what's the rush?

I WANT HIM TO KISS ME!!!!!

Right. So anyway, while I was waiting for the kiss that never came, Jason showed me how to work Dalton's camera, which is almost as old as our camera, but different enough to make it confusing. Okay, so all I've got to do now is wait for the battery to charge. But for some reason, I feel uneasy. I decide I need to take a quick peek into Chachi's room. I take off my sneakers and slip into the hallway. Doodles is on her bed, sorting through her candy orders and putting money she's collected in neat piles. Fortunately, she doesn't look up as I pass. And I don't have to worry about her hearing me, because her headphones are on and she's blasting her *Freaky Friday* soundtrack CD so loud, I can hear it buzzing.

Past Doodles's door, I stop and listen. Dad's still rustling the paper downstairs. I don't hear Mom anywhere, so she must be out saving the world. Now I'm up the stairs and in front of Chachi's door. I turn the knob. Locked. My heart starts to race. Is she in there? Was her schedule changed? I hazard a faint knock. Nothing. This can only mean that she left and locked the door on her way out, which definitely confirms that she knows I've been in her room. It's one of those easy-open push-button locks, so I wonder what the point is. In a matter of seconds, I get a bobby pin from my bedroom, stick it into the lock, and hear that satisfying pop. That must be how she gets in, since there's no key.

I head straight for the drawers. Empty. Crap crap triple crap. I turn and pull open the closet. Just clothes. What could she have done with all that food? I imagine her stuffing it, wrappers and all, into her mouth. Maybe Chachi's the bulimic. I imagine her in a paper gown at Dr. Dander's office. Dr. Dander saying, "I'm afraid it's a classic case." Chachi saying, "No. Think again. I must know."

All right, so there's no more food evidence. What about the money? I sort through the junk on the desk and dresser. Just letters and catalogs and scraps of paper. Great. I bite my thumb. The mattress, I think, and look under the left side of it. Nothing. But on the right side, I find a small leather-bound book. Must be her diary. Okay. Maybe this is cold and nasty of me, but I take it. I tuck it in my back pocket and straighten the bed. I pause as I notice Chacha's picture on the wall, staring at me. Never mind. I hit the lock and pull the door shut on my way out.

Now my mind is buzzing like Doodles's headphones. I need a new plan, and I need it fast.

I lean into Doodles's room. "Hey, Doodles." She's so into her CD, she doesn't hear me. I pull down her headphones. "I said, hey."

"Go away." She pulls the headphones back up, but I pull their plug out of the CD player and the buzzing stops. "I'm not talking to you ever again."

"Yes you are," I say, and sit at the foot of her bed. "Come on, Doodles. You don't really think I took your Christmas money, do you?"

Doodles scoops up the candy money and tries to storm out of the room, but I snag her by the arm.

"Let go of me." She tries to shake me off, but it's no use. She's crying now. "I was saving to buy you a *Lord of the Rings* computer game, but you don't deserve it. You don't deserve *anything.*"

"You were? Oh, Doodles, that's so sweet." My grip relaxes. She almost slips through my hands, but I grab her just in time.

"You got your stupid money, now just leave me alone!"

"Not until you listen to my story."

"I'm not listening to your dumb stories, ever."

"Just this one last time, Doodles. Then, if you want, I'll leave you be. Deal?"

She wipes her cheeks with the back of her hand. "Do I have a choice?"

Still holding her arm, I lead her back to the bed and we both sit. "Okay, Doodles. It's like this. Remember how Rani had to undo the power of the evil genie? And how she had to break into the genie's high tower to find all the power and secrets that had been taken there? Well, Rani did make it there, and she was followed by her little faithful friend," I say, and search for a name, something close to Cherise. "Her friend Scheherazade. The tower was a terrible and frightening place, but Rani didn't care. She knew she had to stop all the evil and hurt the genie had caused, not only to her but to everyone she cared for. Like Scheherazade. See, Scheherazade had this special sparkling jewel, and now it was missing. And Rani knew the genie was to blame. You following me?"

Doodles gives a small nod.

"Rani doesn't see the gem in the genie's tower, but she sees all this shiny stuff in this trunk. Rani thinks it might be everyone's joy and happiness the genie has taken away. But before Rani can take it all back, she hears the genie returning. Rani and Scheherazade escape just in time.

"At least they think they do. The very next night, a dark figure is seen scurrying through the alleyways of the city shouting, 'Thief! Traitor!' and pointing toward Rani's room in the palace. Guards search Rani's room, expecting to find someone hiding there, but instead they find Scheherazade's jewel, hidden among the gowns."

"So Rani was the thief," Doodles says.

I shake my head. "That's the way it looked. That's the way the evil genie wanted it to look, and that's why the gem was planted there. To punish Rani and Scheherazade for entering the tower. To spoil their friendship and joy forever. Now, the question is, Did the genie succeed? Or will Rani and Scheherazade band together to bring the monstrous genie down?

"That's it," I say, and release Doodles's arm. "That's the whole story so far."

Doodles is thoughtful for a moment. "Chachi's the genie?"

"Yes."

"You mean she planted my purse in your dresser?"

"That's exactly what I mean."

Doodles rolls her eyes. "Then why didn't you just say so?"

28

We are having another dinner without Chachi, since she is still at Super Fresh. God bless Super Fresh. We're having burgers and fries. Mom makes her burgers with ground chicken, and they are so juicy. I'd like another one, but I can feel her eyes on me. See, if a suspected anorexic is eating, everyone can see that she's doing better. But if a suspected bulimic stuffs herself, well . . .

I sigh. I guess there'll be other meals, other chances to have a second burger. Soon enough, I think. I glare at Doodles, but she is too into rolling her fries in catsup to notice me. I clear my throat and she looks at me, but so do my mom and dad.

"Yes?" my dad says.

"Throat's dry," I say, and take a sip of milk. I glare at Doodles again and am thinking of kicking her, even though I don't think my legs will reach her, but she finally gets the message.

"I need to turn in my candy money soon," she says, and nods at me. "So Sunday night, I'm gonna put my money on the table in the living room, just so we don't forget to bring it to school on Monday."

"Sounds fine," Mom says.

I hazard a wink at Doodles. So far so good. I knew we had to give Mom some reason to leave something on the coffee table all night or she, anti-clutter queen that she is, would immediately neaten it away.

"So, Sangeet?" Mom says. "Did you eat enough?"

No! I want to stuff my face with lots and lots of burgers!!!! "Yes, I'm fine."

She nods, wipes her mouth with a napkin, and turns to my sister. "Actually, I was thinking. Instead of leaving the candy money on the table, why don't we just put it in your backpack tonight so we don't forget it? It'll be much neater and simpler."

"You can't," I say. Crap. Why not? "Uh, she has to do it her way. Her teacher's doing this lesson on responsibility, and wants her to make her own decisions. Isn't that right, Doodles?"

"But Mrs. Mertle never said—"

"Yes, she did. *Remember?*" I glare at her again.

Doodles looks all serious, and I think she really is trying to remember. Great. So I say, "Remember how it was all part of that lesson about Scheherazade?"

Doodles's eyes widen. "Oh yeah."

Oh brother.

Mom says, "Okay, then. We'll do it your way, Cherise," and starts to collect the plates.

Dad is studying me and Doodles and rubbing his chin like he's suspicious about something. Before he can speak, I excuse myself and head to the bathroom. It's Evasive Tactics all over again, but I also do have to pee. The freaky thing is, when I'm done and I open the door, there's Mom.

"Everything okay?" she says. "In there?" I guess she means in the bathroom, but the way she gets real close to me and studies my face, "in there" could just as well mean in that whacked-out head of mine.

"Yeah."

"Great." She's wearing's a thin-lipped false smile, and she's wringing her hands.

"God, Mom. I wasn't purging. I was peeing."

"I know that. I know that," she says, still wearing that weird insincere smile.

The phone rings. It's Jason, I'm one hundred percent sure. I shout, "I'll get it," and race to my room.

"Is it Jason Crawford?" the voice says, which totally throws me. "Sara's Jason?"

Then it clicks. It's Megan on the phone. And she's hit a nerve. "What do you mean, *Sara's Jason*?"

"I just mean, he was with her in the library that time. Is it him? He's pretty new, right? Didn't he move in like the end of last year? Because I couldn't find him in the yearbook. Or was he from the other middle school? Well?"

"Well what?"

"TELL ME!"

"There isn't much to tell." Which, really, is true. Sort of.

"Are you going out with him? Because he is pretty hot, you know? And what about Sara? And do you think he has any hot friends? Oh, please tell me he's got hot friends. You could introduce me," she says in a breathless voice. "W-we could double-date."

"I don't know."

"You don't know about what? The friend doesn't have to be sizzling-hot. Promise you'll introduce me. *Please.*"

"Megan, relax."

"I can't! That's the problem. You know what would really help me relax? A boyfriend. I think that would fix everything. What do you think?"

"I think my mom's calling me," I say. This is a lie, but I can't exactly say what I really think—that Megan's a terrifying lunatic around guys, and the last thing I'd want to do is to introduce her to Jason and his friends. I know that's harsh, but I hardly know Jason and I don't know any of his friends, and Megan would totally ruin everything with one of her embarrassing scenes. "I gotta go."

"Hey, you doing anything tonight? Like going out with Jason?" She giggles.

She's hit another nerve. "Not exactly."

"Oh. A bunch of us are going to the football game. You want to come?"

"I can't." I could, but I've got this whole filming thing set up. And suppose Jason does call? "But thanks for asking."

"Sure. What are friends for?"

Now I feel guilty. Megan is my friend. If I can introduce her to Jason's friends, then I should, shouldn't I? Maybe she'll forget she ever asked. . . .

We hang up, and now I'm listening to Q102 (on low, so Dad won't go nuts), hoping to catch some more music by the Stinkin' Monkeys. If I were to go to that concert, which I know is totally impossible (but you never know), then I don't want to be a total loser and not recognize a single song.

While I do this, I load the fully charged battery in the video camera and practice by filming my room. I zoom in on my mirror, and for an instant I can picture myself as a movie director shouting, "Cut!" and "Action!" Orlando Bloom, of course, is the star of the film, and Jason is the co-director, but he keeps messing up his shots since his camera keeps straying over to me—because, let's face it! I look totally amazing with this camera in my hand. I lower the camera and stare at myself in the mirror for a moment. And it's still just me staring back. I shake out my hair like they do on those shampoo commercials, but it doesn't flow and sway like it does on the model. More like it flops and tangles. And just by my hairline are the dreaded beginnings of three zits. Ugh. And my nose, did it grow? What if I had a growth spurt and only my nose grew? I know that's stupid, but I push my nose back in a bit, just in case.

Forget all that. I squint my eyes so my face looks blurred and imagine I really am exotic and mysterious, and not just some average girl from Doylestown, Pennsylvania. Pretend that I know how to use this camera, and that I'm allowed to date guys and go to concerts. What's the harm in that?

I return my eye to the camera and quickly scan my room in a dizzying rush of images. I zoom in on Orlando's face. And up close like that, he doesn't look like a poster on a ceiling but like somebody real. Like an actor in my own film. Cool.

I've got to see if it looks as real as I think, so I sit up and hit the rewind button, which stops immediately. Then I look through the viewfinder and push PLAY. Nothing. Great. Is this stupid camera broken too? I shuffle through the manual, and, duh, I didn't hit the record button. I bet a digital camera would work like a dream. But we'll never get one.

Feeling restless, I sit at my computer and scan my buddy list. On top is Gina's screen name, Dare2Dare732. Guess she's not grounded anymore. There's a funny feeling in my stomach: dinner mixed with sadness and loneliness. I want to IM her, but she hates me. She totally hates me. I mean, it's Friday night. We should be hanging out, or at least chatting. Jason is the most incredible thing that might, just might, be happening to me, and

I'm dying to share this with Gina like I've shared everything forever, but . . .

I swallow hard and look at the rest of the names. Hari's not on. Jason's not on. So what is Jason doing tonight? And why didn't he at least ask me to join him? I mean, *are* we going out? He did hold my hand in front of everyone. If that doesn't mean something, I don't know what does. I guess I'm really busy this weekend anyway. There's the presentation on Monday, and of course the Chachi trap. Still, it would have been nice if he had asked me to hang out this weekend, you know? Even though I'm not allowed to. My thoughts immediately jump to Slutty Sara. Slutty Sara and Jason.

Now I feel really crappy. So crappy, in fact, I decide to do something completely and horribly lame for my Friday night. Something that will have me totally wallowing in self-pity: my homework. And this is what I do until it is nearly time for the next part of the trap to begin.

29

It's a raw Saturday morning. More winter- than fall-feeling. The wind is cutting through my sweat-pants, my nose is already running, and I've only biked to the end of my street so far. I think about turning back. I mean, what's the point? If Gina shows up in the cemetery, she'll probably treat me like I'm a ghost or something. But biking/running on a Saturday morning has become such a habit. Gina and I have done it in rain-storms, with mud splattering up my back and around Gina's ankles, and in the snow (which, with a bike, can be real tough). Sometimes we've seen freshly dug graves standing empty, and once we even saw a casket being lowered into a hole. We were quiet a long time after we saw that. But we shared that quiet. We did it together. The quiet between us now, there's no togetherness in it at all.

I guess I keep hoping everything will somehow turn

out okay. Some things do improve, don't they? After all, didn't the next step in the Chachi trap go good last night? I've got to give Doodles a lot of credit, because she could have totally screwed it up, but she didn't. When Dad came back from picking up Chachi, I told Doodles to go downstairs. She did, wearing her most serious expression. I listened as Chachi came into the house too, and as Doodles announced again that she'd be keeping all her candy money on the living room table on Sunday night so she wouldn't forget to bring it to school.

"Cherise, baby," my dad said, "you told me this already, remember?"

Then I heard Chachi stomping up the steps, so I backed into my room. Say it, Doodles, I thought. Say it while Chachi can hear. And then, just like we practiced, Doodles said, "It's just such a lot of money, Daddy. More than two hundred dollars."

At that moment, I heard Chachi's feet stop.

Now all Doodles and I have to do is to spend the rest of the weekend talking up all the money she's collected, to tempt and tempt and tempt Chachi until there's no way she can resist the lure. Then, *BAM!* She's busted.

I bike up to the Elmer mausoleum. No sign of Gina. I rub my icy hands together and wait. The wind shakes the branches of the old maples around the graveyard. Brown, brittle leaves scuttle around the grass till they are pressed against the tombstones. A golden banner spelling out MOTHER, loosened from its memorial wreath, tumbles past me. I'm about to give up on this entire bike/run thing when over the hill I catch sight of a pink knit hat bouncing along.

I try not to smile and it's a good thing, because she marches right past me. She tucks a strand of her sandy-blond hair back into her hat and starts her stretch beside the mausoleum. So I'm a ghost after all.

I set down my bike, and the next moment I'm mimicking her stretches. Suddenly I'm talking, and I don't care if she's listening or not. And at first she isn't, or doesn't seem to be, but when I tell her about the bulimia appointment, she stops in mid-stretch. "Not that it was horrible," I say, studying her face. "What I mean is, if you needed help, it would have been great, you know?"

She touches her toes. I decide to change the subject. When I explain about how Chachi stole Doodles's purse and set me up, Gina mutters, "That bitch."

We start to bike/run, and I begin to feel that things might end up okay between us. Except for the fact that Gina is running much faster than she usually does. Maybe she's trying to burn lots of calories. That's something a bulimic would do, isn't it? As always, I do extra laps around the cemetery paths. Each time I reach Gina, I slow down, coast by her side, and talk. Each time, I tell her a little more about Jason. Dissing him, kissing him, and the whole Stinkin' Monkeys saga.

"You have to go," Gina says.

"I wish."

Gina stops. I brake. "You know how much a concert costs?"

"Thirty bucks?"

"More. Sometimes much more. He must be really into you, Sang, to take you along. You have to go. All you need is a plan."

"Yeah?"

Gina puts her hands on her hips. She twists her mouth as if she's chewing something, then says, "Good luck with that."

"What? Wait."

But she's jogging again. I'm riding beside her. She looks angry. Better change the subject. "So are you ready for the presentation Monday?"

"Afraid I'm going to screw up your precious grade?"

"No, I didn't mean that, what I meant—"

"Everything is under control," she says in a cool voice.

"You know," I say, "bulimics usually try to control everything. Or do they feel out of control? I can't remember. Which do you think it is?" I watch her closely, expecting some sort of reaction.

Gina just rolls her eyes.

I take another lap, half expecting her to be gone when I round the bend, but there she is. I tell her about my hippie research. About how hippies were mostly middle-class kids. And how they wanted total freedom. "In a way, that's kind of like us, right?" Gina doesn't say anything, but she doesn't tell me to shut up either, so I babble on about how the hippies didn't like anything organized, like religion, or school, or government.

I take another lap, feeling even more certain that she won't be there when I round the bend again. That I've lost her. I see she's still there, jogging along, but I can't shake the feeling that she's somehow gone.

"Hey, Gina," I say when I'm at her side. "We need to talk."

She looks at me through the corners of her eyes. "What do you think we've been doing?"

"You know what I mean. I just, well, I really miss you." I wait for her to say something. She doesn't. "Don't you miss me? A little?"

"That's not the point," she says.

"Then what is the point? Would you just tell me so I can say 'Sorry' and we can move on? Whatever I did or said, I'm sorry. I'm really really sorry, okay?"

"It's not about you."

"Is this all about Dalton? Because if you spent some time with him, you know, working on the project this weekend or something, I bet he'd totally be into you in a flash. He'd be crazy not to be, because you're—"

"Don't," she says.

Crap. I bite my lip. Just say what you mean, Sang. "Well, is there something else wrong? Something you can't control, maybe? Because if there is something wrong, you can tell me. You know, bulimia isn't anything to be ashamed of."

Gina stops, and so do I. Her cheeks are an angry pink. "You are out of your frickin' mind, you know that?"

"Nobody's out of their mind," I say pointedly. God, I'm sounding just like my mom. Maybe I should shut up. But how can I? What if, unlike my mom, I'm actually right? "It's totally curable, Gina. But you need help."

"Me? Need help? Because you think I'm bulimic? What an ego you have! You think you've got me all figured out. That I'm poor pathetic Gina, who can't survive without you. That I must have a goddamned eating disorder, because why else would I not be talking to you, right? It doesn't even occur to you I'm just not into being your friend anymore."

"Okay." Tears sting my eyes. "So you're saying you're not bulimic."

"I'm saying people change. They grow apart. So get your own life."

She turns off the paved path, races across the street and onto a wood-chip trail through the forest where she knows my bike can't follow. The wind howls, and leaves swirl behind her, and for a minute all I see of her is her hot-pink cap bobbing. She reaches a twist in the trail and disappears.

30

I can't help but think Gina would have approved of my trap. The way I took it step by step. The way I dangled temptation in front of the nose of my prey. The way I waited and waited.

It's Sunday night, and Doodles and I are still waiting. We're hiding behind the living room couch with a decent view of her candy money, which is resting on the coffee table. Of course, all of this would probably work a lot better if Doodles wasn't hiding with me, but she wouldn't take no for an answer. Now she keeps squirming and talking about stupid stuff in what she thinks is a hushed voice. She's getting louder and louder as she talks, and I have to keep elbowing her and telling her to shut up.

I look through the camera for the zillionth time, praying that Chachi will come down. Maybe "praying" isn't the right word to use. Especially with today being Sunday and with my mom, the occasional Catholic, deciding that this Sunday we all (minus Chachi, thank God) had to go to mass, what with "all the difficulties we've been experiencing of late."

So I sat on the hard pew, with Doodles on one side of me (squirming there too) and Dad on the other side of me, his eyes closed and his lips moving in some silent Sikh prayer. My mom was flipping through the mass book, desperate to not lose her place or be caught not knowing all the words to the Apostles' Creed or when to stand up, sit down, fight fight fight (yeah, team!). Anyhow, during the homily, the priest stepped off the main altar area and walked in front of the pews, talking about what it means to be honest. Really honest. How hard that is, and how important it is. "Jesus was honest, and look." He gestured toward the giant Christ on the cross that is hanging behind the altar.

I gulped and glanced at my dad, who was nodding his head like he agreed with everything. My dad is not Catholic, he's a Sikh. He believes in one God, and that it's right to be good to others, be moral. That kind of stuff. But Jesus on a cross? Somehow I don't think that's written about in the Guru Granth Sahib.

I spent the rest of mass staring at light shining blue and red through the giant stained-glass window, and thinking about how my trap was okay because, while sneaky, it was to expose the real truth. And even though this is not very "turn the other cheek," it's still the right thing to do, isn't it? Of course it is.

So after that I was totally convinced. That is, until

lunch. While we four were eating grilled cheese sandwiches, Chachi came and sat at the table and stared at my dad. Our conversation just stopped.

"Are you working today, Kajal?" my mom said.

Chachi didn't answer, just kept staring at my dad.

My dad continued to eat as if nothing weird were happening, but I could tell by the way he chewed and chewed and chewed his sandwich and stared at nothing in particular that he felt kind of strange. And I could feel something about to happen, like just before a storm, when the air gets all still and heavy and uncomfortable. Doodles and I were wolfing down our sandwiches, gulping our milk. Doodles finished first and bolted from the table.

I was almost done. I had one swallow more when Chachi pointed her finger at Dad. "You have forgotten your dead brother," she said. "You have forgotten all about him."

Dad slowly put down his glass and set his jaw.

"How dare you?" Chachi said.

Dad's nostrils flared as he took a deep breath.

"You're all done, honey?" Mom asked me. "Why don't you just scoot on upstairs?"

But before I could scoot, the action began. "This is his death anniversary, and what do you do? Laugh, eat. You should fast. You should mourn. You should suffer." I hazarded a look at Chachi. Crap. Tears filled her eyes. "He was a good, good man. But you? You do not care at all."

My dad slowly pushed his plate away. "You think I

don't remember his death anniversary? You think I don't remember my own little brother with sorrow every single day of my life?"

"No," Chachi said, her eyes now dry. She poked her finger toward my mom. "Her, I don't blame. She doesn't know any better. But you. You are no good."

I was dying to run out of there, but afraid that Chachi would then start pointing her finger at me. I decided it was best just not to move. Besides, my dad was glaring at Chachi. I didn't want to miss him ripping into her.

"Your brother would be ashamed to see you now." Chachi swayed her head from side to side, obviously proud of what she'd just said.

I braced myself for the explosion. For my dad screaming at her. Instead, he spoke in a calm voice, in Punjabi. I thought maybe he was saying something soothing to her, but when he stopped, Chachi banged the table with her fist, threw her chair to the ground, and stomped upstairs. My heart thundered in my chest as I sat, waiting for Dad's next move. After a minute he stood, picked up his plate, and placed it in the sink. He left the house to take what turned out to be a long, long walk. Mom and I cleaned up the kitchen. Neither one of us talked.

So now I'm still not totally sure about this whole trap thing. I'm sitting in the dark, holding this camera and wondering, What will happen when I show everyone this film? How will Chachi react when I catch her red-handed? Will she cry? Will she throw furniture? And whose side will my parents take? I mean, if they let her treat my dad like that, maybe they won't mind a little bit of money taken here and there. Maybe being a widow is a free ticket to being nasty.

Be strong, I tell myself. And I remind myself of the only thing I know for certain: things can't keep going the way they've been going. Our family is falling to pieces.

So I look through the lens at the steps. Doodles finally has stopped squirming, and I think she's asleep. Then I hear a door open. My heart is pounding again. This is it. I hear Chachi's bare feet rasping against the wood floor. In a moment I see the beam of her flashlight. She is wearing her dark blue sweat suit, and her black hair is covering most of her face. I worry that the flashlight won't make it bright enough for filming. I worry that nothing will show up on the video at all.

Just keep the camera trained on her, I think. She goes straight for the money. She's reaching for it. Now I realize the camera isn't making any sound. Crap. Press the record button, idiot! I do. But instead of the gentle whirr I usually hear when the tape is moving, there's nothing. Nothing! I hit the button again. Damn it all to hell. NOTHING.

Chachi's got her hand on the money. She'll take the money, I'll have no proof, and Doodles will be screwed again. So I elbow Doodles hard.

"Ow!"

Chachi drops the money. "Eh?" She shines the flashlight on us just as I ditch the camera behind the couch. "What is this?"

"W-we fell asleep," I say. "Right, Doodles? We were telling ghost stories in the dark to be spooky, and must have fallen asleep."

"Get out, you stupid girls." The flashlight casts deep shadows on her face, and I can see her fury. "Sneaky bad brats! Eh!" She's shouting. "Get out, NOW!"

I push Doodles up the stairs, and I grab the money. No way she's getting her hands on this, I think as I rush past her. She grabs my arm and whirls me around. "What do you think you are doing? Eh?"

"Nothing," I say.

She pulls at the wad of cash, and I snatch it back. Her hand slaps me hard, leaving a burning sensation across my cheek.

The hall light comes on. "What is going on down there?" My dad, his pajamas and hair rumpled, is at the top of the stairs.

Chachi starts rattling off something in Punjabi. Dad comes downstairs and turns on the living room light. He looks at me, at the money in my hand. His expression says it all.

"Dad, I—"

But he just looks away.

Hands trembling, I hand him the money and take a step back. Chachi is beside him. I turn and run to my room and lock the door, and wish I could just disappear.

31

"The fifties may seem like a happy time when everyone was polite and respectful," I say, and point to the time line I'd hung on the wall behind me. I'm wearing a tie-dye shirt and a peace-sign necklace and a pair of old bell-bottom jeans Gina handed to me this morning. She gave outfits to all of our team. Army fatigues for Dalton, platform shoes and a glittery silver disco pantsuit for Megan, and a hideous striped maxiskirt for Sara that she absolutely refused to wear. Gina changed into her mom's red hot pants (which Mrs. Finelli said she must change out of the very moment her presentation is done), a fake-fur top, and a pair of shiny black boots, and she put on white lipstick and white eye shadow.

"In the fifties," I tell the class, "it seemed everyone had a house with a white picket fence and life was perfect. But when you look past the bobby socks and poodle skirts, you'll find a time when, like Megan just told you, women didn't have equal rights, and people of color couldn't share the same school or even the same water fountain with white people. Things had to change. And in the sixties, with Vietnam raging"—I nod toward Dalton, who has just finished his segment on that war—"the young were paying the highest price in the battles. So they wore their hair long and dressed differently, and talked about peace and love. They were rebelling not just against their parents but against everything organized. Everything that told them what to do or think. And the protests, the sit-ins, the marches, were huge. Like the one in D.C. in 1967. One hundred and fifty thousand people protested. Can you imagine?" I talk about how antiwar protests went on well into the seventies. How sit-ins and demonstrations on college campuses resulted in demonstrators being shot to death. I explain how riots followed, and how colleges all across the country were closed. "But hippies let everyone know how horrible the war in Vietnam really was, and this surely helped end the war faster. Hippies did step out of what was considered normal by society. They were rebels. And, in a way, many of them were also heroes who dared to be different and helped change the world."

I'm totally relieved that's done. I take my seat, and Dalton gives me a bright full-dimple smile that I hope Gina doesn't see. Not that anything I do matters to her anymore.

Next is Sara, who is supposed to talk about space

exploration. "It was really cool," she says. "Lots of people watched it on TV and stuff." She chews her gum and stares out the window like she's the one in outer space.

"And . . . ?" Mrs. Finelli prompts her.

"And," Sara says, and giggles, "well, there was this space mission, and the guys almost died, but they didn't." She shrugs. "They made a movie out of it."

Dalton sinks into his seat. I'm biting my lip hard. It's Gina's turn, and sure, she gave us costumes, but none of us have seen her work. What if she never did her research? That would be just like her: all big ideas with nothing to back them up. What if her part is as lame as Sara's? I imagine my transcript arriving at a college with a C under "History" and being immediately put into a shredder.

I'm chewing on my thumbnail now. Come on, Gina. I know you don't like me anymore, but please please don't shred my future.

She sashays in her hot pants to the front of the room, and as she passes Dalton's desk, he sits up. Gina pulls down the movie screen, flicks off the lights, and sashays to the back of the room, where a computer is rigged up.

Her presentation turns out to be on the protest songs of the sixties and the seventies, with graphics and pictures of hippies clasping signs, and rock groups jamming on guitars, and Beetle vans plastered with flower and peace-sign stickers, and the music of the day playing. When a photo of our cemetery appears, Pete Seeger sings:

Where have all the soldiers gone?
Gone to graveyards every one.
When will they ever learn?
When will they ever learn?

It's incredible. It's creative and says it all and puts all of our other presentations to shame, and I knew, just knew, she'd pull it off, because she's amazing. Okay, so maybe I didn't know. How could I? She's never done something this polished in her whole life. Not without my help, that is.

The last thing she presents is a verse from "The Times They Are A-Changin'," by Bob Dylan:

Come mothers and fathers
Throughout the land
And don't criticize
What you can't understand
Your sons and your daughters
Are beyond your command
Your old road is
Rapidly agin'.
Please get out of the new one
If you can't lend your hand
For the times they are a-changin'.

32

"Thanks anyway, Dalton." I hand him back the video camera. "I couldn't get it to work right. It kept getting stuck or something every time I tried to film."

"Really?" He takes it from me and sets it on his locker shelf. "That's weird. Sorry about that."

"Oh, don't apologize. It was nice of you to lend it to me." I hitch up my backpack on my shoulder. "See ya."

"Sang, wait. I'll walk with you to the bus." He pulls out his coat and bag, and slams his locker shut. "Think we got an A today?"

"Yeah. I think we did."

He smiles at me. "Me too. It was dicey for a while there, and I was thinking, Why did I ever sign up for this stupid project in the first place? Then I remembered." He stops and faces me. "You."

"Me?" Gulp.

"You must feel it too."

"Man, it's hot in here," I say, dramatically fanning my face. "Is that what you feel? Maybe it's an Indian summer. You think? Not Indian like me, you know, more like Pocahontas, but that should be a Native American summer, then. Right?"

Dalton touches my arm and leans toward me. Right there in the hall, in the middle of everyone walking to the buses, he's coming at me with his lips! "I'm gonna be sick." Did I say that out loud? I must have, because Dalton looks completely stricken. "I—I haven't been well all day," I say. "Maybe that's why I feel so hot."

He touches my forehead. "You are a little warm. But I don't care," he says, and again leans close to me, but I lean back like we're ballroom dancers doing a dip.

"Dalton!" I push him away and take a giant step backward.

He takes a giant step forward, leans closer . . .

"Wait!" I hold up my hands. "Don't get too close. It might be that throw-up bug that's going around."

"Throw-up bug?" Now he steps back. "Well, I just wanted to tell you . . ."

I cover my mouth with my hand. Make a gagging sound.

"Oh." He turns pale and holds his stomach. "Like to help . . . I'm not good with . . . Oh God." He covers his mouth and rushes to his bus.

Phew. Okay, so that didn't totally solve the problem, but why deal with today what I can put off till tomorrow?

Gina whooshes by me on the way to our bus, dressed again in what's become her typical all-black look. I wonder for a moment what would have happened if she'd seen Dalton actually kiss me. Part of me is relieved this didn't happen, but the other part of me? Well, let's just say that now I wouldn't completely hate it if she felt as miserable as she's been making me feel. I know that's not the nicest thought in the world, but there you go.

Of course there's no way I'm taking the bus. Hey, exercise is good for me, right? I make my way out of the parking lot.

"Sang, wait up." Megan is soon beside me. "We so got an A today. Don't you think?"

"I hope so. Can you believe how pathetic Sara was?"

"What do you expect from someone like that?" Megan asks. We exchange a knowing look. "So? How's your hun-bun?"

"Megan, he's not my hun-bun, okay?" Jason hasn't talked to me all day, although he did wink at me once in the hall between classes, which counts for something, I guess. Lame, right? He wasn't at lunch at all. Maybe the throw-up bug is real and he got it. Maybe that's what he was doing all weekend. Maybe he's bulimic. This makes me wonder, Can guys be bulimic? "Let's not talk about it."

"Sure. But you two do make a cute couple," she says.

We shuffle through some leaves while I think about this one.

"Everyone says so," she adds.

"Megan, please tell me you didn't say anything to anybody."

"Is it a big secret or something?"

"Listen, for the zillionth time, there's nothing going on between Jason and me. Not really. Get it?"

"Sure, I get it. But then why is he running this way, right this very minute?"

I spot him over my shoulder and turn away fast, trying not to smile. Megan nudges me and grins.

Jason rushes up to me just as we reach the road. But he isn't rushing *up to* me, he's rushing *past* me. "Got work," he says as he hurries on.

My cheeks burn and my eyes drop to the ground. I feel Megan's stare.

Then something truly incredible happens. *Jason stops in his tracks. He turns and runs back to me, and grabs my arms. "Visit me," he says, "okay?" and kisses me on the lips. The kiss leaves me stunned and openmouthed.*

Okay, so that's a lie. What he actually does is continue jogging into town, his black backpack bouncing behind him.

"Wow, I believe you," Megan says. "There really is absolutely nothing going on."

Oh God. She's right.

"You okay, Sang?"

I give a weak nod.

"Well, who needs him anyway?" Megan says. "I mean,

he's kind of weird, isn't he? First of all, I heard he used to live in New Jersey. That can't be good."

I nod again.

"And so what if he has a hot earring?" she says.

"Yeah. Big deal," I say. "Anyone can go to the mall and get one of those."

"And what about at lunch?" Megan says. "He sits with all those snooty populars and a bunch of freaky-looking kids, like that Brandon Gables."

She's right. Brandon Gables always wears the same blue T-shirt. That's pretty strange. And those size-zero girls who hang around that table, flipping their hair and reapplying their lip gloss. What does that say about Jason? And Slutty Sara is sometimes hanging around him too, right? So all in all, I'm lucky to be done with him.

But what about the Stinkin' Monkeys concert? I tell myself a guy like Jason probably doesn't even remember asking me about it. Or maybe he did it like some mean joke. Like I'll show up at the train station and he'll be there with Sara and they'll just be laughing at me.

"So you okay, Sang?"

"Yeah. Great." I try to sound cheerful.

We walk on, talking about this and that, and I ask Megan if I can borrow her camcorder. She says she'll talk to her dad about it, and pretty soon I'm updating her about Chachi.

"She actually hit you?" Megan stops. Her eyes get all big and seal-ish. "Did you call the police?"

"No."

"Oh, you have to. That's child abuse, you know. My parents see cases like this all the time. You know, maybe you should talk to my parents."

"It's not like that. Anyway, I'm handling it."

"What did your parents say? You did tell them, didn't you?"

I shake my head.

"Sang!"

"There's no point. My parents don't believe a word I say. That's why I need the camera."

"Okay, I'll ask my dad tonight."

"Only about the camera? Promise?"

She hesitates for a moment. "Promise."

I squeeze Megan's arm. "You're a really good friend," I say, realizing for the first time how true this is.

When we reach Planet Smoothie, Megan offers to treat me to a Lunar Lemonade with a Booster Blast. It's supposed to be a mood elevator, but I say, "No thanks." Megan decides to stay. Apparently she needs her own daily Blast before going home and facing her parents, whose probing questions must make her feel like a patient with an appointment that never ends.

So I go on alone. That's okay. I'm actually getting used to being alone. Alone is good, right? It lets you think, it makes you strong. In fact, I'm feeling so strong I plan to march right past Jason's ticket booth and just ignore him. Yes, that's just what I'm going to do.

Only I don't, because he sees me and calls me over.

Despite my best intentions, I'm soon talking with him. Well, he doesn't have any customers. So he must be bored in that booth. I'm just a little diversion. That's all I've ever been, right? Crap. So much for being strong.

But you know what? If he is just talking to me because he's bored, or just playing around with my feelings and then laughing at me behind my back, he's doing a pretty convincing job of being the nice guy. I mean, he's all smiling and joking with me, and when somebody does come to buy a ticket and I say, "See ya," he's like, "Wait a minute."

My heart speeds up as I wait, and he goes from the booth into the theater's lobby. A moment later he comes out of the lobby door onto the sidewalk. "I've got a break."

"Really?"

"Not really," he says in a low voice.

"But you'll lose your job," I whisper, trying not to smile.

"Nah. It's only for a quick coffee, right? Anyway, I asked Gretchen at the concession stand to cover for me. I've done it for her before."

In Coffee & Cream we order from Michelle Baldarasi. I try to be all nonchalant in front of her, but she smirks at me and Jason, and reaches for her nose ring. I can just feel she is about to say something embarrassing, like "Hey, who's the hunk?" or "Wanna hear how many times Gina went to the bathroom last night?" Fortunately, she glances at her manager, drops her hand to the counter, and only tells us what we owe.

I rummage through my backpack for some money. Jason offers to pay, but I say, "No, I've got it in here somewhere." I unzip my bag's small front pocket and Chachi's diary falls open onto the ground. The day I found it, I tucked it in there just to keep it safe. I totally forgot about it.

Jason picks it up. "Keeping a journal?"

I feel my cheeks sting. "Sort of." I take it from him and am about to close it when I notice it's written in English. Interesting. I'm tempted to read it right now, but force myself to put it away till later.

It's not too chilly, so we sit on the bench outside the shop, and Jason is telling me about the train times to the concert and how I'm going to be a complete Stinkin' Monkeys fan before the night is through. I'm staring at him. At his soulful hazel eyes. And I'm wishing I could sit with him like this forever, all relaxed and close. I'm thinking if this is for real, if he really does like me and really is thinking I'm going to go with him to this expensive concert, then I should tell him the truth now. "Jason, I . . . well . . ." I wriggle on the bench. "You see, it's like this. I don't . . . God, this is hard."

"Oh," he says, and chucks his half-full cup into the garbage. "I get it." He scratches his neck. "No problem. See you around, I guess." He stands and starts back toward the theater.

"What?" I catch up and pull his arm. "What exactly do you get?"

"Look, it's okay, Sang. You're not really into me. I get it. Later, then."

"Wait, that's not what I meant at all."

He closes his eyes for a moment and shakes his head. "So what exactly did you mean?"

I look around at people passing on the sidewalk. I pull Jason to one side. "See, what I meant was . . . well . . . ," I say, and swallow. God, this is so *unfair*. I like this guy. I really really like him. And he actually, for some bizarre, unexplained reason, likes me! Isn't that an incredible miracle? Shouldn't everything else be easy? You know, all happiness and joy and passion and kissing . . .

"Hey, Crawford." A woman with spiky red hair is in front of the theater, waving at Jason.

He waves back. "Crap. I'd better go before I get in trouble."

"Sure," I say. "Go. No. Wait." My mouth is totally dry, my palms are sweaty, and I'm starting to feel a little dizzy. How can I possibly say it? I just can't. But if I don't, he'll think . . . "Listen, I—I don't want you to think that. You know. The whole 'I'm not into you' thing. Because that's not the way it is." I hold my breath.

He digs his hands into the pockets of his jeans and smiles, and I swear to God, his eyes actually sparkle.

33

Some things feel right, you know? And you have to trust your gut. For example, my mind keeps telling me there is no way Jason really likes me, but my gut, when he says he does in fact like me, just knows he's telling the truth.

I'm thinking about all this as I'm wandering toward home. I'm so wrapped up in wonderful sweet gorgeous Jason, it takes a while for me to remember Chachi's diary. I grab it from my bag and look up and down the sidewalk with guilty eyes before I start to read.

Each entry is dated and begins with a hokey "Dear Diary." This should be entertaining. I stroll along and flip through the pages. Nearly every one is full. Some entries are printed in green felt-tip marker, others are scrawled in pencil, still others are smudged, having been written in script with what must have been a leaky blue ballpoint pen.

August 12, 1975
Dear Diary:

    He's coming over today. This might be it, but you never know. I'm scared but I'm excited too. Swam at the pool all morning, which was freezing. It rained, which was a bummer. Susie said I should be ready. Write more later.

Whoa. Who's "he"? Must have been Chacha. Must have been when Chachi's parents had Chacha meet her for the first time as a possible husband. I try to imagine my parents picking out my future husband. I picture a lineup of guys, all complete dweebs.

I flip the page. There's a bunch of dull stuff about the weather being crummy, about getting new clothes for back-to-school, about trying to go to the movies with friends but nobody's parents could drive. Jeez, growing up in India sounds pretty boring. You'd think there'd be something different, like, I don't know, a cobra sneaking into the house, or something like that.

August 20, 1975
Dear Diary:

    We almost did it today, but my stupid mom came home early. Billy left, and mom screamed at me and I cried, but later Billy and I secretly talked on the phone for hours. He loves me and I love him. More later.

Okay, now I'm confused. What exactly could "did it" mean back in India? No way could it mean what "doing it" does here, could it? And Billy isn't exactly an Indian name. Maybe Chachi had a seedy fling before she met Chacha and was forced into marriage, and that's why she's so bitter and strange now. Juicy stuff, I think, and eagerly flip the page.

August 21, 1975
Dear Diary:
    We did it. I tried not to let Billy see me cry, but he saw and was so sweet. I still hurt a little. Susie told me it's not supposed to hurt next time. I love Billy sooooo much.

I'm surprised, and more than a little creeped out reading this about my aunt. But what I read next completely stops me. Stops my feet, my breath, my heart, everything.

Billy + Lena
2 B
+ 2 Gether
4 Ever

34

"Hello, is Lena there?"

I cover up the phone mouthpiece and yell, "Mom, phone!"

She pokes her head into my room. "Who is it?"

"Probably somebody from one of your goody-two-shoes charities."

Mom gives me a look as she takes the phone and walks downstairs with it.

Saint Mom. The do-gooder. Making all these rules for me to live up to. What crap.

I close my door and lock it. I pick up Mom's diary again, but I can't bring myself to read any more. I should show it to her. I imagine her face dropping from a smile to one of horror as she realizes I know what a phony she is. She was thirteen when she wrote in that thing. She was a Slutty Sara.

I chuck the diary into my backpack and fall onto my

bed. With arms crossed, I fix my eyes on Orlando Bloom like we're having a staring contest and the first one to blink is going to be shot.

What do you do when everything you've been told, everything you've been measuring yourself up to, turns out to be a lie? I close my eyes and breathe deeply. Don't think, remember? Feel. Go with your gut.

But what if you're not sure what you feel? What if your gut's all mixed up? Maybe I feel too much of everything at once, you know? I'm furious with my mom and my dad for never taking my side, and I'm disgusted with my mom for being such a liar, and I'm freaked out that my parents think I'm a bulimic and a thief, and I hate hate hate Chachi for making my life a living hell, and I'm sad about Gina stepping out of my life, and I'm worried about her maybe being the real bulimic, and I'm excited about Jason, and I'm stressed about telling him I can't go to the concert.

Well, at least I feel okay about my grades now. That's under control. If only I could get these other things under control too.

Maybe it's time to bend the rules. I mean, why be such a good girl and dutiful daughter? Who exactly am I trying to impress? My mom? Ha.

Suddenly I feel focused. I've got ideas.

In a matter of minutes I'm on the Internet. Hari's not on. He's never on when I need him. I page down my buddy list and find WILDnSAFE. Megan's on. It's fate.

We IM each other, my computer blooping with every reply she sends. First we chat about the sorry state of her love life:

WILDnSAFE: id do anythin 4 luv
WILDnSAFE: tru luv
SINGSANGSUNG: hang in there
SINGSANGSUNG: itll happen
WILDnSAFE: how do u know
SINGSANGSUNG: cuz I do . . .

So I tell her all the good stuff about Jason and about the concert. She's so excited for me, and it feels really good to have someone to really talk to. I tell her not to get too excited, because I'm not exactly allowed to go with him.

Next Megan tells me she doesn't have a camcorder anymore. Her dad lost it at some conference. She's all apologetic, but I tell her not to worry, and I mean it. Anyway, I have a huge favor to ask her. She lives pretty close to the train station. If I can sleep over at her house the night of the concert, I can slip away, go to Philly with Jason, and be back before her parents notice anything. My fingers fly over the keyboard as I explain my idea. Finally, I type:

SINGSANGSUNG: u dont have 2
SINGSANGSUNG: i wont be mad if u say no
SINGSANGSUNG: k?

After a minute, I get her reply.

WILDnSAFE: id like 2 help but . . .
WILDnSAFE: u know
WILDnSAFE: my parents will kill me

She's right, of course. But only if we're caught.

SINGSANGSUNG: its ok . . . nevermind
SINGSANGSUNG: sry
SINGSANGSUNG: cya

Oh well, it was worth a shot. I sit back and stare at the screen, but you know, it's funny. I don't feel like this is the end of the world. I probably should, but I don't. I just feel like somehow I'll work everything out. I guess it's because I don't plan on giving up.

Time for some action. I flip open my datebook. Chachi's at work for another hour. Good and bad. Bad, because she'll be home for dinner. Good, because I've got some things I'd like to do in the meantime. I stand, and that's when I hear a bloop.

WILDnSAFE: ok
WILDnSAFE: lets do it
SINGSANGSUNG: u sure?

There's a long pause, and I hold my breath. I'm about to type again when *bloop!*

WILDnSAFE: yup

WILDnSAFE: anythin 4 luv

Yes! Yes yes yes!!!!

SINGSANGSUNG: u r the BEST

I stand and allow myself approximately one minute to
do a little dance of joy.

Okay, enough of that. Time to get down to business. I
pull the bobby pin from my dresser drawer, and I stop at
my door to listen. I hear Mom helping Doodles with
homework at the table. Dad isn't home from work yet.
All clear. I head upstairs and there's a moment of worry
when I pop open Chachi's lock, but Doodles and Mom
obviously don't hear because they continue to talk.

I pull the door shut behind me and it's pitch-black in
here. I hate these short November days. This gets me
thinking about Chachi's flashlight. I flick on the lamp
switch and start rummaging through a few dresser drawers packed with newspapers and letters and handkerchiefs
and, ugh, giant white underwear. By the time I get to
the bottom drawer, I'm looking through traditional Indian salwar kameez suits, filmy white and pink polyester
chunis, one-size-fits-all drawstring pants in garish pur-
ples and reds, and papery silk *kurta* pajama tops. I never
see Chachi wear this stuff. She's usually in jeans or sweats.
At the back of the drawer, I finally find what I'm looking for: the flashlight. I take it, imagining Chachi's face

when she looks for it the next time she plans to do a midnight raid.

Hmm. Big deal. Stealing a flashlight hardly seems like anything. I look around the room, wondering what else I can take, and when I see Chacha's picture, a moment of inspiration hits me. I unhook the portrait and slide it into the drawer, just where the flashlight had been. I arrange the chunis around Chacha's face so when the enemy opens this drawer, she will see only eyes staring back at her.

It's a start.

35

Tonight we're eating spaghetti and meatballs. It's one of my favorite dishes, especially with hot garlic bread on the side. Of course the best spaghetti and meatballs I've ever had was at the Baldarasis'. Mrs. Baldarasi makes her sauce from scratch, peeling the tomatoes herself and everything, and her meatballs are so tender. She told me the secret is to mix in saltines that have been soaked in milk. Mom's meatballs are the pre-made frozen kind and the sauce is straight from a jar, but still, pretty tasty.

So I wolf down my food. When Mom rises to get the salt from the counter, I ask for seconds.

Mom gives me a worried look. "I think you have had enough, Sang," she says, like I've been drinking beers all day or something.

"I'm really hungry, Mom. And it's really good."

Mom shakes her head and returns to the table, then puts some salt on her meatballs.

"For goodness' sake, Lena. Can't she have a little more?" my dad says.

"I don't think that's such a good idea, *considering*." She's still shaking salt. Her meatballs are starting to look snowcapped.

"Here. Take some of mine," Doodles says, pushing her full plate toward me. Doodles is one of those kids who is only hungry when it isn't dinnertime.

"Nice try," I say, and stand. I pick up my plate, and Mom and Dad exchange a look. "I just want some more dinner, okay? If you want, you can follow me the rest of the night, even into the bathroom. Deal?"

"Gross," Doodles says.

"Sangeet," my dad warns, "watch your tone."

At this moment, Chachi comes into the dining room. She's scowling, but that's nothing unusual.

"Hello, Kajal," my mom says.

Chachi doesn't respond. Just makes a beeline past the dining table into the kitchen, throws open a cabinet, and slams a pot on the stove.

Mom looks flustered by the snub. Dad cuts his meatballs into little pieces. Doodles starts shoving food into her mouth and chewing fast, spaghetti strings hanging from her lips. She's clearly bent on getting away from the table ASAP.

"Anyway, Mom," I say, "if you didn't want me to have seconds, you shouldn't have made such a delicious dinner." I smile.

BAM! Mom jumps as Chachi slams the utensil drawer shut.

"Dear God, must you break my house?" my dad shouts.

Mom pats his arm to calm him. "Is everything okay, Kajal?"

No response. Chachi is now chop-chop-chopping a mound of onions. Seeing her with a knife is a scary thing indeed.

The pot of spaghetti is on the stove beside her. Has a plate of seconds ever been harder to get? I decide I'm going for it. Holding my plate up like a shield, I edge beside her. I dare to serve myself. Chachi gives me a cold glare.

"You want some?" I say. "It's good."

She continues her frantic chopping.

"I'll take that as a no," I whisper, and return to the table. I don't like turning my back to her, but I sit anyway.

"So," my mom says in a forced cheerful voice, "the holiday food drive is well under way. We're collecting for more than two hundred needy families in our area."

"Nice," my dad says. We continue to eat, with Chachi's slamming as background music.

"Oh, I forgot to tell you!" Doodles beams at us, looking festive with a beard and mustache of sauce. "I won the candy competition. I'm the top seller!"

"You did?" Dad says. "That's great." He wipes the sauce off her face with a napkin.

"Yeah," I say. "Good job."

"I won a humongous chocolate bar. I should get it any day now."

"Are you going to share?" I ask. "Like Dad always says, family takes care of family."

"Weeeeeeell," Doodles says, "I was thinking I'd—"

I feel my chair shake. Chachi has surged into the dining room and is clutching the back of my seat and yelling at my father in Punjabi. My dad moves back from the table as if the words have pushed him away.

"What are you going on about?" he says. "No one's been in your room."

Gulp.

"Where is my husband's picture?" Chachi says. I see her hand like an ax over my head as she points at Mom. "I demand to know."

"Kajal," Mom says, "I assure you, I don't—"

"Stealing. Lying." She pushes my chair. "Ask this one where it is."

Dad sets down his fork. "Sangeet?"

My heart is throbbing fast. "I never took the picture from her room." That's the truth.

"You see?" my dad says. "She says she hasn't taken it."

Chachi bangs on the back of my chair and marches away. After a moment, we hear her bedroom door slam.

"Phew," I say, suppressing a smile. I notice Doodles

hanging her head, her shoulders shaking. I drape my arm around her. "Why are you crying?"

"It's s-scary."

I kiss Doodles's head. My dad stands, comes close, and rubs my cheek. "My good girls," he says, but he's staring at me. Then he casts a dark look upstairs.

36

"I don't know, Sang," Megan says as she pulls her lunch bag from her locker. "Are you sure this is gonna work?"

"Sure," I say. "It's perfect. Your parents and my parents will both know I'm sleeping over at your house, which I am."

"If they discover you're not there—"

"Don't even say that. Look, I'll only be gone for a few hours. If your parents check in on us, you can just say we can't come to the door because we're busy trying on clothes, or that I'm asleep already or something."

"Right. That'll definitely work." Megan sounds confident, but she's turning her lunch bag round and round in her hands. "The train station's only like, what? Two blocks from my house? You'll be back as fast as you can. It'll be great."

"I know!"

"And even if we *are* caught. So I'll be punished. So what? Nothing I can't handle." She bites her lip. "You know, just the usual stuff. Of course my parents know every mind game in the book. They'll reverse-psychologize me and manipulate me until I'll beg for mercy, then they'll be super-nice until I explode with guilt." Her eyes become huge. "It'll be great," she says in a shaky voice. "Fun. Anything for love, right?"

"Wait. I can't make you do this," I say, feeling my own measure of guilt. "It's too risky."

I expect Megan to say it'll be fine. Instead, she says, "Oh thank God," and practically collapses with relief. Oh crap! "I'm so glad," Megan says. "But, Sang, what about the concert? You can't miss it. Isn't there anywhere else you can sleep over?"

We both instinctively look down the hall, at Gina's locker. She's surrounded by goths. Even from this distance, I can see the white shine of her newly unbraced teeth. Or maybe they just seem so bright next to all the black clothing she and her new friends are wearing. I see her reach into her locker and pull out the bag of candy that I snuck in there this morning (I may not know what's on her mind these days, but I *do* know her locker combination). The bag is full of sticky, gooey stuff, like caramels, Milk Duds, and lots of bubble gum. All the things she couldn't eat for the past two years.

I know, it's stupid of me to even get her anything.

But somehow, when I saw in my datebook today's date marked *Braces OFF!!!!* in Gina's pink marker, I couldn't resist.

So Gina glances at me and pretends to barf into the bag. Her creepy friends burst out laughing.

The hell with her.

Megan and I walk to the cafeteria. I head for the cappuccino machine, and Megan tags along. After I grab a pizza slice and pay, she says, "You're not mad at me or anything?"

"No, of course not. Really." I try to give her a reassuring smile.

"You sure?"

"I'm fine." Okay. There's something I really have to do, and I can't put it off a moment longer. "See ya," I say to Megan. I walk past our usual table, heading toward the far side of the cafeteria. The table where Jason is. He sits with a mix of guys in concert T-shirts and sports jerseys and girls wearing cotton-candy pink and blue, their hair straightened and highlighted. I swallow and study my own clothes. Jeans, a long-sleeved maroon top, sneakers. God, I'm dressed like a three-year-old or something. I clutch my cappuccino tight, and hesitate.

Megan catches up to me. "You're ditching me? I can't believe you're ditching me."

"I'm not. I just . . . well, I think I'd better tell Jason the truth."

"Oh, Sang. I am so so sorry about all this. It's all my fault."

"It's nobody's fault. Well, maybe my mom's." I take a step forward.

"Wait," she says. "I'll come with you."

"Oh." I'm trying to come up with a nice way to tell her not to, because, well, let's face it: There are guys at that table. Lots of them. And Megan and guys, well . . . "I don't think you should—"

"Sang, I'm your *friend*. Of course I should. For moral support."

Now I don't know what to say, so I say, "Right."

"Is there anything in my teeth?" She gives a toothy smile.

"Perfect," I say. "How 'bout mine?"

"You're good," she says. "Don't worry. I'm right by your side."

So we make our way to the table. I have to admit, it does feel good to have Megan next to me as we walk its length, past some of the most snooty girls and hottest guys in the school. Of course, not one of them notices us, which makes me wonder for the umpteenth time what made Jason ever notice *me*. I mean, what have I got that they don't?

Shut up shut up shut up! Smile, I tell myself. Be confident. Or at least don't be pathetic. And pray that Megan won't be, well, Megan.

At last I'm standing next to Jason, who is in the middle of telling some super-popular Miss Cheerleader about how a football connected with Henry Paddy's nose in gym and blood came spurting out.

Jason notices me. "Hey," he says, and slides over to make room for me and Megan.

"Hey," I say, sitting beside him.

"Hey hey," Megan says, giving a goofy wave and sitting on the other side of me.

Miss Cheerleader rolls her eyes.

"Jason, this is my friend Megan."

Jason nods at her, and Megan says to him, "Oh, hot." Her eyes touch on guy after guy at the table as she says, "Hot, hot, hot."

I kick her.

"Hot in here," she squeaks. She uncrinkles her paper bag and pulls out her lumpy sandwich. She stares at the jock sitting to her right. He's a giant, with a square jaw and bulging biceps that bulge even more as he lifts his sandwich to his mouth. "Hey," Megan says to him.

Oh God. No.

"I'm muscles," she says.

Oh God oh God.

The jock sets the sandwich on the table and looks down on her like she's a tiny bug.

"M-Megan. That's me. So what's in your pants?" she asks. "SANDWICH. I mean sandwich."

At this point, everyone around them is staring. The jock stands. Megan's face is level with his pants.

Megan's cheeks burn red as her harp-seal eyes dart around the table. "I—I've got tofu and bean sprouts in my pants. SANDWICH. IN MY SANDWICH." She covers her face. Forget talking to Jason. I've got to get her out of here before she completely self-destructs.

"Like, gross," a girl named Amelia Flemington says. "That sounds so disgusting."

Megan focuses on Amelia, who has gone back to reading a chemistry textbook with super-brainy David Jovanovich. "At least no animals were harmed in the preparation of this lunch," Megan says. "Which is more than I can say for that." And she points to the brown fur collar on Amelia's sweater.

"Chill," Amelia says. "It's totally fake." She rolls her eyes again. "What a loser."

Megan drops her eyes to her tofu, and I open my mouth to defend her. But David Jovanovich beats me to the punch, saying, "I think she's cool."

Megan stares at him.

"You would. You can tell the tutoring center I want a new tutor," Amelia says. She slams the chem book shut. "Come on, Kermit." Kermit, as it turns out, is the name of the giant football player. And I bet nobody kids him about it either. He dutifully follows Amelia down to the far side of the table.

Meantime, Megan is still staring at David Jovanovich. David Jovanovich is so smart, he's a little strange. He's been drinking black coffee since he was in fifth grade, and he does the *New York Times* crossword puzzle every day, and he can talk about logarithms and genetic engineering, and he plays the harp and likes to skip when he's happy. He wears ratty university sweatshirts, and his hair is always sticking up in the back. But he doesn't smell bad or anything. Before I know it, David Jovanovich and Megan are deep in conversation. And it's not about pants or being hot. It's about the desperate plight of the grizzly, and about the radical approaches of Greenpeace. Megan is actually talking. With a boy. Like a human being. I wonder how long this will last.

"Listen, Jason," I say. "About the concert . . ."

"Right." He pushes aside his soda. "We can meet at the train station around six-thirty. It's six-thirty, right, Gary?"

Gary is the guy sitting on the other side of Jason and the one who was supposed to go skating with him on that no-show night a zillion days ago. Only I was sure his name was Glen. Gary nods and smiles at me.

"Six-thirty," I say. "Right." I don't know if I'd ever feel comfortable at this table. I glance back at my old table. Dalton's there with the usual crowd. He's looking around the lunchroom, so I sink down a bit, hoping he doesn't see me here with Jason. I mean, I really don't want to hurt him. A roar of laughter comes from the goth table as Gina and her dark lord–like friends chuck candy at each other. One guess where the candy came from.

I suck down my cappuccino and say to myself, Stop putting things off. It simply isn't fair to keep pretending. Maybe he can use his ticket for someone else. Or maybe he'll decide not to go without me. "See, Jason, the thing is, I really need to tell you—"

"No you don't," Megan says.

"Yes, Megan, I do. I really do."

Megan looks at David Jovanovich, who winks at her, and a wave of blush washes over her cheeks again. She giggles and snorts, but David Jovanovich doesn't look frightened by this. Instead, he beams at her like she is the cutest little harp seal on the planet.

"It's okay," Megan whispers in my ear. "Everything is okay. I'll cover for you. For love, right?"

I study her for a moment, but her eyes are all for David Jovanovich, who is grinning at Megan while attempting to comb down his stand-up hair with his fingertips. Wow, will you look at this? Megan has found love, or at least "like," and I'm *so* going to that Stinkin' Monkeys concert. Wahoo! I feel so fantastic, I give Amelia Flemington a friendly smile. In return, she makes a face at me like she's just bitten into a tofu-and-sprouts sandwich.

"So?" Jason says.

"So?"

"You need to tell me something?"

"Oh. Right." Um. Er. "Can you lend me your camcorder?"

"Oh," he says, and winces. "Hmm."

"Let me guess. It's broken. Or is it lost?"

"Actually, neither." He swallows the rest of his soda. "The thing is, Sang, I have a policy of not lending it out."

"Oh," I say, feeling a bit stung. "Well, if you have a policy and all." I bite into my pizza.

"Listen, it's nothing personal. It's just that I worked for a long time to save for that camera. It's really expensive and cool." He looks at me and his eyes are sparkling again, but I think this sparkle is for his stupid cool camera. "Isn't it cool, Gary?"

"It's cool," Gary says.

"Gary and I are going to make a film this spring," Jason says.

"Hey," Gary says to me, "you could be in it if you like, Sang. I'm sure there's a part for you. Right, Jason?"

Jason shrugs.

I take another, larger bite of my pizza and wonder what kind of guy doesn't lend his own girlfriend his camera. Well, I guess the whole "film Chachi in action" idea is a bust. Unless, that is, I ask Jason to do the filming for me. I imagine him in my house, saying, And . . . action! Chachi coming at me with her hand raised, and Jason shouting, Cut! This time let's try that with a little bit more anger, okay?

Suddenly I'm choking on my pizza. It's like there's a wall of mozzarella sealing off my throat. I reach for my cappuccino, but it's empty. Jason hands me his soda, but of course that's empty too. Megan shoves her drink in my hand and I take a huge swig of it.

I can breathe again, but at what price? "Blech! That's horrible."

"Sorry, Sang." Megan takes her drink back. "I guess soy milk isn't for everybody. I'm lactose intolerant," she tells David Jovanovich.

"Me too!" he says. I half expect him to grab Megan's hand and go skipping off into the sunset, or at least to the next class.

37

The world has flipped upside down, because now I've got my dad sticking up for me, while my mom tries to be super-strict. Get this: When I ask to sleep over at Megan's on Saturday night, Mom is all, "No way," but Dad says, "Oh, for goodness' sake. Let the child have some pleasure in life, already." Mom finally relents when Dad points out that I'll be staying with a pair of shrinks, so if I start freaking out or anything, they'll know what to do. So yeah!

That was Wednesday evening. Later that same night, I sneak Chachi's beets from the fridge and stick them in her bra drawer. One in each bra cup. Beet bras. The newest rage.

Thursday afternoon, Chachi's in a rage, screaming that I've put all her puddings from the fridge into my closet. Sure enough, there they are. Mom's upset. She threatens to call Dr. Dander. And my father? He just shakes his head and says it doesn't seem like I've eaten any. He tells me to put the puddings back into the fridge. That's it. End of story.

At dinner that night, Chachi has obviously retrieved her beets, because she chomps them all throughout dinner, and in between chomps she slurps up her dahl soup. She follows this up with three puddings, her pudding-brown eyes staring at me the whole time.

Thursday night, Chachi's on night shift again. I go to the kitchen and scoop up a handful of *masoor dahl.* These are little orange lentils. Upstairs, I spread them neatly between the sheets of her bed. Of course these are dry uncooked beans, not wet and mushy like cooked ones would be, but they'll do. Thursday night, I tell Doodles more of Rani's story, and it goes like this. . . .

Rani knew the evil genie had framed her, and made her out to be a thief. The evidence against Rani was overwhelming. The genie demanded justice, and so Rani found herself in prison, and there she sat. She wept bitter tears into her chuni, wondering how such a horrible fate could befall someone who had only tried to do good. Still, she had faith in the justice system, and was bound by the laws of the kingdom. She believed good would win.

At last Rani's trial came about. She was glad, for she thought she only had to speak the truth to be free. But she was wrong, for the genie cast a spell so that every person in that desert kingdom would hear Rani's words as lies. On that first day of testimony, the jury of wise men and women frowned and shook their heads, and Rani despaired.

On the second day of testimony, the evil genie spoke, and even Rani began to be affected by the wicked words, thinking perhaps she did steal from the genie. Hadn't she been in the genie's tower, opening trunks? Who does such a thing but a thief?

Rani knew the penalty for theft: beheading. The henchman always kept the scimitar blade dull so that he would have to hack at the convicted neck over and over again. Still, so powerful was the evil genie's magic that Rani felt like she was about to throw herself on the cold marble floor and confess to the crime.

Something made her stop. It was her little faithful friend Scheherazade, who smiled, not at the genie, as did the others who were so mesmerized by evil, but at Rani. Scheherazade smiled at Rani with trust and love and friendship.

So Rani knew then she mustn't give up. She had to fight hard, not for herself, but for the sake of truth, for the sake of her friend. That night, with the help of Scheherazade and some faithful servants, Rani escaped from her prison. This is how it was done. The friends dragged into the prison a large wicker basket filled with masoor dahl, Rani's favorite food. The guard was touched, knowing that she would never be alive long enough to eat all that dahl, would never see all those beans cooked and served. So he let them in. Her friends placed Rani in the basket, gave her a straw to breathe through, and covered her with dahl. When the guard stopped them on the way out, they sadly explained that Rani only wept when she saw the present and had wanted it removed. The guard gave the dahl a quick glance and let them go. That night, while the genie was flitting about celebrating the soon-to-be death of Rani, Rani and her faithful followers climbed the genie's hideous tower. They took away the *trunk that was filled with everyone's joy and happiness, and in its place left masoor dahl: piles and piles of it, which they spilled all over the floor, in the closets—even in between the sheets of the horrid creature's bed.*

It's Friday afternoon. I get home feeling so incredible. The week's over, I have almost no homework, and my only real worries are, one, what will I wear tomorrow night? Two, will my twenty-dollar bill be enough money for a concert T-shirt? And, three, have I died and gone to heaven? Because I am so excited. Seriously.

The amazing thing is, this wasn't really such a great day. What happened today? In a word, Dalton.

I'm at my locker, pulling out my books for my next class, when I feel this presence behind me. I turn and there he is.

"Hey," he says. "Have you been avoiding me or something?"

"No," I say. Unless you count diving for a drink at the water fountain when I see him coming, or that time yesterday when he waved to me and I suddenly made a U-turn for the bathroom. Anything to avoid a lip-lock.

Dalton smiles, full dimple. "Great. I thought you were mad at me or something."

I close the locker and hold my books in front of my face. "Mad? Me? Why?"

"What are you doing?"

I peer over the top. "Nothing. See ya." I hug my books and hurry to my next class, but Dalton hurries beside me.

"Sang, you doing anything tonight?"

I again put my books between my face and his. "Tonight? Me?" Duh. Ask enough questions? I quicken my pace. So does he.

"Go with me. To the movies." He says this in spurts because we're practically running now. "Just go out with me. Okay?"

Crap. There's no running from this situation. I stop. Lower my books. "I can't."

His dimple disappears. He looks really crushed.

"What I mean is, I can't date," I say in a hurry. "I'm not allowed to till I'm sixteen."

"Oh." He purses his lips as he considers this. At least he doesn't look crushed anymore, which is good because I really don't want to hurt him, you know? "So when will that be?"

"Summer. Sorry." I give him a friendly smile.

"That's okay," he says. "I'll just have to ask you again, then." He grins, pushes up his glasses, and goes.

Great.

Of course this isn't the end of the matter. At lunch I'm back at our regular table (somehow I couldn't bring myself to sit at Jason's table again), and Dalton is there being really nice and not weird or anything. And David Jovanovich runs over to the table and sets his soy milk beside Megan, and pretty soon the two of them are talking about the mating habits of lampreys. That's about when Jason comes by, and leans over me, and says, "Stinkin' Monkeys!"

"Right," I say.

"Stinkin' Monkeys," Dalton says. "You like them, Sang?"

"She's crazy about them," Jason says. "Can't wait till tomorrow night."

"Yeah," I say.

Jason waves, and heads to his own table. I think I'm in the clear, but Dalton says, "Wait, you're going out with him? Tomorrow night?"

"Oh, it's nothing," I say. I take an extra-huge bite out of my hamburger.

"But you're going out with him?" Dalton asks again.

I point to my mouth and chew and chew. Mouth's too full to answer. Sorry.

"Yo, Dalton," David Jovanovich says. "Sang and Jason are together." He holds up two fingers and crosses them. "As one."

Megan elbows David, who says sheepishly, "But everyone knows."

Dalton throws down his napkin. "Not everyone," he says. "Sang? Is this true?"

I point to my mouth. Still full. Sorry.

"So you lied to me. That's great. That's just great."

I finally swallow. "Dalton, wait."

But he's not waiting. He's over by the goths, talking

with Gina. Pretty soon they're both casting evil looks my way.

Then David apologizes more times than any average kid would. The only way I can make him stop is by taking the seaweed snack bar he offers me, which I tell him I will certainly eat, but just not right now.

Well, what's done is done. I tried my best to be nice. Not to hurt his feelings. So I shouldn't feel bad, even though I do.

Now I'm lying on my bed, thinking all this over, when the phone rings. It's Megan. "You weren't online. Why weren't you online?" she says. "We've got lots of details to work out, you know?"

"Okay, I'll sign on. Just wait a sec."

"It's okay. I can talk now. My parents won't be home for another half hour."

I hear the TV from downstairs. I listen carefully, but there's no sound from Chachi's room. I know she's up there. But there haven't been any outbursts about the dahl in her room, which makes me a little uncomfortable. Maybe she's dead from shock. I close my door and lower my voice. "Okay, let's talk."

"Okay, we rendezvous at seventeen hundred hours."

"I thought it was seventeen hundred thirty. Is that how you say it?"

There's a click on the line. "Hold on a sec," Megan says; then she's back. "Sorry. It was call-waiting, but no one was there. Or if they were, they were too paranoid to respond." Megan's parents get lots of strange calls from patients with problems. Even though they're supposed to only call the office, sometimes they do get the home number. Sometimes they even stop by. Like one time I was over at Megan's on a Sunday and this woman showed up at the door, eating a head of lettuce like it was a giant green apple. Apparently it was her eighth head and she couldn't stop. Personally, I would have picked chocolate.

"Okay," I say. "We meet Saturday at seventeen—let's just say five-thirty at your house, okay? We hang out for a while, and then figure out a way for me to sneak out."

"How?"

"I don't know. We'll think of something. Then I'll go to the train station, meet Jason, head to Philly for the concert, take the train back, and sneak back into your house, which should be really easy, since your parents go to bed so early."

"Sounds easy enough, but—" There's another click. "Hold on again."

I study my nails, wondering if I should paint them red or leave them clear-coated.

"I'm back."

"No one again?"

"Yeah. Listen, I'd better get off and put on the answering machine. Dad says sometimes patients who are too timid to talk to a person can still talk to a machine. It's because a machine can't ask questions or something."

"Okay. I'll be online later if you think of anything else. I can't wait till tomorrow!"

"Me either. I mean, I know it's not me going, but still, it's pretty exciting. And maybe someday it will be me."

"You and David Jovanovich?"

There's silence on the other end.

"Are you blushing?"

"A little."

She's so funny. Okay, time to focus on tomorrow night. The concert! I open my drawer and pull out shirts, one after another. I'm sure I should wear something black. Maybe black and red. Everything I have is so dorky, somehow. All high-necked and long-sleeved and plain-colored. Not even tight at all. Not that I want super-tight or low-necked.

I bite my lip and pull Mom's journal out of my backpack. What am I hoping for? Tips on how to be a first-class slut? But what if things tomorrow night do, you know, *progress?* Do I follow my gut? What if I inherited my mom's tendencies? What if, in my gut, I'm a slut?

I fall back onto my bed to have a good long think, and I'm faced with something horrible: white ceiling. Where. Is. Orlando.

I bound out of bed. "Mom?" I shout. "Mom!"

38

It's Saturday morning. The morning of the big concert. Of me and Jason together on our first real date. I can't let the enemy get to me. Not even when I find both Orlando posters shredded to bits in my garbage. Not even when my mother claims I'm ridiculous and asks me, "Why in heaven's name would Chachi do a thing like that?" Not even when Chachi is all smiling, saying, "Hell-o, Lena, how are you this morning? Hell-o to darling little Cherise," and moving to grab Doodles in a hug, which she avoids at the last moment by dodging past her and racing to the bathroom. Good trick.

"You're in high spirits today," Mom says to Chachi.

"Yes, yes. Why not, eh?" the enemy says, her eyes resting on me, a smirk resting on her face.

Grrrrrrr. I'm not going to let her get to me. Orlando wouldn't have wanted it that way.

"I need the iron. I need to iron my best salwar kameez. Now," Chachi says.

"Oh," Mom says, and sets down the newspaper she was reading. "Okay, I'll set up the board for you." She puts down the cup of tea she's just poured.

"You iron," Chachi says. "I cannot do this. I will burn myself."

That'd be a shame.

For a moment, I can see Mom about to object to doing Chachi's grunt work, but she takes a deep breath and says, "Sure. I'd be happy to."

"You are wearing something not cheap tomorrow?" Chachi says to me.

"Sure," I say. Whatever. "Tomorrow?"

"For the *gurdwara*," Mom explains. "Didn't Daddy tell you?"

"Tell me what?"

"He's arranged to do a special *kirtan* for Chacha's death anniversary."

"Kirtan?"

"You know, the music program of the temple service, with the tabla and the harmonium. The works. We'll go Sunday morning."

"But I'm sleeping over Megan's," I say. I'm starting to seethe. There's no way I'm missing my sleepover/concert just so I can go with Chachi to the gurdwara in New Jersey. I glare at her, and her creepy smile deepens. She's obviously thrilled to be messing up any plans I have.

Obviously pleased at the thought of me being trapped in the car with the family for an hour and a half each way, and spending another two hours sitting on the floor in the gurdwara, my head covered with an itchy scarf, listening to words I can't understand and music I can't sing to, and touching my head to the ground when everyone else does, and saying *"Sat Sri Akal!"* on cue.

Don't get me wrong. I usually like the gurdwara. We only go a few times a year, and each time it feels so exotic and so very Indian. I fit in and I don't. I mean, I look the part, with my hair and eyes and all, but I'm obviously not as Indian as the other girls, who are all dressed in traditional salwar kameez outfits, speaking Punjabi and waving to friends. We don't know anybody there, and my mom gets lots of stares as the only "Westerner" in the temple, just like when we would go places in India. It makes me feel like I can rise from the gurdwara's Persian carpet and walk to the beat of the tabla drum out of the gurdwara and find myself not in New Jersey, but in New Delhi. And outside would be not a blacktop parking lot full of minivans, but white marble terraces and long, shallow pools where the faithful come to bathe before entering the temple, and beyond that would be stalls of vendors selling silver bangles and marigold necklaces.

But this time it would be different. This time it would be for Chachi. I'd be bowing and touching my head to the floor for Chachi's husband, but really for Chachi. "I'm not going."

"Disrespect," Chachi says to me, her familiar frown re-appearing on her face. "How dare you refuse to—"

"Why don't you get your outfit, Kajal," Mom interrupts, "and I'll iron it right away."

"Hmm," Chachi grumbles, and leaves.

"Mom, there is no way I'm going."

"Oh, you're going, all right."

"I'm sleeping over Megan's. I already told her I would." I'm whining now, and I don't care. I imagine Jason waiting for me in the train station, the train starting to move. . . . "Chachi ruins everything. *Everything.* I hate her."

"Sang! Don't say that."

"It's true." I cross my arms.

Mom takes a deep breath. "I'm sure you don't mean that."

"And why are you always so nice to her?"

"Sang, everyone deserves kindness."

"Do they, Mom? Or are you just trying to prove something?"

"What is that supposed to mean?" When I don't answer, she takes a deep breath and says, "Look, I'm not going to argue with you. Family is family, and that's that."

"But—"

"Calm down," she says, holding up a hand. "You can still sleep over—we'll just need to pick you up a little earlier."

"Really?" I uncross my arms. "But do I still have to go to the gurdwara? With *her*?"

"What would Taoji think if you don't come along?"

"Taoji? He's not coming till Thanksgiving. How would he know?"

"Dad called Taoji and asked him to change his plans. Now he's coming Sunday morning instead of on Thanksgiving, just so he can go to the gurdwara."

"Then he's staying all week? That's so great!"

"Not so fast. He had to rearrange his flight plans at the last minute, so he's only coming to see us for the day. Then he'll have his business meetings, and he'll actually be on his way back to India by Thanksgiving."

"So because of Chachi, he's missing Thanksgiving?"

"This death anniversary thing is a big deal, you know."

"Thanksgiving's a big deal too, you know?" I feel tears well up in my eyes.

"It's okay, Sang." She reaches her arms out to hug me.

"No it isn't." I race to my room because, really, where else can I go?

I try to calm myself, which is hard because when I lie on my bed I can't help but notice Orlando is gone.

I deep-breathe for a while. Even though Orlando's gone, I can still feel his solid stare, I can still be strong like Legolas, determined like a pirate. Think positive. Try. At least I'll see Taoji, and now we'll have to take two cars to the gurdwara, so I won't have to ride with you-know-who. I think of Jason and remind myself that this is going to be the very best day of my life. Except I'm starting off completely on edge.

What if I've overlooked some important detail? I keep

running the plan through my mind step by step. Of course I haven't figured out what to wear tonight.

I know someone who can help.

Soon I am biking around the cemetery, pretending to get exercise when, let's face it, I'm just waiting for Gina. It's a bright morning, and sparkles of frost still glitter on the grass despite the rising sun. My breath comes out in frosty puffs, and this makes me think about snow, and Christmas, and Hari. Over the past week I've sent him e-mails saying "Urgent" and "Call Me" and "Need Some Advice Quick," but he never e-mails back. And he's never, ever online. But Hari will be back next week. I'll have a few days to hang out with him and catch him up on all that's been going on. It'll be good. And by Christmas, he'll be home for a few weeks. Then I'll really have someone on my side, a big brother to stick up for me.

I do a few more laps and stop by the Elmer mausoleum. No sign of Gina. I wanted to tell her I was going to the concert, that I'd come up with a plan all on my own. I wanted to tell her how good her teeth look without braces. I wanted to ask her if I could borrow one of her punk-rock T-shirts for the concert, and maybe some black nail polish. I wanted to say sorry I thought she was bulimic.

But I still think she could be. I can't help it. Bulimics lie and deny, right? I *hate* this wondering and worrying.

I do only two more laps; then I slowly ride toward

home. To the left is Fonthill Castle, with its long, sweeping lawn bordered by giant trees. Today it doesn't seem romantic, just a large lumpy building of cement and glass. I ride into my neighborhood, past my driveway. I'm not ready to go home yet.

I glide down Maple Avenue, past Victorian mansions with wraparound porches and brass mailboxes, and before I know it I'm setting down my bike in the Baldarasi driveway. I'm ringing the bell. I'm hearing all sorts of wonderful commotion inside. People calling out to each other, "Get the door!" and the sound of feet stomping down stairs. The door flies open and it's Angela Baldarasi in her black leotard, her hair in a bun, looking every inch the elegant prima ballerina.

"Sang, hi," she says in her soft voice. She opens the storm door and lets me in. I step in and inhale the rich smell of baking cookies. Or is it cake? "Is Hari back yet?" Angela says. Blush rises up her long neck and reaches her cheeks. "Michelle wants to know."

"Tell Michelle he's coming Thanksgiving morning," I say.

"Giiii-na!" Angela shouts, now sounding more like a Baldarasi than a ballerina. She waves me to the couch, and again screams, "Giiii-na? Get your butt down here!"

Mrs. Baldarasi comes out of the kitchen. She's wearing black polyester pants and a black-and-red flannel shirt, the tails of which she's knotted just over the middle of her stomach. There's flour dusting her cheek, and more on each pant leg, where she's obviously wiped her hands.

"Angela, what are you doing still home? You're going to miss those expensive dance lessons."

"I'm waiting for Michelle to take me."

"Miiii-chelle!" Mrs. Baldarasi screams. "Get your butt down here!"

A muffled "I'm in the bathroom" comes from upstairs. I love this place.

"Sang? When did you sneak in?"

"Hi, Mrs. Baldarasi. Just a minute ago."

"I already called Gina, twice," Angela says.

"That one," Mrs. Baldarasi says. "She's out jogging. Didn't you see her?" She gives me a worried look.

"I guess we just missed each other," I say. I shouldn't have come.

At that moment there's a flush upstairs, the bathroom door is thrown open, and Michelle comes clumping down the steps in a pair of oversized work boots. She grabs a set of keys from the shelf and heads out the door.

"Your coat!" Mrs. Baldarasi shouts, too late.

"Bye, Mom," Angela says. "See ya, Sang." She grabs her ballet bag and jacket and follows, with much lighter footsteps.

"Well, bye, Mrs. Baldarasi," I say.

"Stay, Sang. Maybe Gina will be back in a minute."

"That's okay. I'll see her Monday."

"Sang, can you help me in the kitchen first?"

"Oh. Sure." I think of how weird it would be for Gina to come home and find me helping out her mom.

The kitchen is a mess of dirty mixing bowls and

rolling pins dusted with flour and sugar. The green kitchen towel hanging over the oven-door handle has two floury handprints on it.

Mrs. Baldarasi waves at the mess. "Thanksgiving," she says, by way of explanation. "Just hang your coat on a chair and sit."

I do as I'm told.

"Now mix in a cup of these chocolate chips, gently. Here." She puts a bowl filled with white creamy stuff in front of me and hands me a bag of mini-chips and a rubber spatula. She hurries to the counter, where she starts moving pots from one side to the other and wiping the counter beneath with a sponge. "They all used to help me," she says. "Especially with the cannolis. It's like a tradition, you know?"

I pour in some chips and start to stir with the spatula. In an instant it is snatched from my hand.

"No no no. Not so hard. Fold them in," she says, and moves her hand like she's winding a crank. "Sideways, okay?"

I do this a few times, and she nods and scurries back to the counter. "Used to be, all three of my girls would fight to fill the cannolis for the holidays. Now look. Too busy." She wipes her hands on the towel, making it even whiter. She comes at me with a spoon, dips it into the mix. Before I know it, she plunges the spoon into my mouth.

Oh God, that's good. Sweet and tangy, with little bits of chocolate crunching about.

"Well? It's okay?"

I swallow. "It's fantastic."

Mrs. Baldarasi nods. "Tasting is the best part of cooking," she says. She puts a tray of hollow tubes of cooked pastry in front of me and grabs a cloth bag. "Now I'll put the filling in the pastry bag, pipe it into these shells, and . . . ta-da!" With a few quick flicks of her wrist, Mrs. Baldarasi fills a cannoli shell with swirls of creaminess, each side ending in a point. I'm wondering why she would possibly need my help. She sets the cannoli on the tray, picks up another empty shell, and fills that too. Clearly, I'm not needed.

"Well, guess I'll get going."

"Sang, wait." She touches my wrist, leaving a dot of filling. "Can I ask you something? You know, woman-to-woman." She crosses her arms on the table and leans close, and I pray she isn't going to talk about feminine hygiene or something equally awful. "Gina. What's going on with her?"

"Oh." I lick the filling from my wrist.

"You can tell me," she says, her voice lowered to almost a whisper. "No one will know. I swear."

"Well, I don't really know anything."

This is the truth, but Mrs. Baldarasi raises a skeptical eyebrow. "How about a cannoli to take home, okay?" She's not looking at me now. Just filling up cannoli after cannoli and stacking them on the tray.

"I'd tell you if I knew, Mrs. Baldarasi." No I wouldn't. *Best friends keep best-friend secrets.* Besides, Gina did say she wasn't bulimic. If only I could be sure.

Mrs. Baldarasi shakes her head in obvious disappointment.

So I say, "Gina just stopped talking to me about two weeks ago. Just like that." No secret there.

She sets down the pastry bag and looks me square in the eyes. "And?"

"And that's it. It's like she just doesn't want to be my friend anymore." I squint at my hands. "It wasn't my idea. It's like she doesn't need me or something."

"And these so-called new friends of hers, with the hardware sticking out of all their body parts, and their clothes torn, and their hair all spiky and weird—you know them?"

"Not much," I say.

Mrs. Baldarasi frowns, and a deep crease appears between her eyebrows. "Any drugs or nasty things going on?"

"I don't know," I say truthfully.

"This is trouble." She picks up an empty pastry and holds it like a cigar. "Bad friends equal bad news. That's always the way." She raises the cannoli shell to her lips as if about to take a puff, then quickly sets it down. "Maybe Gina's just going through something. Believe it or not, I was a girl once. I had my share of wild times."

I think of her hot pants, I think of my mom's diary, I think of tonight's concert. I think I'm tired of thinking.

"I've been watching her like a hawk, though," Mrs. Baldarasi says.

"You have?"

"Sure, sure. In the house, at least."

"And you haven't seen anything unusual?" I hold my breath.

"Nothing. Except she is wearing ugly clothing. Why?"

"She's eating normal and all?"

"Of course. *Why?*"

At once I feel somewhat relieved. I mean, this is the closest I'll get to proof that Gina is in fact *not* bulimic. If anyone would notice appetite and things related to food, it'd be Mrs. Baldarasi, right? But it's no guarantee. If I say any more, I'll be betraying Gina, won't I? I drum my fingers on the table a few times, thinking this over.

"Mrs. Baldarasi? See, there's this stomach flu going around. Changes in appetite, throwing up, that kind of stuff. So just watch Gina, okay? It could be serious."

Mrs. Baldarasi stares at me, as if looking for deeper meaning. "This *flu,* do only girls get it?"

Oh God. She probably thinks Gina's pregnant. "No, not only girls. At least I don't think so. And I'm not saying Gina's definitely going to get it. But it's *possible.*"

Mrs. Baldarasi nods slowly. Message received. And without me officially betraying any former-best-friend secret trust.

"You're a good friend, Sang." She pats my arm. "The kind of friend Gina needs. How 'bout I give you a dozen cannolis, okay?"

While Mrs. Baldarasi puts the cannolis on a paper

plate and covers them with foil, she says, "Try not to worry." I'm not sure if she is telling this to me or to herself.

"Thanks for the cannolis," I say, and put on my coat.

She's about to grab me in a juicy hug when *BZZZZZ!* It's the oven timer. "Good Lord. The pies," she says, throwing her hands in the air.

39

By 5:30 p.m. I'm in Megan's driveway, with my overnight bag flung over my shoulder and my skirt (for the gurdwara) on a hanger. I wave my mom away even as she reminds me for the bazillionth time that they'll be picking me up at 8:30 a.m. sharp and that I'd better be ready and waiting by the door. Right.

I say a polite hello to Drs. Chung and Chung, and there's an awkward moment when Megan's mom stares at me a bit too long, as if I've got the word "bulimic" tattooed to my forehead. Megan and I dash up to her room, and lock the door, and blast music. She lends me a camouflage-print Greenpeace T-shirt that David Jovanovich gave her.

"I'm meeting him at Planet Smoothie tonight," Megan says, and covers her mouth, as if she can hardly believe what she said.

"Get out! Megan, you're really crazy about him, aren't you?"

Megan shrugs, then giggles, then falls onto her bed, which is covered with stuffed animals. Not teddy bears, but rhinos and leopards and pythons. That sort of thing. Megan twines a stuffed python around her arm. "I think I'm in love." She sighs. "I'm all dreamy and pathetic. Is that how you feel about Jason?"

Well, the pathetic part, mostly. I sit beside Megan and can't help but smile. She looks so happy.

"Sang, just look at us. We both have boyfriends!"

I lie on the bed beside her. A stuffed giraffe tumbles onto my stomach, and together Megan and I and a host of fuzzy wildlife replicas stare at the puffy clouds painted on her ceiling. I sigh contentedly.

"So," I say, "what do your parents think of you and David?"

"Are you *kidding*? No way am I telling them."

I raise myself onto my elbow. "Don't tell me you aren't allowed to date either."

"Oh, I can. I just don't want them psychoanalyzing him. It'd be a complete nightmare. I want to keep this a secret for as long as I can."

I pick up a stuffed kiwi bird and wiggle its fat feet. "So you can act normal and all around David Jovanovich?"

"I don't have to," she says. "He's not normal either."

It's not long before panic sets in for us both. What to wear, how to do our hair, how to get out, and how to sneak back in. But at last we get it all right. Me in the

Greenpeace shirt and jeans, my hair down, and with a pair of black glittery earrings; her with her hair up in a sophisticated bun and a hot-pink SPCA T-shirt and jeans. I gaze at myself in the mirror and I look sort of like a hippie. A revolutionary, out to change the world. Protesting against injustice and evil. I make the peace sign. Megan sees this, flashes a peace sign back at me, and smiles. We slip on our coats, coat our lips with clear lip gloss, and make kissy faces at the mirror.

Megan squeezes my hand. "Let's go."

We race down the stairs to the front door. "Bye, Mom," she yells.

"Wait!" Her mom steps out of the shadows and blocks the door. "Where are you off to?" She's a short, slim woman, but intense. Always so serious. And I have no doubt that if she wanted to, she could wrestle both of us to the floor.

"Just walking downtown," Megan says. "Thought we'd stop by the bookstore and maybe get a smoothie." She's as cool as a penguin.

Her mom crosses her arms and stares at Megan for a moment with the intensity of a CIA agent questioning a spy. "You have your phone?"

"Yes, Mom."

"Is it charged?"

"Yes, Mom."

Dr. Chung breaks into a cheery smile. "Have a lovely time, girls. Don't be out past ten."

"Mom." Megan crosses her arms.

"Hmm. Ten-thirty, then. But no later. I mean it."

"Ten-thirty," Megan says in disbelief.

"Nine-thirty, then," her mother says. Ouch.

"Ten-thirty, right," Megan says, and guides me out the door, whispering to me, "Stupid psychological tricks."

"Bye, Dr. Chung," I call over my shoulder. We trip down the driveway and continue up the block in the direction of town till we reach the corner.

"See? I told you it would work," Megan says. Her mom isn't the only one using psychological tricks. Megan learned from her parents that liars usually look away from the person they lie to, so she made sure she didn't look away when she told her mom what we were doing. And she didn't lie. Not exactly. After all, she is going to those places, just not with me.

"You have my cell number in case you have any problems?" Megan says. "And the quarters?"

I pat my pocket. That and the twenty dollars in the other pocket is all I need. "Don't worry. Everything will be perfect," I say. "And so will you."

"Knock wood." Megan raps on her forehead. "Remember, the back—"

"The back door will be unlocked. You'll have snuck back in alone beforehand during your parents' favorite Animal Planet program. I know. I'll be fine. So will you. Now go!"

I give Megan a quick hug, and she dashes toward town. I turn right and head toward the train station. In minutes I'm in the station parking lot, threading my way through parked cars. Ahead, the track glows with flood-lights, and the platform looks crowded. Well, it's Saturday night. I guess a lot of people head into Philly on a Saturday night. And today *I'm one of them.* The silver train is parked on the track, doors closed. Doylestown is the end of the line, so trains just stop here, unload, and then wait for the next departure time before reloading and heading back out.

I step into the floodlit brightness and feel electrified. Like someone's flipped a switch inside of me and suddenly I'm alive and independent.

The platform is filled with high school kids all dressed in varying degrees of grunge, some wearing Stinkin' Monkeys T-shirts, all with blasé looks on their faces like they head into the city every weekend. Maybe they do. I realize how I must look. All eager and wide-eyed. I tone it down, shrug, even slouch a little.

On the lookout for Jason, I make my way through the other slouching, shrugging kids.

I'm at the end of the platform. No Jason. I turn. I remember my fears. That he doesn't really like me. That he was just setting me up. My eyes dart toward the darkness of the parking lot as I imagine him crouching in the shadows with his friends, pointing and laughing.

I feel pressure building in my head. Like a dam's about to burst. Chin up, I tell myself. Breathe. I'll slowly walk back through the crowd and into town, and I'll find Megan, and that will be that. And I will not will not cry.

Passing an especially grungy bunch of guys, their

jeans streaked with dirt, their hair dripping with grease, I'm starting to think that perhaps this is all for the best. Right?

My eyes pool up; the floodlights swim before me. Who am I kidding, I think, when—

"Sang?"

"Jason," I say, and look away. Rub my eyes on my sleeve.

"You okay?"

"Fine," I blink away crystals of tears from my lashes. "Just something in my eyes. Dust from the train, I think."

Jason looks at the immobile train. "Oh." He's gorgeous tonight. He's got that leather jacket on that I'd love to borrow someday, and his hair is all hip and rockstar-looking. Long on the forehead and spiky, but not greasy or anything. And his earring sparkles like the last tear I'm now flicking off my lash. "Did you get your train ticket?" he asks.

"No." There's a long awkward moment where I wait for him to get me one.

"You'd better hurry," he says.

"Right."

Inside the one-room ticket office, I sidle up to the window and reluctantly hand over my twenty dollars. I get only thirteen dollars back. Still, I can probably get a T-shirt for that, right? I fold the money into a tight bundle and tuck it into my pocket along with the train tickets. If I get desperate, I can always use the quarters Megan gave me too. At least a dollar's worth. I descend the stairs back to the platform just as the train doors hiss open. I see Jason anxiously looking for me, and I wave and quick-step to his side.

"This is going to be so awesome," I say, and he nods. I follow him up the steep metal steps of the train into the back car and he gives me the window seat, very gentle-manly. He slides in next to me; then someone slides in next to him. I lean forward, expecting to meet his brother, but instead I see it's his friend Glen—or is it Gary? I didn't know he was coming along. Jason doesn't seem surprised. I sink into my seat. This makes the whole thing feel a lot less date-ish.

Then again, maybe I'm overreacting. I sit up. "Is your brother coming?"

Jason points to the front of the car. Among the sea of greasy dyed-black hair, I see one head that looks washed, and the same brown as Jason's. Then I see a flash of hot pink by the door. For a moment I almost think it's Megan; then I realize it's actually Gina.

Gina? She's shouldering this overstuffed backpack, and wearing her hot-pink hat and a hot-pink T-shirt un-derneath her blue ski jacket. She's like a flash of neon light among all the black clothing. She scans the train car and catches my eye, but when I give a wave, she spins on her heel. I crane my head and can see her in the next train car now, jamming her backpack onto the metal rack above the seats.

Well, guess she's into the Stinkin' Monkeys too. I stare

out the window, which is blurred by countless scratches and gouges, and hope she's not sitting near us at the show. Deep down I wish she would have at least nodded at me, or given a small thumbs-up. Some acknowledgment of how cool it is that I've pulled off going to this concert. I try to tell myself, Whatever.

The train tugs forward and starts to move, the train yard sliding away as we glide into the night. After we show our train tickets to the conductor, Jason pulls something out of his back pocket. It's an envelope, and from this he removes our tickets and hands me one. "You might as well take this now. Check out the seats." He points to number 329 CCC on the bottom. "They're right on the floor." He turns to his friend. "Mosh pit!" they both say, and pump their fists.

I picture myself getting body-slammed by some fat sweaty dude with man breasts. Jason and his buddy are looking at me expectantly. "Mosh pit," I say faintly, and try to pump my fist, but it looks more like a toot-toot motion, and at that very moment the train blares its whistle.

"Do that again," Glen says.

I do it again. Nothing. He grins and settles back into his seat.

"So that's forty-five bucks," Jason says. "Not bad, huh?"

"Not at all," I say. Wow, forty-five bucks. This guy *really* likes me. "I'll keep it safe." I tuck the ticket deep into the back pocket of my jeans. I double-check that my thirteen dollars and return train ticket are in my front pocket.

"So," he says.

"So," I say. We're both leaning back against the seat, face to face, and it's like there's no one else in the world but the two of us. My dimple is doing overtime here, because I'm smiling and smiling.

"So," he says, "you can pay me now if you want."

"W-what?" Dimple is fading.

"The forty-five bucks," he says simply.

And the dimple is gone. "But, Jason," I say. My mind is bouncing all over the place. I mean, this is a date. He asked me out! The reasonable part of my brain is saying, Well, there is no law that says a guy has to pay, but the reasonable part of my brain is pretty small. "But, Jason," I say again, "I've only got like thirteen dollars on me."

"Okay," he says. "You can give me that and I'll take the rest later."

My cheeks are burning as I dig into my front pocket.

He starts to laugh. "I'm just kidding, Sang. Keep your thirteen bucks."

"Oh. Ha-ha."

He fixes me with those beautiful hazel-green eyes, and I feel my dimple return. "You can just pay me the money next week," he says.

"Yeah, sure," I say, and snort. "Good one."

He's totally serious.

He starts talking to his buddy about the symbolism in the song "Raunch Rock." And the truth sinks in. He really does expect me to pay him. FORTY-FIVE BUCKS! Where am I supposed to get that kind of money? I haven't had a call for babysitting in forever. My head is abuzz. So much so, I don't notice that Jason and Glen are waiting for me to say something.

"I'm sorry," I say. "What?"

"You don't mind, do you, Sang? The 'Monkeys' part?" Jason says.

I'm lost.

"I mean, 'Stinkin' Monkeys' could seem like an insult or something, you know, to your God?"

Now I'm really lost.

" 'Cause you worship the monkey god and all?"

Oh. "I don't. That's Hinduism. My dad's a Sikh."

"A-seeking what?" Jason says, and cracks up. Glen rolls his eyes.

During the rest of the ride, Jason mostly talks to Glen. They talk about music, movies, guitars, and sports. Now and then Glen asks me something, but mostly I'm left with my own thoughts.

The train trundles along, and I glance at the stations at each stop. They start out small and gingerbread-house-ish, surrounded by trees. These eventually give way to bigger, more modern-looking stations, with large parking areas. Suburban houses are replaced with row houses. Signs are covered with graffiti. Now we're getting closer to the city. Huge industrial buildings are on either side of the track.

I realize how far I am from home. I tuck my hair behind my ears and peer at the next train car. I see Gina's pink hat. She's sitting next to a gray-haired woman. I chew my lip.

Jason and his buddy are talking lyrics again, debating which song is the ultimate Stinkin' Monkeys tune. I wait patiently for a lull in the conversation.

"But 'Hate It All Too Much' really says it," Jason argues. "It gets the whole stinkin' left-out thing going."

Still waiting.

"Yeah, but 'Raunch Rock' hits all the high notes and low notes of . . ."

Blah blah blah. Still waiting. Finally I just interrupt. "Jason? Did you see Gina get on the train?"

He blinks at me as if just now remembering I'm along.

"She's here," I say. "In the next car. Did you see any of her friends get on with her?"

"The goths?" he says. "Going to a Stinkin' Monkeys concert?" He and his friend crack up at this.

"What?" I say.

"Sang, this isn't exactly their style, now is it?" Jason says.

"Oh. Of course not." I feel so stupid.

"That's okay, Sang," Jason says, and rubs my arm.

I try to give him a smile.

The train starts to slow, starts to rock back and forth. The greasy heads in front of us nod from side to side like they're keeping beat with their own "Raunch Rock" tune. Jason's brother gets up, makes his way back, and stops by us in the aisle, bracing himself by holding on to the backs of the seats. He says, "Don't get off until the Suburban Station stop, okay?" He looks a lot like Jason, only with a wider jaw and a goatee. "It's the second stop in the city."

"Second stop," Jason says, "got it."

"From there we'll take the Broad Street subway line to the end, going south. Can you remember that, in case we get separated?" Jason nods and cracks his knuckles. He actually looks a little nervous.

"I'm Sang, by the way," I say to his brother, who nods and returns to his seat.

"Second stop," Jason mumbles to himself.

"Second stop, then subway going south," I say.

He tilts his head toward me and smiles. "I'm glad you're here."

"Really?" I tilt my head toward him and the train suddenly jolts to a squeaking halt. Our heads bang together like two coconuts.

"Stop number one," Jason says, rubbing his forehead.

The conductor walks up the aisle, saying, "Market East. Market East this stop."

Lots of people rise from their seats and start to file out, but the Stinkin' Monkeys crowd stays put.

I look out the window at men on the platform tucking their papers under their arms, at mothers tugging their kids along. At Gina hoisting an overstuffed backpack over her shoulder.

Gina?

I feel a flutter of panic. She's alone. Maybe she got off

at the wrong stop. And what's with the pack? Why would she need so much stuff for a concert, unless . . .

I'm on my feet, pushing Jason. "Come on. We have to get off."

Jason stands, but doesn't move. "It's the next stop, Sang."

"I know, but Gina's out there."

He sits back down.

"Don't you get it? She's pulling a Pretzel. Alone!"

He looks at me as if I'm speaking Martian.

"A Pretzel," I say. I climb over his legs, and Glen's legs, and into the aisle. "Means running away. Come on, Jason. Gina needs me, and I need you."

"But the concert! I've paid a lot of money for this ticket."

"We have to hurry." I rush down the aisle.

"Sang!"

Soon I'm out of the train and on the platform. I can't see Gina. Other people step off the train. I wish Jason would hurry. I wait for him like a runner in a relay race waiting for a team member to hand off the baton. The minute, the very second Jason comes through that door, I'll grab his hand and together we'll run to find her.

Come on, Jason. Come on!

There's a snakelike hiss. The doors slide shut. The train starts to move. With a whirr, it disappears into the dark tunnel.

40

The platform is coated with soot and tattered bits of grungy paper. People head toward the exits. And I think, This must be some kind of joke. I laugh, but when it comes out as a horrible sob, I clap my hand over my mouth.

Jason didn't mean to leave me here. He couldn't have. He couldn't have.

I turn. No Gina. Oh God oh GOD OH GOD.

There's a square wooden bench behind me, and I collapse onto it. Inside, I feel as dark and empty as that tunnel. Tears wet my face. People pass by me. No one notices me. No one cares. No one.

Try to pull yourself together, I think. Okay, what would Rani do? Or Legolas? Or . . .

Who am I kidding? I'm nothing like them.

A pigeon with a mangled foot hobbles past me and stops to pick at a dried wad of gum. I wipe my cheeks with the back of my hand while the bird's beak pecks and pecks at the gum. It's crazy, because the wad is as hard as the pavement, and even if it did get a piece off, it'd just be nasty old gum. How long can a bird live on gum, anyway? I stand. The bird flaps its wings and flutters to the opposite side of the platform. At least its wings still work.

Suddenly I wish I had wings. I'd soar over the passengers stepping onto the escalator and fly out of the train station and over the city until I found Gina.

I don't have wings. Still, I have to try, don't I?

I dig my hands into the pockets of my jacket and muscle past people. I get onto the escalator, which is way too narrow for the huge woman in front of me. This ride is taking *forever*. I tap my foot. I bite my pinkie nail. The woman in front makes Mrs. Baldarasi look like a swimsuit model, and there is no way I can squeeze past her to run up the escalator stairs. As we rise, I get a large and nasty view of her lumpy bottom squeezed into a pair of purple polyester slacks.

At last we're at the top, and for one awful second the fat lady is stuck, and I imagine myself and everyone else behind me trapped in a fleshy buttock bottleneck.

Thankfully, she unsticks her hip and waddles off, but so slowly that I can't help banging into her.

"Sorry, ma'am," I say.

"Who you calling 'ma'am'?" The woman turns, and suddenly she's a he, with stubble and a bulldog face. "Do I look like some kinda woman to you?"

"Um," I say, and back away.

"Do I?" He's yelling now.

I spin around and speed-walk away. Please don't follow me please don't follow me please don't follow me. I hide behind a flower stand. I peek out, and he's gone. Deep breath.

I scan all around for Gina and realize I'm inside this huge indoor shopping mall, which would be cool, except I realize Gina can be in any of these boutique-y stores lining the sides. I also realize my legs are shaking.

Just find Gina.

This mall is so much more crowded than the one near home. I walk along, trying to spot her, wishing I was taller, wishing *she* were taller. I pass a pizza place, a Chinese restaurant, an ice cream shop, Claire's. I halt.

Gina loves Claire's. At least the old Gina did. It's cheap and has everything from really cool toe rings to rhinestone tiaras. So I dive into the store, which is jammed with kids my age, just like at home. But at home almost everyone is white, and here there are all types of kids, including a cluster of Indian-looking girls. I would be struck with the coolness of this if I weren't so struck with terror. *No Gina.*

I rush back into the main mall. Stand on my tippytoes. It's no good. I don't see her. I spy an empty bench and stand on it. I scan the shoppers from back the way I came, in case I passed her. Nothing.

"Miss, get off the bench," says a police officer. He's

super-tall and round, and adding to his heft is a belt loaded with a gun, billy club, cuffs, and a radio.

Good, he can help me. "I'm looking for my friend," I say. "She's short and is wearing a pink hat."

But Mr. Police Officer puts his hands on his waist and says, "Listen, I don't care if she's eight foot nine and wears rhinestone-studded sneakers. Step off that bench before I haul your ass down."

He makes a grab at me, but I lunge to the left. My eyes make a quick sweep of the shoppers fanning out in front of me. Oh my God. I see Gina's hat ahead in the distance. I'm filled with a whoosh of relief. "Found her!"

A meaty hand grabs my wrist and yanks me off the bench. "You're gonna find a piece of this in a minute," he says, tapping his billy club.

"R-right." I back away and make a run for it.

"Hey!" he shouts, but I'm outta there. I slalom past people, dodging shopping bags and strollers. I see my goal: Gina riding up yet another escalator. Now I'm really running, my stride long and catlike. I'm almost at the escalator; I can see Gina almost reaching the top of it.

"GINA!" I shout, but my voice is nothing in this colossal mall. I step onto the escalator and catch my breath. A finger is jammed into my back. I spin around, expecting the cop.

But it's that fat angry guy again, the one with the huge butt stuffed into the purple polyester pants. He's saying, "You got a problem with me? Hmm? You got some kinda problem?" He spits when he says "problem," and it's clear who's got one. Suddenly I'm a quivering mass of fear.

The escalator here is wider, not so packed. "Excuse me," I say to the elderly woman in front of me.

"Why, surely, dear."

I wind my way up the escalator steps, and at the end I'm outdoors, on a sidewalk. Gina's across the street, studying a map.

I race to the corner, but the light's changed. "Gina!" I scream. I cup my hands by my mouth. "Giiii-na!" With the cars zooming and the rattle-bang noise of a passing bus, there's no way she can hear me.

After the bright mall, I'm almost surprised to find it's still night outside. But store lights and streetlamps and car lights seem to keep the sky's real darkness from entirely reaching the ground. I shift my feet like a jogger trying to keep her pace. The streetlight changes. I'm off. And in a minute, I'm right behind her.

41

Maybe it's because I'm thinking Gina would be none too glad to see me. Maybe it's because I don't know what to say to her. Or maybe I'm just dying to see what she has planned out for herself. Whatever the reason, instead of calling out her name again or reaching out and tapping her on the shoulder, I stay behind her, silent.

People around me have determined looks on their faces. They know where they're going, and they want to get there fast. Some people seem worn and are lugging shopping bags. Others are made up for a night out on the town, like the man and woman to my left. She with her long legs and spiked heels, he with his broad shoulders and leather jacket and—what's this? He has a diamond stud earring.

I can't help it. For a moment I imagine I'm the woman with the legs and the shoes, and Jason's the guy, and we're all grown up and successful and in love, and I'm clutching his arm just like that woman is now, and I wonder where we're going. To an elegant dinner? To take a horse-pulled carriage ride? To dance close and slow? And here we are, surrounded by the glitter of streetlamps and neon signs—an urban Diwali with a magic all its own.

The man puts his hand in the air, and a battered red cab screeches to a halt. He opens the door for her, and she gives him a dazzling smile as she slides into the backseat and he follows. The cab pulls away.

Like the train did.

I realize I've stopped, and I rush to catch up to Gina.

There are fewer people around us now. Some have gone to the plastic bus shelter at the corner, and others have turned down side streets. Gina pauses to look at her map again. So I turn and pretend to study the window of a Wawa. That's when I see the pay phone by the door. That's when I think of my quarters, and of calling Megan. But before this thought goes any further, Gina is across the street and I'm scurrying to follow.

There's a light flow of cars and cabs along this street, but the sidewalks ahead of us are quiet, and a little spooky. No stores here. Just office buildings, closed and dark. Here I had thought cities were always alive and full of action, not dead like this.

Gina halts. If I know anything about my ex–best friend, she's drawing a deep breath before taking the plunge into this dark block. She took a deep breath in third grade before jumping off the ladder into a pile of snow (and breaking her arm), and in fifth grade before kissing Shawn O'Brien (and him giving her a bloody nose). And every time, I saw the bad things coming and I warned her.

And I've got a bad feeling now.

But she's trotting ahead, her footsteps echoing against the marble buildings, and I'm trotting behind her, my footsteps just as loud.

Gina breaks into a full run, and I'm right on her heels. She crosses a street, and ahead everything is bright and floodlit. I try to follow but twist my ankle on the uneven cobblestones. I groan and hop-step to the other side just before a minivan veers and peels past me.

Gina hazards a glance over her shoulder. "Un-frickin'-believable!" she screams, and marches up to me, swinging her arms fast. "You? You're the one following me?"

"No," I say, and bend over to rub my ankle. It's pretty sore, but I can still bend it.

"No? You just happen to be chasing me down a dark alley? Scaring the crap out of me? What the hell is wrong with you?"

I stand and see Gina's face all flushed. She's breathing fast.

"I thought you were some sort of rapist or something," she says, pushing my shoulder.

Okay. Now I'm pissed. "So you'd rather I was a rapist?"

Gina bares her teeth at me like a growling dog. Her teeth do look good. All straight and white.

"Listen, Gina, I didn't plan to follow you. I just saw you get off the train and I thought—"

Gina holds up her hand. "I'm not interested in what you thought. Just leave me alone, okay?"

"But you can't pull a Pretzel. It won't work. It's not realistic. The police will be looking for you. And besides, you can't really make a living off selling pretzels to tourists. And even if you could, you're too young. There are laws against you working without going to school, right?"

"See that?" She points at me. "That's the kind of crap I'm getting away from. People judging everything I do. Planning everything out. Get this: I don't want you or anyone else to plan my life, okay?"

"But going into business *takes* planning," I say. I'm trying to be helpful.

"Shut up, Little Miss Perfect." She hoists her backpack higher and walks away.

I follow, even though my ankle is sore. I have to. It's the right thing to do. Plus I don't know where else to go.

She says something, but all I hear is the rumble of a bus zooming past us. When the bus taillights are a block away, I can finally hear her. She's saying, "Leave me alone. Leave me alone. Leave me alone."

We walk on like this for half a block more, until Gina stops. "Are you gonna leave?"

I walk up really close to her and stand tall. "Doesn't look like it."

She raises her hand and I flinch, but she's pointing at the building behind us. "Look where we are. In America, in front of Independence Hall, where the Declaration of Independence was signed." I look to my right, and sure enough, there's the brick building we visited on our fourth-grade class trip. "And see over there?" She points to the opposite side of the street, where there's a long lawn ending at a glass structure.

"The Liberty Bell," I say.

"Right. So leave me alone."

I stare at her.

"Liberty. Independence. Freedom," she says. "That's what I want. So just go."

I open my mouth to argue, but before I can speak, Gina says, "Look, Sang, I don't want to spend the next few years killing myself to get A's and B's. And I don't want to just grow older only to find my biggest achievement is that I can wear my mom's fat slacks. And most of all, I don't want to spend the rest of my life making these huge, fantastic plans that I never have the guts to carry out because I let everyone else shoot them down. For once in my life, I just want to create my own destiny. I mean, is that so wrong?"

"No. No, of course not. But I don't think running off to Philly is the answer, Gina. I think you need to go home." I reach out for her arm.

She takes a sharp step back. "Don't judge me. Just go."

"But what are you going to do?"

"That's my business."

"But what if you get hurt, or in trouble? Or what if you have a problem and need help?"

"Stop with the bulimia crap, already. I swear, you are so—"

"That's not what I meant."

Gina rubs her forehead like she's got a wicked headache. "Look, what do you care? It's not about you, Sang. In case you haven't noticed, we are not friends anymore."

"Fine. Okay." I start to walk away. But I stop, and stride back. "You know what? It's *not* okay. Gina Flora Baldarasi, you have been nasty to me," I say, counting my points on my fingers, "and rude, and obnoxious, and you've made it incredibly clear that you don't like me anymore, even though I'm the same person you've been best friends with forever. So I'm nothing to you. Well, fine. You win. I'm nothing!" My voice echoes against the bricks of Independence Hall. "Like you said, that's your business. But it doesn't change what you are to me. See that?" I wave my hand at the building. "I'm independent too."

Gina laughs. "You? You've never been independent in your life."

"Shut up."

"All you ever said to me was, 'Gina, what should I wear?' or, 'Gina, what should I say?' or, 'Gina, what should I do?' And what did I get out of it? Everyone thinks of you as the smart one, the tall one, the exotic one. What was I? Your stupid little sidekick?"

"That's not true. You are so—"

Gina holds up her hand again. "I don't care what you or anyone else thinks I am or am not. No one's gonna tell me what I can or cannot do. Can't you get it?"

"But what about your parents?"

"Mr. and Mrs. Average at Everything and Taking Care of Everyone? What do they know?"

"I meant, what about your parents worrying about you?"

She digs her hands into the pockets of her jeans. "I'm gonna call them." Her eyes shift to the left. "I am. I just need a little time alone first." Suddenly she grabs my arm. "Sang, promise me you won't tell anyone you saw me. Promise."

"But I can't just—"

"You have to, Sang. This means everything to me. Besides, best friends keep best-friend secrets."

"Don't you dare pull that on me." I shake my arm loose.

"God, you're right." Gina tucks some hair by her ear into her hat. I see she's got three new piercings, with tiny silver hoops. "Look, Sang, I'm sorry, okay? I—I never wanted to hurt you."

I cross my arms.

"Sang, I'm trying to apologize here. I'm trying to be honest with you, okay? You asked me once if I missed you. Remember? And truthfully? I did miss you." And in a small voice she says, "Still do."

I'm staring at her, totally convinced she's playing me, but then I notice something. Tears are shining in her eyes. Gina can't do fake tears. She just can't. "You actually mean it, don't you?"

Gina shrugs awkwardly.

So I grab her in a hug, and say, "You *are* my best friend." Tears prick my eyes. Gina hugs back and nods, and at last everything feels like it's going to be okay. Like it's going to be the way it used to.

She lets go, her eyes suddenly dry. "So don't tell anybody you saw me. Okay?"

"But, Gina, how can I—"

"You have to. I trust you." She hooks her thumbs under the shoulder straps of her backpack. "And don't follow me," Gina says as she backs away. "Thanks, Sang. You're the *best.*"

I feel frozen to the pavement as I watch her reach the corner. "Gina?" I shout. "How can I contact you?"

She just waves, hesitates at the curb long enough to let a car speed by, and crosses the street. She continues down another empty sidewalk. I see her pass the Olde City Luncheonette, her form a mere silhouette in front of its glowing pink neon sign. She looks small and strong, and she's leaning forward slightly, either from the weight of her backpack or from her determination to move on as fast as she can. Past the sign, she blends in with the dark stone building. Next I see her as a flash of movement in front of an ATM before she's gone from sight.

I feel that nervous weakness in my knees again. Okay. Think think think. From Independence Hall I go straight back past the dark office buildings. Turn at the Wawa. In through that shopping mall. That's how to get to the train station. Market East. That's what the conductor called it. Remember this, I tell myself, for when I get back here.

I cross the street, pass the luncheonette and the ATM, and continue on Gina's trail.

42

There's a damp, cool breeze tossing my hair in my face. I gather the strands up in the back, twist them into a loose knot, and tuck this inside my collar. I pull the zipper of my ski jacket up and dig my hands into its pockets, but still feel a shiver. But it's not from the cold.

I stay close to the buildings and I pass the brightly lit entrance of a hotel lobby with its brass-handled glass doors and a uniformed doorman, who touches a white-gloved hand to his top hat. Beyond the pool of light by the entrance, the sidewalk seems to disappear into blackness.

I force myself forward, even though it's like leaving the warmth and security of a bonfire to go exploring the dangerous jungle. I tell myself it's just a street, and a straight one at that. No different than State Street or Court Street in Doylestown at around 9 p.m. I'll walk a bit more, but if I don't see Gina, I'll go back the way I came. I turn and memorize the hotel, the ATM, the luncheonette. See? I'm not lost. No worries. Across the street is some sort of a park, with tree branches waving in the wind like the arms of people who are trying to signal rescuers: Help! Over here!

I move on, even though I don't see any sign of Gina. Another block down, the sidewalk becomes busy. People laughing, pulling open doors leading to smoky bars, candlelit restaurants. Not likely Gina's in any of those. I reach the corner. The street sign says I'm at Chestnut Street and Fourth Street. Gina might have turned, but I can't. I have to go straight. Straight I can handle. So I cross.

And I look at everyone everyone everyone that I pass. Men and women in elegant long coats, and guys and girls who remind me of college kids at Hari's school, in their jeans and leather jackets and striped scarves, elbowing each other and talking and laughing. I see a man in a stained and torn brown sweat suit, his gray-black hair matted, his face sunburned-looking and leathery, his stare vacant. His hand is out. His palm is streaked with dirt. His nails are brown and thick.

The elegant people, the college kids, they all pass by him, not even glancing his way. Not even noticing him. How is this possible?

I reach into my pocket. I mean, an extra dollar won't mean much to me one way or another, but this guy could get some food with it, right? So I pull out my money and am about to peel off a dollar for him when his hand closes on the bundle of bills and he takes them all. Okay, so it was kinda rude of him, but hey, he's homeless. So fine. Let him have it, I think. That's when I notice something white between the bills. My return train ticket! In an instant, the money and my ticket disappear into the pocket of his sweats.

"Excuse me, sir," I say, "but I accidentally gave you my ticket."

The vacant eyes turn toward me, as if he's noticing me for the first time.

"S-so," I say, "if you wouldn't mind giving it back?"

He looks away and holds his hand up to the next passerby, who ignores him.

"I need my ticket," I say, a bit louder.

The man snarls, baring yellow teeth. He growls at me, starting low, then getting louder and louder.

I don't wait for the attack. I run. My heart is pounding painfully in my chest. What is this crap? Rules don't seem to apply out here. Cops are nasty. You try to help somebody and they attack you. Nothing makes sense.

I'm stuck at the light at the next corner. Thank God the man hasn't moved. He was just trying to scare me. It worked. I'm still panting with fear. I hold my stomach. Okay, Sang. Breathe slower. Try to relax. Why couldn't that creep just hand back the ticket? It's not like he's gonna go to Doylestown, right? I picture him standing in front of the County Theater, waiting for me. The thought makes my teeth chatter.

I look up at the street sign. Third Street. I still have

my quarters. I can call Megan, and she can figure something out. Or maybe Gina can lend me a few bucks. This thought almost makes me laugh. Almost.

When the light changes, I cross, and up ahead I can hardly believe what I see. Gina, and her map. She's there for a moment, then gone, and I realize she's turned left. I race to the corner. It's a narrow one-way alley, darker, quieter, spookier than the street I'm on now. I can see someone up ahead. It must be her.

So I follow. Of course I do. I get closer and see it really is her. She pauses to look at the map again, so I pause too. At a distance up ahead is the next intersection, flooded with light and the echo of horns tooting and the hum of traffic cruising by, but before Gina reaches this, she stops, looks up at a narrow brick building, pulls open the door, and stands for a moment while a rectangle of light from inside spills onto her and the sidewalk, and in she goes, leaving me in the dark.

At the door, I read the sign beside it: BANK STREET YOUTH HOSTEL.

"Hostile Youth" is more like it.

The door suddenly opens again, and out step five or six grubby-looking twenty-somethings, all shouldering mini-backpacks and speaking a foreign language. French, I think. Before the door shuts again, I catch a glimpse of Gina talking with someone behind a desk.

Okay. I've seen enough.

43

I've made it back to the Wawa. I'm standing in front of the pay phone, a pile of change in my hand.

Should I call Megan? Tell her I'm on my way back somehow? Or should I save this money and see if I can find some more on the sidewalk? Enough for a ticket?

Should I trust Gina? Because if I trust her and give her some time, then maybe, just maybe, things can get back to the way they were. . . .

I lean against the phone and think, If only my life were like a movie. If only I could pick a moment in time, a moment when I was truly happy, and pause. Stay there in that scene and just feel. Feel Jason's warm lips. Or Mom's comforting hug. Hear my dad's laughter while I, as a little girl, dance to the music of a Bollywood movie. Or again feel the closeness of sharing my worries with a very best friend who knows absolutely everything about me, but cares about me anyway.

I'd do almost anything to have that friendship back.

I pick up the handset. I drop in a quarter. Another. Another. They drop like stones, clanging inside the metal telephone. The sound of change.

I press the numbers on the phone. Hot tears wet my cheeks. There's a voice speaking on the line now, but I can't answer. All I can do is think, Goodbye, Gina. I finally find my own voice to say, "H-hello? Mrs. Baldarasi?"

As I tell her everything (leaving out the part where I'm not supposed to be in Philly myself), an ache grows deep down inside of me, and I know for sure nothing will ever be the same again.

When I hang up, I feel more sad and empty than I ever thought possible.

Home. I need to go home.

"Hello, beautiful. Where you been all my life?"

I look up to see a Latino guy in a tank top, with muscles and tattoos bulging everywhere, holding out his arms to me as if he's going to gather me in tight hug. In his left hand is a Wawa bag.

"Why so sad? Come to Papi, sweet thing," he says.

I look past him, wondering who I can call to for help, but all I see are a few of his buddies wearing expectant smiles.

Never mind. Just ignore it. I quickly dry my face and try to move away from the phone, but I'm blocked by Mr. Macho's arm. "Where you going so fast? We hardly got to know each other."

I look around again for somebody to help me. There's nobody. And something wells up in me. It's not fear. It's not panic. It's rage. I turn on him. I point at his chest, and I'm shouting, "Back off, before my foot gets to know your genitals!"

His arm drops and he backs away. And I march on, across the street (thank God the streetlight's green).

"Oooooh! Rodney, she got you good," one of the guys says.

Now I feel like I've become one of the city folk marching along the sidewalk, all of us with a determined step. All of us knowing where we're going, or at least pretending to. It's not long before I'm descending the escalator back down into the mall. I stride directly toward the part where the train station is, ignoring all the shops (I don't have any money anyway) and all the people (there's no one I'm hunting for now). When I reach the escalator that goes down to the tracks, I'm satisfied that I've made it this far.

Of course, what's the point? I don't have a ticket. I don't have money for a ticket. I turn to the right, where ticketing agents sit behind bulletproof glass, talking to commuters through a little metal grate and sliding tickets and money to them through a small slot on the counter. I study the agents' faces. Who will be friendly? Who will care enough to help? My eyes rest on a young black woman behind the window marked INFORMATION. I sigh and get in her line, and I wait. And wait. It's chilly here, so I shove my hands into my pockets. People in front of me are shifting from foot to foot with impatience. One by one, they leave the line, unwilling to wait anymore. Pretty soon it's just me and the person holding things up.

It's some kid in a parka, the kind with a hood that's edged in fake brown fur. His hood is up, hiding his face, but I can tell he's aggravated by the way he's waving his arms about. The lady behind the window is shaking her head. This may take a while. Hey, I can wait. I've got all the time in the world, right? I mean, I'm not going anywhere unless this woman can help me get home for nothing. There's got to be a way. On credit or something. Maybe she can send me a bill—so long as my parents don't see it.

Only thing is, I've got this crummy feeling. If people can walk by that guy on the street, who obviously needs food, and clothes, and a place to stay, why should anybody help me?

Because I'm young and polite. I'll ask nicely.

"Sir," the information lady says, "please step aside."

"But how can you say, 'Wait twenty-four hours'?" Parka Kid says. "Do you know what can happen to a person in twenty-four hours?"

"Please, sir. Step aside."

Poor kid probably missed his train. But I've got bigger problems than a long wait. I've got no way to get home, and never mind the usual crap that's waiting for me when I do get home. I have to get back to Megan's on time. That's the most important thing.

I step up to the window. Parka Kid has moved aside

and is drumming his fingers on the counter next to me. I try to concentrate on turning on the charm.

"Hello, Stella," I say, reading her name tag. "I've run into a bit of a problem and I was wondering if you could help."

"What seems to be the problem, miss?" She sounds all-business. Maybe I should have tried the man at ticket window number two.

"Well," I say, and give a full-dimple smile, "I had my train ticket for home, and this homeless man—"

"Excuse me. Pardon me." Parka Kid rudely shoves me aside. "Look," he says to Stella, who seems pissed, "this is urgent, okay? I can't wait twenty-four hours to talk to the police. I can't wait twenty minutes."

Police?

Stella's saying, "If we reported every missing person, sir, well, the police wouldn't be able to do their jobs. I am sorry."

Parka Kid leans in toward the bulletproof glass, his mouth practically touching the grate. "Just let me give you a description. In case you see her. She's tall, and has this long shiny black hair. Her skin's kinda dark. Not like yours," he says. "More light-coffee-ish. She's Indian, you know? And she's got these big brown eyes with really long, dark lashes. And when she smiles, she's got this dimple."

I peer at Parka Kid's face. Oh. My. God. "Glen?"

He keeps talking to Stella. "And she's wearing this jacket. I think it's black. Or is it blue?"

"It's dark blue," I say.

Glen turns. "Sang?" He pulls me aside as Stella calls for the next person. "Where the hell were you? I've been looking all over the station, and the mall."

"You have?" I tuck my hair behind my ears. "You guys have been looking for me all this time?"

His pale blond eyebrows are knit together. He takes off his hood and runs his hand through his stand-on-end strawberry-blond hair. "I was going totally nuts here. Why'd you go off like that?"

"I thought Gina needed help."

"Gina Baldarasi?" He rubs his mouth and gives this some thought. "And just like that you ran off? What if you got into trouble? Didn't you think?" Glen studies me with his ice-blue eyes. He's thin, and I never noticed how tall he is. Probably taller than Hari. In fact, I feel like I'm being grilled by my big brother.

"Look, Glen," I say, "it's really sweet of you to worry."

"I'm a sweet guy," he says, and shrugs. "Stupid, huh?"

I look at him, really look at him, and I see a gentleness in his eyes I hadn't bothered to notice before.

"I can see why Jason likes you so much."

If Glen is this worried, I can imagine how Jason must be feeling. I'm anxious to see him. I picture a joyous re-union with lots of emotion. I look past Glen. "Where is Jason? Down by the track? We'd better tell him I'm okay."

Glen gives me a funny look.

"Glen?"

Glen's mouth tightens into a thin line. He reaches into the back pocket of his jeans and pulls out his Stinkin' Monkeys ticket, and waves it in my face. "He's there, Sang. At the concert."

I'm stunned.

He tosses the ticket into a wire trash bin. "And the name's *Gary,* by the way. Gary Westbrock."

While he walks to the escalator that descends to the train platform, I'm bombarded with images and sounds. Of Jason refusing to leave the train. Of him yelling, "Sang!" Only now that I think of it, it wasn't his voice at all. It was Gary's. Gary Westbrock's. I'm picturing Jason at the Stinkin' Monkeys concert, without a care in the world. I'm picturing Gary racing back to this train station and searching everywhere for me, arguing with that Stella lady. Searching for me, even though I didn't know his name.

"Gary!" I shout. "Gary Westbrock. Wait!"

44

Turns out Gary Westbrock is this really nice guy. He gives me money for the return ticket home and tells me not to worry about paying him back, even though I totally will. On the train ride home we talk, and he's a little awkward at first. Maybe he's a bit shy, or maybe he's mad at me. But after a short while we're both relaxed, talking like old friends.

I tell him about me and Gina, and he tells me about Jason. About how he argued with Jason all the way to the next train stop, trying to convince him to take the train back to Market East to find me, but Jason didn't even consider not going to the concert, even after Gary chewed him out and told him what an ass he was, abandoning me like that.

"He just said, well . . . ," Gary says, and stops.

"What?"

"It's hot in here." He takes off his parka and sits on it.

He's wearing a baggy black Stinkin' Monkeys T-shirt. His arms are pale and covered with a sprinkling of light freckles. He pulls out his cell phone. "I'm calling my parents for a lift home. Need a ride?"

"Gary, tell me. What did Jason say?"

Gary looks uncomfortable. Crosses his leg and starts tapping out a beat on his black sneaker. Next he's talking on the phone to his mom. When he's done, he flips it shut and sees I'm still staring at him.

"Please tell me, Gary."

"It doesn't matter what he said, Sang."

"It does to me."

"Crap." He uncrosses his legs and leans forward, staring at his hands clasped between his knees. "Here's how it went. I said he couldn't leave you on your own, and he said"—Gary sighs—"he said, 'Easy come, easy go.' " His pale eyebrows immediately pucker. "I'm sorry."

"Oh. No. That's okay." I turn to the window. "I made you tell me."

"Listen," Gary says, "he's a jerk, and I'm never hanging with him again."

I turn back. "But I thought you were best friends or something."

He shrugs. "Things change, right? Some for the better." He gives me a smile.

"Right," I say, and smile back. I grow serious. "Listen, I'm really sorry you missed the concert because of me. I messed up your entire night. I'll find a way to pay you back for the ticket, okay?"

"Forget it," he says.

I nod, but I know somehow I will make this up to him. Gary and I talk some more, and I find out he's the oldest in his family and he's got two younger sisters, one around Doodles's age. And I find out that he plays electric guitar, loves video games, and used to play basketball but wasn't tall enough to get on the varsity, so now he's totally out of shape.

When he offers me his phone to call my parents for a ride, I tell him about how I snuck out to go to Philly, and how Megan was covering for me. I'm tempted to call Megan, but see we're almost in Doylestown by now.

The train slows. Gary puts his parka back on. The train comes to a stop, and we file down the aisle behind a handful of people. "I'm so glad this horrible night is over with."

"Thanks a lot," he says, and laughs.

I laugh too. "You know what I mean."

We climb down the train's metal stairs to the platform. "There's my mom," he says, waving to a woman standing by the edge of the parking lot. "So I guess this is it."

"Thanks again," I say, and give him a hug. My face reaches his chest.

"Hey, no prob," he says.

"There is the good-for-nothing loose girl!" a loud, harsh voice says.

I pull away from Gary as Chachi and my dad march toward us. Oh. My. God.

"Dad, hi!" I put on a false bright smile.

"When your chachi told me, I didn't believe her," he says. "I said to myself, This is a lie. My good sweet Sangeet would not do this. I believe in her. I trust her. And look."

I take in the crushing disappointment on his face, the satisfaction on Chachi's face, the discomfort on Gary's.

"This is my friend Gary." My eyes plead, Please don't make a scene.

"You." Dad points at Gary's face. "What have you done to my daughter?"

Gary raises his hands like he's under arrest. "Nothing, sir."

" 'Sir.' Don't 'sir' me, you derelict. Did you come to my house? Did you talk with me? No. If you did, you would know she's not allowed to date."

Gary's face turns deep pink.

"Dad, it's not like that. *Please* believe me."

"Get in the car."

45

"**M**y good, sweet girls," Taoji says, and wraps his arms around me and Doodles. Doodles's eyes are shining as she smiles into his face. My eyes are burning and sore and all cried out. I rest my face on the shoulder of his freshly pressed dress shirt. Taoji is looking sharp today, wearing a deep blue turban, his mustache and beard neatly combed. We are sitting in the backseat of our car on the way to the gurdwara. Mom is driving. Dad and Chachi are in the other car, ahead of us. Taoji would certainly have fit better in the front seat beside Mom, but insisted on being in back with us.

Doodles is chattering on and on about her school and her friends and what she does at recess each day. I just rest on Taoji and breathe in his scent of sandalwood and just a hint of cumin, my hands resting on my lap. The car feels chilly, mostly because I'm wearing a nylon skirt and panty hose instead of my usual pants. At last there's a lull in Doodles's talk.

"And what of my big girl?" Taoji asks me.

To my surprise, I feel tears forming again. I close my eyes and shrug.

"Tired, darling?"

I nod. I am tired. I am so, so tired.

"Rest, then."

He pats my head and I feel myself relax, grateful for his warm arm around my shoulders, his warm voice as he speaks in low tones to Doodles. Grateful that he, at least, doesn't know about last night, and isn't judging me. Because my parents were so concerned that this visit with Taoji go smoothly, that this death anniversary thing be observed in a solemn and honorable way, and that tradition and respect for family be held above everything else, nobody is to mention what went on last night or all the horrible things I've supposedly done. Not until he is safely gone from our house.

I try to rest. Time passes. Images flit by. I see Megan crying, her parents stern as they hand my overnight bag back to me. I see Chachi so pleased she had overheard me and Megan making plans on the phone the other night, so pleased she was able to blow the whistle on me. I see her nodding with approval as my father yells and yells and yells in the car on the way home from the train station. Telling me I'm grounded indefinitely. Talking about private school. I see my mother at home, flying toward me, her eyes red, making sure I'm okay, then shaking with anger, saying things are going to have to change, saying how phenomenally disappointed she is in me. I see myself sitting in my room, the phone gone, the computer gone, lying in my bed with Orlando gone. Everything gone. No friends to turn to anymore anyway. My head throbs. My eyes burn. I realize someone is calling my name.

"Come, darling," Taoji says. "We're here."

I open my eyes and smile, so grateful to see him. He reaches out his hand, and I take it and slide out of the car. I just have to get through this day. Avoid Chachi. Enjoy Taoji. Then a few more days of school, and then Hari will be home. I need my big brother.

We cross the parking lot and head toward the gurdwara. It doesn't look like much from outside, just a long stucco building with a glass door. The only thing to distinguish it from the small office buildings is the steady stream of Sikhs making their way in. The men wear bright-colored turbans, the women wear rich silk salwar kameezes, the girls wear either salwar kameezes or dresses, and the boys wear dress slacks, but instead of turbans they are wearing *patkas,* cloth wraps that cover the bun of their hair. Because traditional Sikhs don't cut their hair, it can be pretty hard to tell the little girls from the little boys. Many of the boys and men, like my dad, have cut their hair, though, and inside the gurdwara they must cover their heads with a handkerchief or a bandanna or something.

Dad and Chachi are waiting by the entrance. I think about turning on my heel and walking away, through the parking lot, down the busy street, and on and on and on until I'm far away from everything and everyone. But then I think perhaps it would be braver to move forward. To worship at the gurdwara. To do this for my deceased chacha, for my taoji, and for my dad. And perhaps for me too.

So I steel myself and walk by my dad and Chachi in silence, Chachi sniffing at me as I pass. In the cloakroom, we all kick off our shoes, leaving them among piles of expensive sneakers, elegant high heels, and worn old sandals.

I put a red chuni on my head, glad that its fabric is hiding most of my face. I follow my family, padding over the thick Persian carpet as we make our way to the main room. I can already hear the music. The rhythmic tabla drums, the sawing melody of the harmonium, the chanting of the singer. Now Chachi is standing by the doorway to the inner room.

I pause.

"Come, come, darling," Taoji says, and guides me by the elbow. He reaches Chachi and lets go of me. Holds Chachi's arm, and leads her inside.

I follow, down the fancy carpeted path. The room opens up, the ceiling double height. Worshipers are already seated on the rugs—females to the left, males to the right. I fold my hands in front of me. Mom and Dad and Doodles are the first in our group to reach the altar, where the holy book rests beneath a cloth awning. Doodles is wearing a stiff golden chuni draped over her head, Mom has a green silk scarf tied beneath her chin. Dad looks funky, with a blue bandanna knotted on his head. Sort of a Springsteen-meets-Gandhi look. They kneel, touch their foreheads to the ground, toss some money into the box at the foot of the altar, and rise. Mom and Doodles find a spot to the left, while Dad goes to the right.

Next come Chachi and Taoji. I'm touched to see how difficult it is for Taoji to kneel. He seems so much older than he did when I saw him last. He is getting on in years. Chachi makes a smooth bow, then instantly I see her whip out a wad of tissues and start crying. She touches her forehead to the ground, her bony butt shiny in her silky salwar kameez. If only I had the guts to give her a kick. . . .

It's my turn. I go on my knees. I turn to see my father watching me. I carefully hold my skirt down as I bow, but don't dare touch my head to the ground in case it rides up too much, and I pray: God, whichever God you are, make everything okay somehow. I look up at the holy book, toss the money my parents gave me earlier into the box, and dare to hope for the best.

I sit on the rug by my mom. There are no chairs in a gurdwara. Chachi is on her other side, sniffling into her tissues. Mom pats Chachi's shoulder. People stare at Mom, some even turning around to take a closer look. Like they've never seen an American before. True, she is the only total non-Indian in sight, but so?

The service continues. It's long, but I'm determined to not fidget or whisper with Doodles just to pass the time. Instead, I try to concentrate. In the front, a man in white flowing pajamas and a white turban, with a long white beard, reads from the book. There's no English, so I can't follow a word, but I know it's all very serious and religious and holy. And all the while the man waves what looks like a feather duster over the pages, I guess to keep bugs away or something. Every now and then we have to stand. Every now and then we have to say *"Sat Sri Akal!"* and touch our foreheads to the rug. Mom and Doodles dutifully do so, but I can only go partway down because of my skirt. Still, each time I do this, I pray to God to help me somehow, if he can.

Chachi soon notices my partial bow and clicks her tongue. The next time we bow, she points to the rug and whispers, "Down."

I ignore her.

"Disrespect," she says, and crawls beside me. Before I can again start my silent prayer, my face is slammed onto the ground.

I grasp my nose. Blood drips onto my hand. I move to rise, but her hand is strong on my neck.

I push hard against her till I sit up. Chachi is squatting beside me. Just the slightest push would knock her back. But I think of the holy book so nearby.

I stand as Doodles and Mom are lifting their heads from the ground. Chachi yanks my hand from my nose and pulls me by the wrist downward. I throw her off me.

Now I'm stumbling between worshipers to the carpet pathway, blood pooling in my hands. The music pipes up as I run. My chuni drops to the ground, women gasp, and all eyes are on me. I run out of the temple area, through the hallway, and to the ladies' room. Inside a bathroom stall, I shut the door and pull off wads and wads of toilet paper and cover my nose with it. I snivel and think, So this is what praying gets you.

"Sang?" It's Mom.

"Go away."

"You okay, honey?"

"What do you care? I'm such a disappointment to you anyway." I blow my nose. Blood's still flowing freely. I drop the paper into the toilet and grab another wad of paper and hold it to my nose. "I ruin everything."

"Is it bleeding bad? Let me see, honey."

"You don't want to see. You don't want to see *anything* bad."

There's a moment's silence. "Let me help."

Mom's feet are beside the stall door. They're only covered with panty hose, and she's wiggling her toes and putting one foot on top of the other. Probably cold from the bathroom tiles. Mom's probably wishing she had a pair of thick socks to put on.

"Sang? Did you hear me? Open the door, honey."

I hesitate. My hand turns the lock. I slowly push open the door.

"Oh, honey," Mom says. Her voice is so warm, so caring. Her arms are held wide.

"I'm so sorry," I say, and dive into her deep warm hug.

My tears and blood spoil her purple silk shirt, but she holds me tight anyway and says, "Never mind, honey. Never mind."

46

"Get your chachi more chicken vindaloo, *beti*," Taoji says to me. We're at the Indian restaurant halfway between the gurdwara and home, sitting at a large round table. Soft sitar music is piped in, the walls are covered with framed prints of dancing goddesses, and over the door leading to the kitchen is a limp HAPPY DIWALI WISHES banner, looking as sad and forgotten as Christmas decorations at the end of January.

The restaurant is holding its all-you-can-eat buffet lunch. Imagine taking a bulimic to an all-you-can-eat buffet. Kind of like taking an alcoholic to an open bar, isn't it? But I don't say this out loud. My plan is to just quietly taste all the wonderful food and hope nobody thinks twice about me.

Our table is littered with dirty plates the waiters haven't bothered to remove yet. The pile in front of Chachi grows by the minute, the prospect of unlimited free food inspiring her to try a taste of everything, then push it aside. It seems everyone is supposed to take care of her, the long-suffering widow. She does these dry fake sobs between bites, and Taoji pats her on the shoulder protectively, saying, "Poor dear. Brave, brave lady."

Dad has already filled a plate of assorted appetizers for her: samosas and koftas and kebabs. Taoji has brought her salad and raita, and little bowls filled with flaming-orange and lime-green sauces. Mom delivered Chachi a platter of veggies and meats, each in a thick sauce of its own. Even Doodles had to get her some rice and naan bread, though she almost dropped the plate twice on the trip from the buffet to our table.

Chachi eyes the dishes steaming on the buffet table. "Vindaloo is almost gone." She glares at me.

"I'll get it," Mom says, and stands.

"See how spoiled that child is?" Chachi says.

Mom clenches her cloth napkin.

"It's okay, Mom," I say. "I'll get it." Mom sits. I stand and straighten my skirt. Chachi rubs her dry eyes, and Taoji pats her shoulder yet again. At the buffet table, I grab a plate, still hot from the dishwasher.

Doodles is beside me. "Sang, get me one of those." She points to the white squares of super-sweet burfi up against the wall. Her golden chuni is wrapped round and round her neck, one side dangling low and stained brown from where it dragged on her food.

"Fine, give me your plate." I set the empty plate for Chachi down and take Doodles's. I place a burfi on it.

"One more."

I put one more on it.

"What is taking so long?" Chachi says over her shoulder. She turns to Taoji. "So disrespectful."

I tighten my mouth, and take the plate to where the entrees are lined up and start scooping chicken vindaloo onto it.

Doodles pulls on my sleeve, and whispers to me, "Spit on it."

"Doodles!" I say, with mock shock. Doodles waves her chuni at me and skips back to our table.

I follow with the plate.

"Ah, finally," Chachi says, as if she hadn't eaten all day. She pushes aside an almost completely full bowl of rice pudding.

I set the plate in front of her.

"No pickle?"

I take a tiny bowl filled with brown pickle that is beside Dad and place it in front of her.

She shoves it away. "Not that one." She nods to me. "The other."

I roll my eyes.

"See that?" Chachi points to me. "See the disrespect?"

Taoji pats her arm. "She is tired, is all. She meant no disrespect. You love your chachi, Sang, don't you?"

There's a hush at the table.

"You girls are lucky to have your chachi with you. Pampering you. Playing with you. Isn't that right?" Taoji smiles at me.

I press my lips tighter and tighter.

"Eh?" Chachi grabs my wrist. "Answer."

Mom sets down her napkin. "Please, Kajal. Don't force her."

Chachi lets go. Dusts off her hands. "Hmm. See how they let this one get away with this and that? Let her lie and steal?"

"No, no," Taoji says. "Nothing like that. Get the pickle for your auntie," he says to me, and winks. "There's a good girl."

Indian pickles are nothing like the pickles Americans are used to. For one thing, they aren't made with cucumbers, but with funky things like mangoes, limes, chilies, and peas. Also, they are fiery hot. So hot you can't eat them straight, and a mere dot of pickle mixed into a cup of rice is enough to set your tongue on fire.

I fill a saucer with an oily blood-red pickle while Chachi tells my dad, "You must be firm with this girl, I tell you. Punish her. Slap her. That is best." She waggles her head from side to side. "You spoil. This is why this girl is doing the things she is doing. Filthy loose things." She picks up a chicken leg.

"Children grow best with kindness and gentleness," Mom says. "How dare you—"

"Shh," my dad says to her, and shakes his head.

Now I'm standing beside Chachi as she drags a piece of naan through the sauce on her plate and says, "If a loose daughter went with a boy to Philadelphia and did who-knows-what, it is the fault of the loose mother. That is what."

"Stop it!" I slam the pickle down on the table.

"Sangeet!" Dad says in a sharp voice. "That's enough."

"Tell *her* that," I say.

"Don't speak about your auntie that way," Taoji says to me sternly.

Chachi looks me up and down, and sneers. "Turning just like that mother of yours. Disgusting."

"I'd be proud to turn out like my mom! Where do you get off talking about her that way? She's done nothing but put up with you and work hard to make you feel at home, and what did you do?"

"Sang," Mom says, "it's okay. Forget it."

"How can you say that? It's not okay." My whole body is trembling with anger.

"Quiet, darling," Taoji says. "Sit now."

"No. I'm not going to sit. I'm not going to be quiet. Not anymore. Taoji, you should know the truth. She steals things. Not just money"—I shoot a glance at Mom—"personal things too. She—"

"Eh, I know the truth," Chachi says, raising her voice over mine. "I know all about your mother. Doing nasty things with boys when still a schoolgirl."

"Don't," I say. I see Mom's face flush.

Chachi raises her voice. Says, "No. I have read all her dirty secrets."

"What are you going on about?" my dad says.

"No," I say. "Just stop."

"So proud. So proud, she wrote it in her book." She

points at my mom. "Wrote all about how she did the filthy sexual act when she was only—"

Chachi suddenly stops. For a moment it is as if she's been shot. Her mouth is wide open, her eyes staring wildly at her chest, where a blood-colored pile of slime has just hit her. It's like her guts were ripped out of her and are oozing down her front, onto her lap. It's the pickle, of course. There's an eerie bit of silence when all is still and I set the pickle saucer back onto the table. A roar of action follows this. Chachi trying to lunge at me, and Dad holding her back, and Taoji shouting in Punjabi, and waiters tossing cloth napkins at us, and Mom furiously calling Chachi a thief. It's scary. What have I started? I wish it could all stop.

Then I notice something. Something bright and shimmering like a pile of golden treasure on the opposite side of the table. It's Doodles's golden chuni, which she's pulled over herself; light from the window is sparkling on it as she trembles beneath it.

This is my fault. Why couldn't I shut up? I go to Doodles. Pull off the scarf, ready to wipe away her tears.

She's not crying. She's giggling.

I look back at the chaos. At a waiter scrubbing Chachi's chest, making the red spot grow bigger. At Chachi hitting his hands away from her.

Now I start giggling too. And pretty soon Doodles and I are side by side, laughing, laughing so hard it hurts. We're not even making any noise, except for the sound of our hands repeatedly slapping the table.

47

It's Monday, and I'm riding on the bus to school.

Gina gets on the bus, walks up to me. "Thanks for ratting me out, bitch." She flips me the bird and moves to the back of the bus.

If she were my friend, I would tell her how many times her mom blessed me when I called to tell her where Gina was. How much her mom loves her; how much I, in my own "I'm not Gina's friend anymore" way, will always love her.

I stare out the window at the Victorian houses we pass, my mind full of the weekend. Did it really happen? When I stood up to Chachi and told everyone how I felt, it was like pulling the finger out of a dam. Doodles told my parents about witnessing Chachi stealing money and seeing the food in Chachi's room. She said she was afraid to tell them sooner, because "every time Sang told you something, she got in trouble." Dad admitted he was furious that Chachi only bothered to tell him about my trip to Philly *after* I had already left. And Chachi kept saying it was all lies and weeping like she was dying. Taoji was most surprising of all. When we got home, he ordered Chachi to her room. Told her to pack her things.

Seeing that her tears were doing no good, Chachi stomped up to her room and slammed the door shut. We all sat in the living room, listening to things crashing about upstairs. Taoji sighed and told us he was sorry things had gone this way. "She was never quite right," he said.

"What do you mean?" Dad asked.

"You were in America when they wed, but I remember she made a beautiful bride for your brother. It seemed like a good match at first, but always she was cold and strange. Her entire family. After our dear brother died, not one of her relatives came to console her." He shook his head. "I'm afraid love and kindness are things that must be taught. And at an early age. Come here, my darlings." He held his arms out to us, and Doodles and I went to him and hugged him.

"We did our best. You know that," Dad said.

Taoji nodded. "Perhaps more than you should have."

Dad rubbed his forehead. "This is not how it was supposed to play out, you know? I wanted to teach my children generosity, and to involve them in family and tradition. Bring the family closer together," he said, interlocking his fingers. "Not tear it apart." He pulled his fingers apart. "Nothing good has come of this."

"Not true," Taoji said. "*We* are all family, right? Perhaps closer than ever, eh?"

"And I can see just how strong and brave my little girls have become," Dad said, his voice thick. "My little Cherise." He squeezed her hand. "And my Sangeet. My good sweet young lady." He pulled me near to him and whispered in my ear, "I am especially proud."

I could only smile and nod. Then something wonderful occurred to me. "So, Dad, we're okay? All is forgiven?"

Now it was Dad's turn to smile, and for the briefest of moments I thought I was off the hook. That the whole lying-to-my-parents-and-running-off-to-Philly stuff was over and done with. But then my dad said, "Forgiven? Perhaps. But not forgotten, Sangeet. You are still grounded for at least a month, maybe two. After that, we'll put you on a sort of trial parole, I think."

"Oh," I said in a very small voice.

" 'Oh' indeed," Dad said, and kissed my head.

Mom winked at me and handed Taoji a cup of tea. "So what happens with Kajal now?"

Taoji shrugged. "I'll cancel my meetings, take her to her son, and arrange a place for them to stay. If that doesn't work, perhaps it is back to India for her. And as for you two?" He gave Doodles and me a squeeze. "You all get on with your lives, and miss me."

○   ○   ○

I'm at my locker, hanging up my coat. Somebody shoves me from behind. I turn and see a cluster of goths giving me the finger. "Narc," one says. "Loser," says another.

I try to ignore this. I take out my datebook and my history textbook. The diary isn't in my bag anymore. Last night I gave it back.

It was about 8 p.m. and Mom was up in Chachi's room, only it wasn't Chachi's room anymore. Mom had been dusting and vacuuming and had the windows cracked open to air the place out. "Sang!" she called. "Come see."

I went up there and found the room looking almost normal. Furniture pushed up against the walls again, and two trash bags stuffed with all the papers and garbage Chachi had left behind. But no sign of Mom.

"Hello?"

"In here," came a voice from the closet.

"What are you doing?" I said, and looked inside.

"Hungry?" Mom asked, and pointed to the open crawl-space panel in the closet wall. The inside was packed with all the cookies and granola bars and chips and junk food one could ever dream of. "I found the panel ajar and pushed it aside."

"Wow," I said. "Bulimia cured."

Mom nodded. "About that, Sang . . ." She emerged from the closet, and tucked some of her auburn hair behind her ears. "I'm really sorry. I should have listened to you. Trusted you."

"Well, I guess I kind of understand. You were worried." I pulled her diary from my back pocket and handed it to her. "And I guess I should have given you this right away."

Mom took the book and sank onto the bed. "This is so humiliating. I—I never wanted anyone to see this. I just kept it, because . . . ," she said, then shrugged. "I guess I didn't want to forget what I went through, you know?"

"It's okay, Mom. Forget it. I know I sure want to." Then I tried to leave, but Mom called me back, made me sit beside her.

"We have to talk about this," she said.

"That's okay, we don't have to."

"Sang, I need you to understand something. I was ashamed of who I was."

At this point I was looking at the ceiling, at the rug, at my fingernails, at anything but my mom. Let's face it, talking with a parent about sex is awkward, but talking about a parent *having* sex is AWKWARD!

"I was ashamed of what I did," she was saying. "I was thirteen and thought I was in love."

I raised my eyebrows and faced her.

"I know, I know," she said. "Well, I was with this one guy for a really long time. We dated for over a year, and even though there were other crushes, he was my boyfriend. He was sweet, and we were young and stupid, and that was that." She stared at her diary. "After a while, I wanted to be a kid again. Hang out with my friends. Date other people, but not seriously. But, in a way, there was no going back. People found out I wasn't a virgin, and it labeled me. Guys expected things." She looked me in the eye. "I didn't want that to happen to you."

"So that's why you didn't want me to date? Because you didn't want me to have sex?" I admit I was a bit stunned. I mean, dating to me means holding hands, kissing at the movie theater, flirting over coffee. Having sex isn't even on my radar yet.

"You don't know what it was like, Sang. After that, it took me so long to get people to see me as who I really wanted to be."

"But, Mom, I'm not like you were."

Mom tossed the diary onto the bed. "God, what you must think of me."

"Look, what I mean is, you're an amazing mom. I think you taught me well. And maybe that's why it's okay to have a little faith."

"You're right. You're absolutely right." She sighed. "You know, sometimes I feel like I get everything wrong."

"Hey," I said, "I can totally relate. I guess nobody's perfect."

She smiled and smoothed my hair away from my face. "I just thought if I could keep you from getting serious with anyone, at least until you're older . . ."

"So can I date now?"

"Well," Mom said, "it's just that your future children are all there, inside of you. In a way, they're witnessing all the good and bad things you are doing with your life, you know?"

I flopped back onto the bed. "Jeez, Mom. No pressure, right?"

Mom flopped next to me and sighed again. "All the pressure in the world."

I slam my locker shut, and somebody body-slams me. Dots swim before my eyes, and I refocus to see a girl with purple hair and two lip piercings pointing at me with a black-lacquered fingernail. "You're going down, bitch."

I turn and hurry in the opposite direction.

"Sang!" Megan says, hurrying beside me. "Sang, are you okay?"

"Not exactly," I say, clutching my books to my chest.

"What happened? All I know is that your parents found out somehow. And what's all this stuff people are saying about Gina?"

"It's complicated. I'll tell you everything at lunch. But what about you? Did your parents go crazy on you?"

"My parents attribute my actions to peer pressure and say my desire to please others is merely a passing phase of early adolescence."

We stop outside the door of our history class. "So you're not in trouble?"

"Oh, I'm totally grounded."

"Me too. Megan, I am so so sorry. You must totally hate me. I can't believe I did this to you."

Megan shrugs. "It's okay, Sang. It's not like you forced me. Anyway, David thinks my grounding is totally romantic. He sees our forced separation as very Shakespearean. Very star-crossed lovers. He says he's going to wait for me." She grins and covers her mouth. "Ooh, here comes your hottie." Megan waves and dives into the classroom.

"Hey, Sang," Jason says. "You missed a wild concert." He's got on a crisp purple Stinkin' Monkeys T-shirt, and he's wearing that leather jacket, and I'm thinking, It's hot in the school. Doesn't he ever take that damned thing off? "So, like, what was your story?"

"Didn't Gary tell you?"

He shifts his books to his right arm. "Tell me what?"

"Never mind." I move toward the classroom door.

"Sang, wait."

I pause. Is this where he realizes how wrong he's been? That he might have lost me forever, if not in the city, then perhaps to his best friend? That he must fight for me and my love?

Yeah, right.

I pivot around to him, and before he opens his mouth, I say, "It's about the money, right?"

"Well, yeah."

"Well, there's a famous saying. According to Gary, you know it pretty well. It goes like this: 'Easy come, easy go.' "

He opens his mouth wide enough for a pigeon to fly in.

I smile, full dimple, and enter my classroom. For once I'm feeling pretty damned pleased with myself.

48

Flash forward to Wednesday. It's the day before Thanksgiving, and guess what? I'm not dead. Even though every goth in the world has threatened me and pushed me and cast nasty looks in my direction, it turns out that goths are mostly scary makeup and clothes, and not actually all that dangerous. And it turns out I'm not alone, because not only is Megan one of the truest friends in the world, but her boyfriend, David, is also pretty nice, if bizarre. He keeps things interesting at our lunch table, spouting facts about the exact germs that can be found on the handle of the school bathroom door and inventing miniature Olympic games like the javelin toss (with French fries) and the discus throw (with pepperoni from the cafeteria pizza). And Gary Westbrock has also left Jason's table, and sits with us now. He's official score-keeper for the miniature Olympics. Even Dalton is back, though at first he didn't talk to me much. But after I stuck a pepperoni slice to his forehead and said he looked like an Indian with a *bindi,* and he scooped his finger into his catsup and gave me a bindi of my own, well, the tension between us seemed to melt away.

After school, I decide to pay a quick visit to the Poor Richards shop, where I buy a bagful of discounted candles. Even though I'm grounded and I can't go out at night or on the weekends, I'm still allowed to walk home from school—as long as I'm in the door by around 3 p.m.

As I'm hurrying home, I'm thinking about how everything has changed. Me and Jason, over. Me and Gina, over. My family and Chachi, *so* over. Even the Rani story I always tell Doodles seems, after last night, to be done. When I went into her room to continue the story, she was bouncing on her bed, babbling about how many slices of pumpkin pie she would eat this Thanksgiving and what movie she wanted Hari to take her to when he got home.

Finally I said, "Get under the blankets or no story."

"Fine." She crawled under her quilt and flopped her head onto her pillow. "Do you think Mom ordered the turkey from the same place as last year?" She crinkled her brows. " 'Cause last year it tasted like cardboard, remember?"

"But the pie was perfect." I pulled her quilt up to her chin. "Now quiet, so I can finish the story about Rani."

"Oh," she said.

" 'Oh' what?"

"Well," she said, her brows crinkled again, "actually, I'd like a different story. If that's okay."

"A different story?"

"Yeah. I want to hear about how you dumped pickle on Chachi and made her disappear."

"You do?"

Doodles nodded, settled comfortably onto her pillow, and hugged Taffy Bear close.

"Well, if you're sure," I said. And so that was the story I told.

When I get to my house, I'm totally out of breath because I practically ran all the way from Poor Richards. Mom checks her watch and says, "Hmm. Three-oh-five. Not bad." She says she's redecorated the attic bedroom. Sends me upstairs to check it out. With a final burst of energy, I run up the stairs, the bag still in my hand, and throw open the door.

The room looks normal, but not any different. Then I see him.

"Hari!" I drop the bag and race into his arms. He lifts me and twirls me around. "I thought you were coming tomorrow. I missed you!"

"Same to you," he says. He looks a little thinner, and a little hairier (he needs a cut and a shave).

I hit him in the shoulder. "You jerk."

He grabs his shoulder. "What did I do?"

"It's what you didn't do. Didn't answer my e-mails. Or call. Or anything."

"Hey, things have been really busy. I had this huge

econ test and a paper due, and I didn't get to check my e-mails till two days ago."

I cross my arms.

"It's true, I swear. I feel really bad about it, soooo . . . ," he says, and digs around in his duffel and pulls out a college-store bag. "I got you some presents. Check it out."

I take a college hoodie from the bag. "Thanks." It *is* pretty cool.

"There's more."

I look into the bag and pull out a beautiful booklet covered in brown leather, with an image of a flowering tree embossed on it.

"It's a diary. In case you want to work things out and I'm not exactly available."

I run my fingers over the cover.

"And I promise I'll check my e-mails more often from now on. Okay? Sounds like things were totally messed up around here without me. But don't worry. I'm here now. So ask me anything."

"Actually, Hari, I'm good."

"You're good? I mean, obviously Chachi's gone." He gestures at the bare dresser and desk. "But what about that guy you wrote me about?"

"Hari, I've got everything totally under control."

"You do? Impressive. Okay, then." He rubs his hands together. "What do you say we go downstairs to see what Mom's planning on microwaving for Thanksgiving to-morrow?" He heads toward the steps.

"Wait. Actually, there *is* something I need help with."

49

"*a* little to the left," I say as Mom and Hari, standing on chairs, tape a banner Doodles has made over the entrance to the dining room. "Great."

I look out our bay window to make sure Dad's car hasn't pulled up. It's already dark, and under the streetlamp I can see the branches of our bare maple being tossed about in the wind. I strike a match and light the candles we've set along the sill. Next I light the ones on the coffee table. When I use up the last match, I rush to get another matchbook from the kitchen cabinet.

"Help me," I say, and toss matchbooks to Hari and Mom. "Dad will be home any second."

"I can help too," Doodles says. "Give me some matches."

"You can't. You're too young," I say as Mom, Hari, and I light candle after candle on the buffet and on the dining table. Some of these are the ones I bought at Poor

Richards, but most of them we found in cabinets, and in the basement, with the Christmas decorations. Red tapers, white pillars, and a cache of short, stubby candles Mom once bought at the dollar store, just in case the electricity ever went out.

"But I want to help," Doodles says, arms crossed.

I wave out a match that has burned dangerously close to my fingertips. "Well, you can't."

"That's so unfair," she says.

"Look out for Dad," Hari says. "So you can warn us."

"Right." Doodles runs to the bay window.

"Don't get too close to the candles, Cherise," Mom calls over her shoulder. She lights the last candle. "There. Done."

"Wait," I say. "We don't have any sweets."

Mom holds up a finger. "I'll get the pumpkin pie from the fridge." She hurries into the kitchen.

Doodles holds up a finger. "I'll get my giant chocolate bar." She races upstairs.

Hari and I move some candles aside on the table to make room for the goodies. "This is a cool idea, Sang," he says. "We should do this every year."

Mom carefully carries the pie to the table, and sets it down just as car headlights shine into the living room.

"He's here!" Doodles practically shrieks as she tears downstairs. She drops a chocolate bar the size of a board game onto the table.

"I'll get the lights," Hari says, and switches off first the kitchen light and then the dining room light.

"Ooooh," Doodles says. "Pretty."

It is pretty. Halos of candlelight twinkle from every surface. The halos are multiplied by their buttery reflections in all the windows. It's like we're in our own little sparkling city of lights.

Hari, Doodles, Mom, and I grab each other's hands and grin as Dad throws open the front door.

"What's this?" he says. In a blink he's with us, shouting, "What a surprise!" and "Happy Diwali!" We are all laughing as he pulls us into a giant family bear hug. That's when I notice something else has entered the house with Dad. Something that is stirring the candlelight, making it bend and flicker. Maybe it is a gust of November breeze. Or maybe, just maybe, Laxmi, the goddess of good fortune, has finally arrived.

Acknowledgments

Wow. Where to start? I'd like to thank my wonderful agent, Jennifer De Chiara, for being such a positive person and believing in my dreams. Also, thanks go to my sharp editor, Lisa Findlay, whose vision for the book inspired its Diwali ending. I'm grateful for the capable staff at Random House Children's Books, as well as Cindy Revell, who created such beautiful and witty cover illustrations. The Society of Children's Book Writers and Illustrators has provided me with endless guidance and inspiration, and the amazing One-on-One Plus Conference at Rutgers helped set me on the path to publication, so I thank everyone responsible for running these.

I have been in a number of writers' groups throughout the years, and I sincerely appreciate the many people I've encountered who have helped me wrangle with my words. I especially want to give thanks to my talented novel-writing group, the Rebel Writers, for their help with *What I Meant . . .* Group members Chris Bauer, Jeanne Denault, David Jarret, Damian McNicholl, and John Wirebach have all spent much time reading, critiquing, and encouraging. I feel fortunate to know you all.

About the Author

Marie Lamba was born into a funny and loud Italian family. To make her voice heard, she turned to writing. A freelance writer for many years, Marie has had many articles published in regional and national magazines. Her current obsessions include romantic comedies, dark chocolate, and exotic travel. Marie's husband, Baldev, is a native of New Delhi, and together the couple has journeyed all over the Indian subcontinent. They live in Doylestown, Pennsylvania, with a tiny, disobedient poodle and two remarkable daughters, who have always said just what they meant. You can tell Marie what's on your mind by visiting www.marielamba.com.